The
COMING
of AGE

VINCENT MONTGOMERY

Fulton Books, Inc.
Meadville, PA

Published by Fulton Books 2020

ISBN 978-1-64654-365-6 (paperback)
ISBN 978-1-64654-366-3 (digital)

Printed in the United States of America

Special thanks to:

Jasmine Monèt, you gave me the idea of writing a book and here we are today. I can't thank you enough for that spark.

My man Casanova, you looked out with that edit and gave me good advice throughout the entire process.

Shanta, you already know I appreciate that edit too. The insight you gave too was very detrimental to the project, I love you for that.

All of my homies involved in this process, I love you guys. Thank you for keeping me hype while writing.

My cousin Riem, I needed your energy throughout this long process. I love you.

RIP to my little brother Lon. I wish you could've been here to see the final project bro. We talked about it and it's finally done. I miss you boy, I love you.

Prodigy of Mobb Deep, RIP. It was your lyrics, along with NaS and Hav's that inspired me to start writing this book. Illmatic, The Infamous and Murda Muzik were some of my biggest inspirations. I went into this book like I was creating an album. So glad the release is finally here!

My parents and Grandmother, I love you guys.

All the people I'm missing, you know it's all love.

Karée, a special thank you to you. You pushed the envelope when I didn't know how to finish the process. I really appreciate that!!

I hope everyone enjoys this as much I enjoyed writing it.

How did I get jammed up like this? This story I'm about to tell y'all is the truth. I ain't lying. It goes further back. Let me take y'all back to where it all started.

CHAPTER 1

Ring...ring...ring...

R   I heard the alarm clock go off, and all I could think is *Damn! I don't want to go to school today.*

I could smell the scent of fresh bread Grandma was baking in the kitchen, wafting toward the back of the apartment.

That shit smells mad good, I thought as I sat up and stretched. The sounds of the neighborhood bustle, horns honking, traffic, and people rushing to the subway reached my window, signifying the start of a new day.

I got out of bed and turned my oldies off and threw on Nas's "Illmatic" to start my day off properly. As I walked out of my room door, I passed Grandma in the hallway. I gave her my regular hug and good morning kiss on my way to the bathroom. I was feeling on top of the world for some reason. This day felt better than most of days. I couldn't put my finger on it, but I was digging the energy already.

I hopped in the shower while "Illmatic" still played in the background. I finished my shower and headed back to my room to decide on which kicks I wanted to wear with the outfit I picked out for the day.

Damn, I see how Q felt in Juice, I thought while laughing to myself. I finally decided what to wear and headed to the kitchen after I got dressed. The freshly baked bread that I smelled when I woke up was sitting on the table, still golden brown and warm.

Grandma smiled as I quickly grabbed a knife to cut a few slices to take with me.

"I made it fresh for you, son."

Grandma knew how much I loved bread. That was one of her ways to show me she cared.

"And this is why I love you so much, Grandma. This is the best bread ever."

She smiled knowingly.

Bread in hand, I grabbed my backpack and headed toward the door. Almost absentmindedly, I checked my bag, more out of habit than any real purposeful action. What I was looking for wasn't there.

Oh, shit… I almost forgot my work!

A small wave of relief rushed over me. I was so lucky I checked before I left. I would have been assed out if I had showed up without the merchandise. I jetted back to my room, closed the door for a little added privacy, and practically dove at the spot where I kept my stash. As I peeled up the wooden tile on the floor, I thought I heard footsteps. I hurriedly put the capsules in my book bag and gave my room a once-over. I mentally scanned over everything to make sure I was squared away for real this time before I left.

I grabbed my bag and rushed toward the door, telling Grandma that I was going to be home a little late. I was going to hoop with my homeboys, and I didn't want her to worry. She acknowledged me with a nod.

I was halfway out of the door when Grandma called out to me.

"Stephen, aren't you forgetting something?"

I patted myself down, slightly confused, because I was sure I didn't forget anything.

"You aren't going to give this old lady a kiss?" she said while looking up from the book she was reading.

With a smile, I went over, kissed her cheek once more, and told her I loved her.

As I exited my building and headed to the bus stop, I saw a chick (or a shorty, as we often called them) that caught my eye. She was standing near a couple of dudes that I knew put in work, who were eyeing her as well. I wasn't the biggest dude on the block, but enough dudes respected me. They knew I had hands and wasn't afraid to put them to work, so I wasn't really bothered much.

I approached her, and up close, she was even more beautiful than I first thought. She had a creamy-brown skin tone, a slim waist with a coke-bottle-shaped body, long black hair, big brown eyes. I slightly hesitated to speak.

Damn, now she's gonna think I'm too shook to speak to her. And these two corny-ass niggas have seen me hesitate as well.

If she noticed it, she didn't let on at all. Shorty seemed to know what was up right out of the gate. Before I could say anything, she addressed me.

"Hey, how are you this morning?" she said kind of flirtatiously.

Her voice is even bad as fuck, I thought while sizing her up. I could feel the other two guys watching with the screw face, and it gave me a slight confidence boost.

"What up, Mami? What's good?" I said confidently.

"Nothing. Just chillin'," she responded with a slight smile, looking at the ground.

At that moment, I knew I had locked in on her. I could feel my confidence radiating from me, and she was feeling it too. The bus arrived, and we made our way to the back of the bus to get to know each other.

"I usually don't even pay attention to niggas," she said as we settled into our seats. "Too many lame niggas out here. They're always saying the same stuff, using the same lines, and trying to impress me with the same moves they use on these other bitches out here. But you're different. Straightforward, but real. I like that."

I half smiled and half smirked in a way that I hoped looked like I was both a player but also the kind of guy she would still be interested in.

"Yeah, you see it, Ma. You already know."

I gave her my math as the bus pulled up to the school and took hers as well. Once off the bus, we had to separate, as her classes were on the other side of campus.

As she waved goodbye, I yelled one more thing to her. "Don't be out here flirting with these two-dollar niggas. I'll see you later."

She smiled and said, "I won't. You got my attention already."

I knew at that very moment she was mine.

As I walked up to the school, I saw my boys Rah and John posted up. They were ready to start wreaking havoc on niggas out here frontin'.

"What's good, fellas?"

Rah dapped me up, and John responded with his usual reply.

"You know how we do, baby. I'm chillin'. Chillin', mackin', chillin', hangin', mackin', mackin' and hangin'."

We all started laughing as he leaned in to dap me up. I then started telling them about shorty I met earlier that morning.

"Y'all know Sabrina, right?"

They both looked at me, crazy surprised. "Damn, how'd you get that?" they both said in unison.

"This is what I do. I'm not new to this. I'm true to this," I replied with a smirk on my face.

We started laughing again and walked toward the school doors. Once inside, I went to my locker and dropped off some of my books and picked others up. The bell rang for class, and I immediately started to get more focused.

I know what you're probably thinking at this point: *Damn, he's pumping. In school, and actually studying?* What can I say? I was a smart hustler.

I walked to my first-period class, and as expected, the trash was full. I used this to my advantage. I didn't want to get bagged in school with drugs, so I put the ex-pills in a crumpled-up piece of paper. I then threw it by the overfilled trash cans while no one was looking. This was smarter, in my opinion. Nobody could pin them to me if they were found. It was the best method I could come up with. I could keep the drugs nearby without them being attached directly to my name. There was a hard part about this method though—watching it throughout the period and making sure no one picked the paper up and threw it away. But hey, this was NYC, and that rarely happened.

Although I had good grades in my classes, the deans and security guys were always fuckin' with me. They had never caught me doing anything. It was all word of mouth, the things they had heard. I wasn't always this young, ambitious drug dealer; however, a few things from my past changed me. This was the hand that was dealt to me.

Ding.

First period was over, and like on many other days, I was relieved that everything was starting out so smoothly. Walking through the hallway to my second period, I saw one of the customers. Now Nate was one of my regulars who normally copped e-pills. He gave me that look like he needed something. He already knew the drill.

There was a routine, and it played out the same every time. He signaled me somehow, usually by making eye contact inconspicuously. I then followed him to the bathroom. He gave me the bread, and I gave him the work. Smooth transaction every time. And then I went about my business.

I walked into the bathroom like normal, but this time, he wanted more. He usually got two, but today he wanted to cop four.

"Yo, don't die on me, bro!" I said with a snicker, half joking and half serious.

Those were problems that I didn't need. I was already moving under the radar. A student overdosing would ruin everything and possibly get me jammed up. However, I was not his father. He wanted four; I'd give him four.

"Nah, bro, it's for my girlfriend. I finally got her to agree to try it with me tonight," he responded while laughing.

I laughed it off as he took out the bread and handed it over. I quickly counted it to make sure it was the correct amount. I gave him a head nod so he'd know everything was good, and I then looked down at my watch.

Fuck! I am going to be late!

"Yo, get at me, son," I said to Nate before jetting out of the bathroom without waiting for a response.

I ran through the hallway, trying to make sure I would not be late to a class I couldn't care less about. I walked in the door, and Ms. Cooley was standing right there. She had her clipboard, waiting to write the late people's names down.

"Not today, Miss. You won't get me today. I'm on time."

She laughed and continued to watch the door. I took off my Jansport backpack with numerous strings attached while slowly dropping my crumpled-up paper by the trash can. Same routine as earlier in my first-period class. The bell rang as I sat in my seat. Ms. Cooley closed the door and began to lecture the class about equations and exponents, with a quick review from the previous day.

I was sitting at the back of the class, thinking about all the money I had saved up and how to expand it. My thoughts were interrupted by Ms. Cooley's voice.

"Steph, can you come up here and show us how to solve this problem?"

I had no intentions of really doing so, but she was one of my favorite teachers.

"Aight, but don't call on me next time unless I raise my hand."

She laughed again and agreed to my slightly serious demand. I went up to the board and knocked out the problem without hesitation. As I turned around, I locked eyes with my homeboy Rocky, and he started clowning me.

"Son, you're the hardest person I know, but you actually do homework and get good grades," he said, laughing.

"Dog, I joke around all day, but I'm not tryna be twenty-one and still in this motherfucker."

I walked past him and dapped him up on the way back to my seat. Rocky was one of my right-hand men that always had my back. No matter what the circumstances were, I knew he wasn't far behind. We grew up together, robbed people together, slept over each other's houses when we were younger. So it was safe to say we were brothers. He was the pretty boy out of us, and he could hoop for real—not just all right, dribbling between his legs and maybe crossing up a rec league player, but hoop *for real.* The kid even got a few D1 scholarships offered his way. He was talented, smart, and charismatic, so you could understand why we meshed well together.

I told him to meet me after class, and he agreed. Thirty minutes passed, and I was just waiting for the bell to ring at this point. I was just ready to move on to the next class and then to lunch. A shrill sound broke my concentration, interrupting my thoughts. It was time to leave and not a moment too soon. I was relieved as I couldn't stand this boring, easy math class much longer for the day. Rocky met me by the door, and I started telling him about my morning so far. I definitely couldn't leave out Sabrina, the chick I bagged at the bus stop that morning.

He knew how I moved, so this was no real surprise to him. Aside from the fact that she was pretty as hell with a banging body, shorty was smart too. While walking and talking, we saw her waiting by my locker with a smile on her face. Rock hit me with a nod as he could see I had business to attend to.

"I'll hit you later, fam," I replied, returning the same head nod to him.

I greeted Sabrina as I approached my locker and said "What's up?" to her.

"Nothing much. I've been thinking about you all day long, and so I wrote you a letter." She kissed me on the cheek and made her way down the hallway.

I yelled to her, "You know I was going to walk you to class, right?"

She looked back and, with a laugh, replied, "I know, but you're about to be late your damn self."

I looked at my watch, and she was right. I was about to be late for my next class.

As I was walking to class, one of my workers was trying to re-up real quick. I really didn't have the time, but I loved money. It was strange to me because he had never wanted to re-up this early in the morning, but fuck it. I let him buy the rest of my packs off me. It was less of a risk for me, and I got my money, so everyone was happy.

The bell rang before I got to class, and I was late. Since I was not really a problem child and my grades were good, I took my time to get to my next class. When I arrived, my teacher told me the dean needed me in his office.

What the hell did I do now? was all I was thinking as I walked to his office.

It couldn't be anything serious, because they would have sent security for me. As I approached his door, I was glad I didn't have any more work on me. I knew I was good, but for the love of God, I couldn't figure out why they needed me in the office.

I got to the office, and Dean Capmani invited me in. I asked what he needed from me. He looked me over as if I should have known what it was.

"Did you forget you asked me for something last week? Remember?"

I wracked my brain, trying to remember, and then it hit me. "Oh yeah, that MetroCard, right?"

Smiling, he said, "Bingo. It came in this morning. You looked nervous, like you were worried about something. You okay?"

I smiled and replied, "You know I hate coming down here, man. You could've avoided all this by just sending it to my class, but you like to mess with me."

"Bingo, Stephen, you're two for two right now."

We both laughed, and I reached out to take the MetroCard.

"Your teachers tell me you're doing very well, so I wanted to speak to you one on one. I wanted to thank you for applying yourself more in class. I appreciate that. I knew you had it in you." He extended his hand again but this time for a handshake, which I obliged him with.

I had a good feeling this morning when I woke up, and today was turning out to be just what I needed.

I walked back into the classroom and took my seat. As I sat down, I heard the teacher talking about Fredrick Douglass, and I quickly become intrigued. I got so caught up in the lecture that I forgot about the note Sabrina gave me earlier. When I did remember, I took the note out of my pocket, and I saw little hearts drawn on the front of it. I smiled as I opened it up. Shorty was feeling me hard, and she wanted to meet up over the weekend, if I was with it.

Hell, yeah, I was with it!

She also told me to call her tonight so she could get to know me better. I folded the paper back together in the same form in which it was given and tucked it back in my pocket.

The bell rang, and I headed to lunch this go around. I walked through the hallway to go see my crew. We met up at the same spot every day. I saw Rah, John, Rocky, and Risk. I called him Risky Business though. This was another brother of mine, same sign as me with the ambition to get it. This right here was the team, and we'd been together for years. We started joking as we walked to the lunchroom.

"Yo, those kicks are fire," John said to me.

"You know me, son. I saw them, and I immediately had to cop. I haven't seen anyone with these uptowns with the bubble check yet."

Risk just shook his head and said, "Yeah, those joints are mean, son, no lie."

My guys knew what I did, but they knew I was low with it. To them, I was the boss or the one, when speaking, folks tended to listen to. I was cool, calm, and collected no matter the situation. I watched the older heads go out and get it. I also saw the mistakes they made too, so I patterned my outlook of the game off their mishaps.

I came up with a new solution with all the OGs out the game. We were young, but we were getting it. The whole team knew ways to eat, but we weren't flashy with it. I made sure they stacked bread in those Nike boxes just like I did.

"Yo, I forgot to tell y'all about the weekend. I came up Friday night after y'all left the court," Rocky blurts out.

"I caught this Mexican cat sleeping, son. Y'all know me. I was getting my shots up, and I see him knocking back some beers, so I knew he was bent. I walked up to him and say, 'Manito, you got money on you?' You wouldn't believe it, but my man pulled out a stack of twenties from his book bag. All I was thinking was 'This man is not leaving this park with that bread on him!'"

I glanced over at him, ready to hear the outcome. "So what did you do?"

Rocky looked at me, halfway incredulous and halfway laughing. "Fuck you think I did, son? I pulled one of the empty bottles out the trash can and hit that nigga right upside his head. I grabbed the cash, and I bounced quick fast."

We all started laughing, and I told Rock he was wildin'. We all knew Rock gave it up, so we weren't surprised. He was always ready for the quick come-up and showed no fear at all.

"How much you get from that, son?" I asked.

"A quick 1200."

"Damnnnnnn!" we all said at the same time.

That was easy money to us. Shit, I had nearly a hundred thousand stashed away from hustling. I had no intentions on hustling forever. I wanted to get a few good years in and escape to the clean life with businesses of all sorts.

I started eating my pretzel from the cage in the cafeteria along with my apple juice I got every day.

Out of nowhere, Rock blurted out, "Yo, Steph, Sabrina is bad, though. How'd you get that?"

Before I could say a word, Risk looked at me in awe. "Hold the fuck up. What did I miss? When did you bag her?"

"This morning, son, on the way to school."

"So you going to hit that or not? If not, pass that to me. She's been on my radar for a minute now!"

I responded with my regular cool tone. "Chilllllll, son. Y'all got all the bad chicks. Tonya, Toya, Stacey, remember?"

We all laughed.

"Yeah, they're bad as hell too," Rah replied.

"My point exactly. Y'all have all the chicks, not me. I'm low."

The bell for lunch rang, and we all headed to our next class. The end of the day was near, and I had so many things to do. I already finished all my homework, so I didn't need to bring any books to the crib. I had to re-up with the connect later on, and then I was going to hoop later. After all that, I needed to find time to call Sabrina. Maybe I should make her wait a few days. I didn't want her to feel I'm jocking her, but whatever. I'd see how I felt once I got home this evening.

School was out for the day, and my first stop was the connect's spot. I grabbed a few extra grand this morning out the stash. That on top of what I usually brought, I was thinking I wanted to cop more pills this time around. I would talk to the connect and see what he thought.

I get to the spot, and the connect, Jose, greeted me. Jose was a different breed—a Dominican cat who had to be in his mid- to late forties. I heard he made a name for himself in the streets in the seventies and eighties. I wasn't sure about that, but I did know for sure he didn't play with the cash. So when I'd come to him, I'd come correct. We had a little history between us. I definitely came a long way. From him fronting me the product to when I started copping my own from him.

"*Dímelo loco. Ya regresaste?* You're back already?" Jose asked me.

Smiling, I answered him, "Yeah, I'm tryna get this money."

He stared at me intensely, as if he was sizing me up. "You've come a long way, from me fronting you pieces to you copping for yourself." I acknowledged his statement with a head nod. Then he asked, "How much are you trying to cop today, manito?"

"Shit, I'm trying to cop five hundred or one thousand pieces of ecstasy," I replied.

Jose looked at me with a shocked face. "*Carajo loco.* You're aren't playing," he said, slightly impressed.

"I'm just trying to get more money."

Jose knew me since I was little. I started pitching nicks and dime bags for him when I was twelve, and this was where I was now. I got good prices from Jose, so I fucked with him hard. The product being great was an added bonus.

Jose looked over at me again. "When are you going to stop playing and start messing with this cocaine, manito?"

As he pointed to it, my mind started racing. I was thinking I wanted to mess with it, but I didn't want to dip in the stash for more bread. I liked that I had come up and didn't need anybody to front me anything anymore.

The look he gave me as I was going over this in my head was like he was reading my mind. "*Loco, mira,* you've been coming to me for years. It's time I do you a solid. I'm going to give you a kilo of this pure Colombian cocaine free of charge. I know you're smart enough to figure out how to break it down and move it. It just like you've done with the weed and pills over the years."

I was trying to maintain my cool, but even I, Mr. Cool as a Fan, was a little taken back by his generosity. Free of charge too? How could I say no to that?

"*Que lo que tiguere?* What's it going to be?" he asked.

His voice jerked me out of my own thoughts and back into reality.

"Shit, I'll take it and break it down. But I'mma be honest. I'm kind of sketchy about it 'cause I've never sold this shit before."

He assured me I wouldn't have a problem at all with it. "If everything goes well, as I know it will, you'll be back buying more in no time. This shit will sell itself, manito, no lie."

"I'll take it! And give me a thousand pills of the ecstasy too," I yelled out.

He smiled and said something in Spanish that I couldn't quite make. I knew I was on to something bigger than pills. I could just feel it. I got my work from him and put it in my book bag. I took my textbook out and carried it in my hand because I didn't want any slip-ups with that kilogram.

As I was walking, my mind started racing. I was thinking of all the ways I could really start getting more money and whom I could get to sell this shit. I headed to the court to play a few games of basketball with my team and tell them about the shit that just happened with the connect.

CHAPTER 2

T he courts were packed. I could already see Rock on the court, crossing niggas up and driving to the rack.

"I see you, boy. Give me more! No prisoners, no regards!" I yelled out to him.

I saw John, Rah, and Risk changing on the sidelines, so I began to walk over to them.

"Son, I came up today and got a way for us all to get it. We'll talk about it when Rock gets off the court."

They were anxious to hear what I had to tell them, but I told them to chill. I changed and started stretching before we hit the court. Funny thing was, these dudes didn't even know we all could hoop. We all just didn't play on the team because we'd rather be getting money.

We got on the court, and immediately following that, we made a splash. Everyone was looking at us because the chemistry we had was beyond crazy. We started blowing this team out, as we jumped to a seven-to-zero start.

We played a few more games until we were all tired and it was just us left on the court. I started up a game of twenty-one but after running full court for a few games, I'm gassed. Rock calls 'game' as he hits the final shot. We headed to the benches to sit down and catch our breath.

Risk blurted out, "Yo, tell us about that money shit you were talking earlier when Rock was on the court."

I started telling them about the connect Jose and what he did for me today. They all were in shock.

"But this is what I want to do. We are all about to eat off this, and I'm going to show y'all how."

On my way to the courts, I had come up with a plan and rules for how we would conduct business. If niggas followed these rules, we could get more cream than the rest. I didn't know much about coke at all. I figured if we cut it just a little bit, we could make even more money. We just needed a spot to set up shop, cut, and bag it up.

I trusted all these dudes with my life. So I told them the plan.

"Cut the shit, and make it where each of us can buy our own keys next time."

I turned to look directly at Risk. "I'm going to give you my half. I want you to flip it for me uptown."

I knew he was a natural-born hustler, and he lived in Harlem—two key factors to my plan. It was the perfect place to move coke. I wanted him to take my half and get some workers to pump it for me. I didn't expect my guys to be on the streets, pumping. Nah. We knew too many people that would line up for an opportunity like this any day.

I turned back to face Risk, Rah, and John. "I know I don't really need to say this, but don't use the shit. Don't be on the corners selling it yourself either. This is really unknown ground for us, so we have to be smarter about it."

Everyone nodded in silent agreement. They were all on the same page. I gave the brick to Risk and told him to cut it down and give it to the rest of the crew when he was done. Everyone was mad excited about this shit. I couldn't front. I was too! My heart was beating fast, but I knew we could make it work if we wanted to. I motioned to get everyone's attention.

They were obviously excited thinking of the moves we were going to make too. I know they were probably already spending money we hadn't made yet.

"All I ask for is 40 percent of what you make off the key. Y'all keep the 60 percent. I am not trying to eat off your niggas." They looked at me like I was buggin'. I just let out a little chuckle. "Like I said, I'm not trying to be greedy with this shit at all. Remember,

I got it for free, so I'm tryna put y'all on. If all goes according to how I've planned, y'all should all be buying your own bricks in no time."

Before we all went our separate ways, I reminded them to follow the rules, especially not to bring anything to their crib, a rule I myself broke this morning. We dapped each other up, and I began walking to the train station to get home.

Today's been a good ass day, I thought to myself. Grandma made fresh bread, I bagged the shorty I been checking out, and I made some cheese as well. Shit, I even got that free MetroCard I've been waiting for. Most importantly, I moved up with the connect.

I was in the big leagues now. It was *go* time. Everything was going to plan.

It was getting late, but I still had all the pills I needed to get off. I swung by my stash spot and made the drop before going home. A thousand pills of ecstasy was major for me. I wasn't even worried about the coke right then. That situation would sort itself out later. I was going to make crazy bread off these white boys, selling this shit, and I knew it. If I sold these pills at, like, sixty to seventy dollars a pop, I'd more than triple my money!

Jose gave me good prices because I was moving the pills faster than other people. I thought that the fact that I was in high school helped too. Kids were always trying to venture out and try new drugs all the time.

I hit a few of my workers up from the pay phone before I got to the spot to give them the re-up. I didn't front anyone anything. My workers knew if they wanted something, they had to come correct or not come at all. I had G, Mike, Ruff, D-Money, and Kev pumping for me. They were loyal and worked hard. They were true hustlers outside of my main family that I fucked with.

Surprisingly, they were already posted up once I got to the spot. It looked like they had been waiting a while for the next batch to come in.

"What's up, fellas?" I asked.

I meant it as a greeting, but I also genuinely wanted to know what was going down. Everyone replied with different but similar-sounding answers. Before I could break the pack down, G started talking.

"Damn, you got a lot of them shits this go around. I'm tryna get like 250," he said.

That was a lot of pills for one person to handle. But if he had the cash, I was with it. I asked, "You have the bread for that, son?"

"When have I not had the bread, son?" he replied.

Now that I thought about it. He was right. I laughed and told him just that. "You don't even know how much is in here though."

"Son, it's more than 250 in there. Stop playing," he replied sharply.

I guessed he could eyeball it and tell. I told him the price, and he pulled out mad cash like he wasn't playing at all. I was selling it to them for cheap too. These dudes were getting these joints off for over a hundred dollars a pop, so my sixty dollars wasn't hurting them at all. The rest of my guys gave me the amounts they needed with the cash and left me with fifty pieces. Damn, I just made mad money that quick, and I didn't even have to stand on a corner or anything. If that coke sold like this, it was game over!

I put my fifty pieces away, dapped everyone up, and proceeded to walk the rest of the way home. As I walked, I went over the day's events in my head. I had never sold out that fast. Business must be picking up for G to buy that many pieces from me at one time. Not to mention he got another thirty-five pieces from me in school earlier. Today was going well for real.

As I walked up to my crib, I patted myself down for my keys. As I opened the door, the house smelled great. Grandma was cooking some food for me.

As I closed the door, I yelled out to her. "Hey, young lady, how was your day today?"

"It was good. And yours?" she replied with a smile.

I told her I honestly had a great day and that the food smelled delicious. "What's on the menu, Grandma?"

She started naming all my favorites: collard greens, mac and cheese… But I stopped her as soon as she said mac and cheese.

"Tell me there's still more bread to go with this lovely meal, Grandma."

"Yes, child," she said, smiling and playfully swatting at my hand.

I laughed back and told her how I felt about her bread, all while kissing her on the cheek and giving her a loving hug from behind.

She directed me to the bathroom to wash up before I came to eat. I obeyed her rules and went to my room to put my cash away in the sneaker boxes. I put my money in the stash, and if my numbers were correct (I saw no reason for them to be wrong), my sneaker box money would be $130,000 at that very moment. I didn't even know how I made that much in a day, but that upgrade of work surely worked in my favor. I grabbed my clothes for the shower and hopped in with Nas's *It Was Written* CD on blast.

I sat down at the table and began to eat the delicious food my grandmother cooked. She was sitting across from me, looking at me eat. She loved to watch me eat and enjoy the food she cooked for me. I thought it gave her a sense of joy knowing she was providing her grandson something he truly loved. The thought of that alone made her proud.

I told her not to cook tomorrow. She made a lot of food, and it was just us two, so I could eat leftovers. She agreed. I finished my food, washed the dishes, and then took out the trash. I kissed her as she went to her room to get some rest. Shortly after, I went to my room and started getting myself ready for the next day.

A few minutes later, the phone rang. It was Risk.

"It's done, son. I already hit the homies up and told them to check me."

I was a little shocked. "Damn, son. That quick?" I replied. I knew he didn't play and he was about his money just like me, but damn! That fast surprised me a little.

"You know I don't play, bro."

"I know. I just didn't expect it to be done that quickly."

He said he was going to handle my half and get it finished completely in a few days. I acknowledged him and told him we would chop it up tomorrow when I saw him. I started to take my belongings out of my clothes, and I saw the letter Sabrina gave me.

Oh shit! She's gonna be mad I haven't called her yet.

But even with that in mind, I still didn't call her. I was tired, and I didn't want to call her house this late at night. She was probably waiting for me to call, too, but I dismissed it and put my oldies on. Then I tried to get some rest after this eventful day. I knew tomorrow was going to be crazier than today. I could just feel it.

CHAPTER 3

The next morning, as I walked up to the bus stop, I could already see that Sabrina was waiting for me. The scowl on her face left no doubt in my mind that she was pissed off. I could already bet as to why, but I'd mastered the art of not showing facial expressions. My face was as blank as a sheet of paper. As she stormed over, I couldn't help but admire her shape and how her pants hugged her hips.

I greeted her with a half smile, trying to maintain my cool but also trying to show her that I was happy to see her.

"What's up, ma? What's goo—"

She cut me off, cursing at me in Spanish. "Y quien carajo crees que tú ere' pendejo?"

Pendejo. The funny thing was, I knew exactly what she was saying to me. I continued to listen and acted like I didn't know a thing about the language.

As she approached me, I snapped back to reality to put together what she was trying to say.

"So I give you my number, only for you not to call?"

I told her I was busy and to not take it personally. "I know I had promised that I was going to call, but I had things to attend to." That answer did not satisfy her. In fact, it seemed to rile her up even more, so I had to snap a little to nip this situation in the bud. "Yo! I said I was going to call, but I got busy. I'm not going to argue with you over this right here. Relax!"

She immediately stopped talking and looked at me almost submissively with her big brown eyes.

Ah, she liked that shit. It was almost as if she was looking for that exact reaction from me. Well, if she liked it, there was more where that came from! I wasn't done yet. I felt like I needed to smooth the situation over. Run some nice words by her ears so she would feel better. I wanted to have full control over the situation. She wasn't my girl but I knew she would be sooner than later. So I jumped out the window and did the unthinkable. I leaned in and gave her a kiss. I wanted to give her something to think about all day in school. Her heart began to melt and I could tell from her facial expression that she was head over heels already.

Sternly but softly I said, "Now relax."

She did just that and grabbed my arm and started holding me. I could tell I had her in the palm of my hand. I told her I would take her anywhere she wanted to go this weekend. I wanted to further smooth over how I snapped at her earlier. She held me tighter and responded with a smile.

The bus pulled up across the street from the school, and we get off together. It was early, and class didn't start for like another half hour. I saw my crew posted up on the block, already waiting for me. Risk had already filled them in on everything. They were just waiting for my for approval to commence business.

"Yoooooooo, we need to talk," Rock said as I strolled up.

I looked at him, then at Sabrina, without her noticing, and then back at Rock. "Nah, it can wait. Give me a few minutes. Let me walk shorty to class, and I'll get with y'all."

They knew I didn't talk business in front of unfamiliar ears and I liked to keep my shit low. As I walked past them, Rock couldn't pass on the chance to be sarcastic.

"Hi, Sabrina," he said with a sarcastic laugh. He followed up with "This motherfucker" as he dapped me up.

"That's the second time today I've been hit with that line," I respond, laughing.

He laughed, and Sabrina looked at me, shocked.

"You knew what I said to you, and you acted like you didn't understand at all?"

I told her I understood Spanish very well, and I just wanted to hear what she was saying. She looked slightly confused, as if she didn't know what to think.

"Wow. Okay, I guess I can't talk bad about you to my friends then, huh?"

I laughed and told her, "It's okay. I'm smarter than you think."

We got to her classroom, and I gave her a hug and kiss once more to fuck up her head.

"I'll call you tonight. I promise."

She hit me in the shoulder and told me I better, and then she leaned in to get another kiss. I had her open, but then again, she had me in her web a little too.

I then turned around and walked back toward the exit, where my homies were. Surprisingly, they were in the same spot, waiting for me to come back. I walked up to them with my regular "Yooooooooooooooo." Now we could formally talk about business.

Risk explained to them how we were going to break down the brick already. If all went well, we wouldn't have to chop any more bricks down to get money. We would have enough for everyone to cop their own bricks after this. It was all risky business, but we were the right crew with the right mind-set.

I could see the excitement on everyone's faces, and I wanted them to get it in, but smartly and wisely. I reminded the guys about the rules I set in stone for them and how if they started using, our brotherhood/friendship would be over. We all agreed on the terms, and I told Risk to give them the work and then we'd see how it went. We dapped each other up and went to class.

The day went by quick as usual, and all I could think about was how fast the coke would sell. I got home that afternoon, and the first thing I did was call Sabrina like I promised. The phone rang once before it was picked up. I started to ask if I could speak to Sabrina, but I couldn't get the words out.

Before I could utter one word, she replied, "I thought you'd never call."

I laughed and told her, "I promised, didn't I? I don't like to break promises."

She responded, "I like that."

We talked for hours on the phone as I asked her question after question, trying to get to know her better. I asked her where she wanted to go Saturday night.

"To the movies."

All I could think was *That's it? Really? The movies?*

I told we'd go to see the movie and I'd take her somewhere else too. She then started telling me I had to get rid of all the bitches I had. I let out a slight chuckle, and I asked her how she figured I had all these bitches. Her reply was a confidence booster.

"You're a handsome guy. You dress nice, and you always smell good. You're smart, charismatic, have a good personality, and speak with a presence I've only seen few ever do. So I know bitches are attracted to you."

I was smiling from ear to ear after that. Who knew she was keeping track of all this? How did she read me so well when we barely spoke?

I asked her where she got that notion from and how long she'd been keeping tabs on me. She told me she'd always had a crush on me but never moved on it. She didn't want to be one of my hoes. I didn't even deny the statement she made.

"Okay, boo, you got it," I politely replied.

She then started talking fast as fuck, telling me not play with her and she didn't have time for the bullshit. I couldn't front at all. I liked the fact that she just put me in my place with ease. I knew she was going to be ill. I started laughing again.

"Babe, I'm serious!"

There was a hint of exasperation in her tone but also a note of humor.

"Oh shit. We must go together if you just hit me with the babe line. Things just got serious," I said, chuckling into the phone.

She started laughing and told me that it did just get serious and that she knew she wanted me. Damn, now how was I going to let all these other chicks go? I was seventeen with nothing but pussy and money on the brain. I wasn't going to press her on having sex because that was not my style. My game wasn't a slam dunk. It was more like a Gervin finger roll. There was no flash to it, just finesse.

At this point, I needed to see her and just take a stroll around the neighborhood. She didn't live far from me, so I told her get ready and that I was going to meet her by the corner store. I put on my sneakers and my fitted and left the house to meet her at the corner store. I asked her if she wanted something from the store or the Mr. Softee ice cream truck that was passing by.

"Let's get some ice cream, babe!" she replied.

We get our ice cream and started walking slowly, with no destination in mind.

She started licking the ice cream, and I started daydreaming about what else she could be doing with her mouth. She caught me off guard, staring at her. She reacted a little self-consciously.

"Stop watching me eat my ice cream!" she yelled as she halfway turned to hide her face and ice cream cone from my vision.

"I would if you'd stop licking it like that," I muttered almost unintentionally without realizing that she could hear me.

She laughed and playfully hit me on the shoulder. She turned to face me and told me she really liked me a lot, and from the look in her eyes, I could tell that she wasn't lying.

Suddenly, she blurted out, "So how many chicks have you had sex with?"

I didn't want to lie, nor did I want to tell the truth. "Why? You've made it clear I can't talk to no one else but you, so why should that even matter?"

She looked at me, surprised that my rebuttal was so fast and on point.

"I'm not sexing you, so let the drought begin."

She looked at me again, staring directly into my eyes. "It doesn't have to be a drought at all," she said while licking her ice cream more seductively.

Although I couldn't see my own face, I knew it had a look of shock written all across it. She must have seen it as well. She almost immediately told me she was a virgin and she'd been waiting for the right guy to give herself to.

"But it isn't easy. I'm not just going to fuck anybody."

I agreed that it didn't look easy. She had way too much class and sass for it to be easy. But I wasn't going to press her about it. I was going to stay on my cool shit, and eventually, she'd let this nigga in. I could see from the way the conversation was going that it was enticing her more and more.

"I heard you're a freak and you know how to put it down."

I smirked and asked who told her that. She told me she had her sources. We talked a little more before I dropped her off at her doorstep. I kissed her and squeezed her ass all in the same motion. She playfully smacked at my hand and told me to stop before she came home with me. Her tone was serious but playful. It was at that moment that I knew I was in. I decided I would wait until the right time to make my move. I gave her another kiss and ass squeeze before I turned around to go home.

A few days went by, and Saturday morning hit. I wake up to a phone call from Risk saying that everything was taken care of. I was a little shocked. I didn't expect them to move so fast, but nevertheless, I was happy. The faster we moved, the faster we made money. I didn't even ask how much a brick cost. I was going out on a limb, especially based on the fact that Jose gave it to me for free. Even so, I knew enough to know they went for a lot more than wholesale prices on the street.

I told Risk to gather the team up and to meet up in Queens somewhere. I wanted to discuss the next plan of action before the re-up. I had a busy day ahead of me because of my date and this re-up shit. It was time to get the show on the road! We met out in Ravenswood on one of my old blocks I used to chill on. Everyone was there except Rock.

I couldn't front. I was a little agitated. "Where the fuck is Rock at?"

John and Rah both answered at the same time. "Basketball practice."

Fuck, I forgot about that. I'm sure he'll be here any minute, I thought to myself I looked around once more and guess who I see running up? Rock's bum ass!

Jokingly, I said to him, "Nice of you to make our meetings on time, *boss*."

He replied, "This basketball shit."

I went in right off the bat, wanting to know how they got all that shit off so quickly.

John spoke first. "Fiends are biting hard for that shit, son, and we cut it down. Whoever you're fuckin' with has that good shit. No lie. Keep fuckin' with him, son."

Rah jumped right in next. "We need to re-up, like, right now. I could have a brick gone by the time night hits."

I looked at him, like, *What the fuck? How?*

He continued telling me that he knew a few good people that could get it off without any problems. Then I asked Risk how many times he stepped on the work.

"Not a lot. That shit was just that good."

I nodded slowly. "I see. Shit! Well, how much did y'all make off it?"

They started blurting numbers out, and I was shocked because these numbers were high. much higher than I anticipated. I didn't know much about selling coke or any of the inner workings, so I asked them what they wanted to do.

All at once they said, "Get more!"

That was all I needed to hear. "Say no more!" I said, looking around and dapping everyone up. "Give me the bread, and I'll take Risk with me to meet the connect. He'll get y'all right with the work. I have a date with Sabrina later this evening, and I still need to get an outfit and all."

They all started laughing and clowning me.

"This nigga going on dates and shit!"

"He about to fall in love with her."

I laughed along with them. The thought of a girl cuffing me up to that point was pretty laughable, so I understood why they found the notion so funny.

"So? Maybe," I said, slightly laughing to hide my annoyance at the fact that they found my situation humorous. "She's tryna make me stop talking to all my chicks. It was, like, a demand." I made sure to make it clear that I wasn't mad though and I thought that she was ill.

They laughed once more. They knew this was way out of character for me, but they were sure I was serious about her. Business was still business, and they knew I wouldn't slack on that. I knew they were wondering why I picked Risk to come with me and meet the connect.

I knew Risk the longest, and he came from a long family of hustlers. His pops used to run the streets with Rich Porter and Alpo in the eighties, but he got out clean. Risk was a direct reflection of me. I always felt like we were separated at birth because of the similarities that we saw in each other.

I didn't want any static between the crew. So I told them that on the next re-up, I'd take everyone to meet the connect and we would go from there. I fed them the line that Risk chopped it down and did all the leg work so he'd gets to meet him first. They agreed with a look of relief on their faces. Risk knew why I was taking him; it was unspoken between us. We all shook hands, and I told them I'd get with them later.

Risk and I hopped in a cab to the spot. On our way, I give Risk the rundown on how we were going to play it. I still didn't know how much these bricks cost from Jose, but we were about to find out.

As we entered the spot, Jose looked at me and greeted me as usual. "Loco, how'd it go?" he asked. The smile on his face said he knew it went just as he said it would.

I smiled back and said, "Very well." Then I introduced Risk. "Oh, this is my man Risk. Jose, meet Risk. Risk, meet Jose. This is one of my right-hand men you'll be meeting and doing business with—if that's cool with you."

Jose nodded and replied, "Of course, man in. I know you run a tight ship. I trust you. I know you wouldn't bring anyone to me that you didn't trust."

I nodded in agreement. I started to tell Jose it went really well and I needed more. I continued telling him how the coke moved much faster than I had expected. Risk dumped the money on the table.

Jose responded excitedly. "Now you're talking my language!" He moved closer to inspect the cash.

This can't all be from one brick, I thought. It was like Risk was reading my mind. He nodded toward the pile of money.

"Everyone pulled money out of the stash and decided to get more. That totals up to $220K. The question I want to know is how much this shit is per ki?"

Jose looked up and answered, "For you, manin, if you say it's selling that quick, for you and your friends, I'll give it to you whole-sale—$28,000 a ki. So right now, we are looking at eight Kis, if my math is right."

Risk leaned over to my ear and says, "Yo, that's a good-ass price. Them joints are going for like 40 a ki at the minimum anywhere else."

Jose laughed because Risk didn't realize that he was talking loudly. "You're right, Mr. Risk. And this is the best product in town."

I was convinced. "We'll take it."

I could see the big opportunity in this shit now, but I was still a few grand short. Jose told me it was okay to pay the outstanding amount the next go-around. He gave me the eight Kis, and I look over at Risk. The little smirk on his face let me know he was happy. I felt like there was more to it, but I wanted to wait until we left the spot to find out.

As we were walking out, I asked Risk why he was so happy. He looked at me with the same grin on his face—only this time, it seemed to be a little bigger.

"Son, we're about to be rich, like, no lie!"

I looked at him, slightly curious. "What you mean?" I asked.

He continued, "Yo, on the streets, that shit goes for like $95 a gram. You can cut that one brick and make two or three if you do it right. And that's a thousand grams in each. So do the math on that, son." His excitement slowly started to catch on as I realized what he was saying.

"Oh, shit, son!" I stopped to look at him. "That's a come-up for real! Who knew?"

He looked back at me surprised that I was just barely catching on. "That's what I'm telling you, son!"

I chuckled to myself and asked him, "Since when did you become a cocaine expert?" It was a rhetorical question because I already knew the answer to that. The look he gave me said exactly the same. I said, "Well, let's get it."

He acknowledged my statement and agreed. We dapped each other up and hopped in separate cabs and went our separate ways.

CHAPTER 4

S he yelled out to me, "This date is crazy!"

I knew Sabrina wanted to see a movie, but she didn't expect me to take her to the Statue of Liberty too. And of course, the fancy restaurant as well.

"Who thinks of stuff like this? Do you always take girls out on dates like this?"

I started to smile. "I don't take chicks out. Period. So for me to do such is out of the ordinary. I didn't want to take you to just a movie, because that's corny. If you're going to be mine—and I assume you will be or already are since you made me cut off all my chicks—it had to be different and memorable."

She smiled crazy hard. "You're doing a good job, baby. I've never been here before after all these years. This was nice and very thoughtful."

She continued to tell me how I'd done things that no one else had ever done for her with this date. I mentally patted myself on the back.

I'm that motherfuckin' nigga was all I was thinking.

"I'm trying, boo," I managed to respond, trying to hide a grin.

She saw the poorly disguised smirk hidden behind my otherwise emotionless demeanor.

"You still ain't getting no pussy!" she responded with a laugh.

"Did I ask you for some pussy? No, I didn't, so save that shit for someone else," I replied while laughing as well.

She started squeezing my arm that was draped over her and said, "You're so different." She had no idea why I wasn't rushing her.

Shit, I didn't even know myself why I wasn't pressing her about it. I thought it was because she was a virgin and I had never had one of those. Plus, I liked her a lot, so why not wait?

The night was going really smooth. Everything was going according to plan, but I wasn't finished. I had one more surprise she had no idea about, which I was sure she was going to like. I let her know we had one more event for the evening as we hopped in a cab. I told the driver to take us to Empire Boulevard, between Bedford and Empire in Brooklyn.

She looked at me, slightly perplexed. "What's over there?" she asked.

I just shook my head and told her to wait and see.

The cab driver pulled up to the Empire Skating Rink, and she started smiling. I wasn't sure if she liked skating or not. The thought of us both busting our ass seemed like fun to me.

She started giggling and said, "I'm probably going to bust my ass. I haven't been on skates in a while."

"Don't worry. I'm in the same boat as you."

As we walked up to the rink, she cast a worried look at the long line of people waiting to get inside the building.

"The line is mad long though."

I grabbed her hand and started walking toward the entrance. "Nah, baby, we don't do lines," I said as we walked to the front.

She didn't know my cousin was the bouncer here, so we were skipping over the whole line. I saw my cousin Jay. I dapped him up and told him I had some shit I wanted to talk to him about. I told him I'd holla at him another time about it. He looked at me, confused.

"Business opportunity, son," I said.

A look of realization came across his face, and he smiled. He caught what I meant because he knew how I was.

"Bet, son. Holla at me, B," he said.

He opened the door, and we proceed into the skating rink. I went to the front desk and took off my shoes, and Sabrina did the same. I looked up and saw a chick named Tiffany. I used to mess with her like a year or two ago. She was still bad, but she wasn't Sabrina.

"Hey, Steph. How've you been?"

"I'm good. Just enjoying a night out with my girl."

I could sense Sabrina was staring at me hard with the "Who the fuck is this bitch?" face. So being the smooth fella I was, I cut the tension before it could even start to grow. Glancing at Sabrina's feet, I asked in an almost matter-of-fact manner, "What size do you need? A 2?"

Laughing, she said, "No. I need a 4, babe."

Whew! Crisis averted. I casually and carefully looked back at Tiffany. I made sure any communication I had with her seemed as benign and professional as possible. I told Tiffany I need a 4 and a 10.5. She gave me the skates, and I could tell she wanted to say more. She was keeping it cute and being respectful enough to just chill—for the moment. I was sure I'd be getting a phone call from her any day, asking me all sorts of questions.

I thanked her and started walking away from the counter. I knew Sabrina was going to ask me who she was at any moment. So before she could get the words out her mouth, I spilled everything.

"Yes, I used to fuck with her. No, I didn't know she worked here. No, I'm not fucking with her now. Are you happy?"

She smiled and said, "Damn, you're a mind reader, too, huh?"

"Nope. I just knew exactly what you were going to ask me." I had no reason to lie to her, and she knew it.

She looked at me and, in her half-playful, half-serious manner, said, "Don't make me fuck you and her up."

I start laughing hysterically. "You're the one. You're crazy."

She looked at me once more and said, "Yes, but you like it."

I agreed and began skating. It was actually nice on the wheels. It came to me like second nature when I got on the floor. Sabrina was doing well too—after her first fall. We both laughed about it as we skated the night away. It was true what they said about time when you were having fun. Before we knew it, they were playing the last song of the night, and then it was time to go home. We headed outside and hopped in a cab. I started to give the driver the directions to her block, but she stopped me.

"I don't want to go home. I want to lie with you."

She laid her head on my chest. In my mind, I was thinking there was no way she was lying in my bed and expect me to do nothing. It was just not possible!

The cab pulled up to my block, and we both get out. I took a long look at her body, savoring every inch. It looked magnificent. The outfit she wore tonight was crazy, and the jeans were hugging every curve on her lower body. Her body, along with everything else about her, like her pretty-ass smile, was enticing me more and more.

She asked me, "Will your grandmother trip if I sleep over?"

"She wouldn't care, and besides, she's asleep. She doesn't bother me like that, nor does she come into my room."

I opened the front door, and we headed straight to my room. I asked her if she'd like to shower, and she replied yes. She asked for a T-shirt to sleep in.

All I could think was, *Damn, that's all she wants? It's going to be a long night if all she wants to do is cuddle.*

She came out of the shower in nothing but my T-shirt, and I was just staring at her. Damn, she looked amazing, and her body was crazy! I tried not to get too aroused, so I grabbed my boxers and headed to the shower. I needed to get out of the room and get my mind right.

When I came out the shower, I saw her watching TV. She turned her attention to me, and her focus was all on me. I locked my door, and she slowly and seductively crawled to the foot of my bed. I could swear I'd never seen any girl do it like that before. I met her at the edge of the bed and started kissing her. She pulled me closer and told me she wanted to give herself to me. I could feel her heart beating rapidly. I slowly took off the shirt I had given her and laid her down on her back.

I wanted to put her at ease. I started kissing her body while listening to the sounds and moans she started making. As I searched her body for all her spots, I found her hot spot. It was her neck. I could tell from how she was breathing when I got close to it and touched it with my lips. I was going to make her mine, and I knew just how to open her up. I kissed her, moving my lips down her stomach while caressing her brown nipples. I listened to her body, trying not to ignore anything, even the slightest movement.

I got to her nicely trimmed pussy, and I started sucking on her clitoris, making her moan. I worked my tongue in circular motions while eating her pussy to the point that I could feel her get wetter. She was about to cum. I could feel it from the way that she was pushing my face into her pussy. The thought of her cumming, as well as enjoying herself, was making my dick hard. Finally, I heard her moan.

"Papi, I think I'm about to cum! Don't stop! Shittttttttttt! Fuckkkkkkkk! This shit feels good! It's cumming, papi! It's cumming!"

I started flicking my tongue against her clitoris more and more as I aggressively pulled her toward me. I wanted to make sure she didn't escape this pleasure that I was giving her. She let out a loud moan as she came. I covered her mouth. In the excitement of the moment, I forgot where I was.

Fuck! I wonder if Grandma heard. I listened intently for several seconds... Nothing. *Aight, cool. We still good.*

I refocused my thoughts on what was in front of me. I started giving her long licks to help soothe her first nut. After she got her composure back, she pulled me up toward her face and started kissing me. I could tell she wanted to taste herself and see why I was enjoying eating her out so much. She could feel my dick against her pussy, but I still had my boxers on. She took my boxers off to get a view of my package.

"Damn, baby, that shit is big. I'm supposed to take all that?" She seemed a little unsure, but I reassured her.

"Yes, you are, but I'll be gentle with you."

I wanted to be prepared, so I laid my towel down under her. I just knew it was going to get messy. I could tell she was ready but still scared. Her facial expression said it all. I laid her back down and began to insert myself into her wet pussy. She let out a sigh and a moan of relief. The slow strokes began, and I could tell she liked it as she pulled me in closer. I found a good rhythm and started killing the pussy. She was moaning and breathing hard, telling me to fuck her. I couldn't front. Her shit was good, and the sounds were driving me crazy. I looked down at the pussy as I was hitting it. I felt as though it was talking to me. The combination of her tight, wet pussy and the friction from my dick was music to my ears.

She started moaning in my ear again. "Papi, I'm about to cum again! Shit, you're hitting this pussy! It's yours! It's all yours!"

I knew it was mine from how she was digging her nails into my back. I start my shit while kissing her neck, telling her she better not ever give my shit away. I went deeper.

"Damn, Papi, you're killing this shit for real! What did I do to you?"

I dug deep, feeling her shake and breathe harder with every thrust. I could feel her body working up a nice sweat. I had no intentions of stopping anytime soon, so I told her to get on top. I wanted to teach her everything about sex. I was the professor, and she was working to get that A in this class.

She started riding me as I guided her on the exact way I wanted her to move. I was going to make a pro out of her in no time. She started shaking again and told me she loved me. I wanted to think it was the sex, but deep down, I knew. I knew she had fallen in love with me in this short bit of time. The dick was just the icing on the cake.

I took her from on top and flipped her on her stomach. As I entered her from the back, I whispered in her ear, "I love you too, baby!"

That shit made her go crazy to the point she started speaking Spanish. "*Que rico!* You better not give this shit to anyone else! *Métele duro, papi! Dámelo, papi!*"

She was staking her claim to my shit, and I had no problem with that at all. I was feeling her, and I really did love her. She was ready for me to cum, so she told me to get up. She wanted back shots, and I was just the man for the job. She didn't know that was my favorite position. I grabbed her small slim waist with a firm grip to let her know I meant business. I started piping her down, all while watching her ass shake. She started speaking in Spanish once more, telling me to cum with her and to fuck her harder.

Her Spanish / New York accent was driving me crazy! I pulled her closer and started to pound her out. She was moaning loud, and I didn't even care who heard anymore. I could tell she was going to cum, and I needed to cum with her. I grabbed her hair and wrapped it around my fist and pulled her neck toward me.

She moaned, "I'm cumming, papi! I'm cumming!"

I thrust harder. "So am I, baby!"

I let out the biggest nut on her ass. She looked back at me while I moan and cum. It was almost like she was reveling in seeing the fruits of her labor come to fruition.

"That shit was fuckin' good, although you probably woke up my grandmother with all that moaning."

We both started laughing.

"That was your fault, papi. You did that. Next time, don't be so good, and I won't be so loud." She laid down next to me and rested her head on my chest. Lying there, she asked, "Did you really like it?"

"Hell yeah. Shit was incredible, babe."

We continued lying down, catching our breath. A few minutes later, I was ready for round two.

CHAPTER 5

A few days later, I started to see things more vividly. As I lay in my bed, waiting for the alarm to go off, I started putting everything into perspective. I was heading into my senior year of high school in a few months, my grades were good, I had some cash saved up, and the work was moving itself. I had no intention of selling drugs forever. I needed a way to get out clean and find a legal way to wash the money. College was also on my mind; however, I didn't want to go out of state. I had so much going for myself here, and to be honest, this was home. I was still hoping to get into St John's University out in Queens. That had been my dream school from day one.

All these things were in my head, and I finally took the time to actually give them some thought. As for the work, that shit was moving on the block real fast, so fast that I wondered if I should take a hundred grand from the stash and re-up with my workers with that and have them pumping coke and pills. My brothers were already moving mine and theirs, so I wasn't missing anything. The money always came back correct. I didn't want to throw all the bread that I'd saved up into one jar because if someone got caught, I'd be left with nothing.

Maybe I should leave the stash alone—just take the 30 from the 130 and whatever I get from the bricks I had on the street now. I remembered Risk telling me the street price for them joints were $95 a gram. I knew for sure I had 3 Kis on the streets right now. He also mentioned he could cut it down to make 1 brick into 3.

With that lingering in the back of my head, I started doing the numbers, and if my numbers were correct, that was $855,000. Shit, that was a lot of money! Could this actually be real? I had to beep Risk ASAP! We had to talk about this shit immediately! I wanted to know everything. As soon as the thought entered my mind, my alarm clock went off. I gained a boost of energy from the thought of all that money. If I were to stop right now, I would have close to a million stacked up.

All I could think was *What the fuck am I going to do with the money? Where the hell am I going to stash it? That's too much money for sneaker boxes.*

I had to do some more thinking and had a million questions running through my mind. However, I pushed them to the back of my mind. I was focused on getting ready to see Sabrina at the bus stop. I threw on some Guess jeans and a Tommy Hilfiger shirt to go with my blue, red, and white Uptowns with the bubble checks. I brushed my hair and put my two-toned Durag around my neck. I was always dipped but low key with it. I had a Jesus piece, but I kept it tucked a lot, but not because I was scared. I wanted it close so that I'd feel protected all the time. I didn't really care for the flash. All I wanted was the money.

I saw Sabrina, and she ran up to me still hyped from Saturday night. Her hugs were so warm and cozy that I couldn't help but lean in and get caught up in her warm embrace. She was dangerous to me right now because I didn't normally move like this. Yeah, she had the kid open. I'd never held hands with chicks, let alone kiss them in public, so this was all new to me. I couldn't front; it felt good, so I was rocking with it.

It didn't dawn on me until that moment, and I started thinking to myself why Sabrina's parents didn't trip about her not coming home Saturday. I found that rather odd, but I didn't bring it up. It didn't seem like a problem to her, so it was no problem for me. All I knew was that I wanted to see more and more of her. I was becoming addicted to her. She wanted to spend the whole weekend together, she told me. I didn't know how I felt about that. A day was fine, but the whole weekend was nearly impossible due to my lifestyle. Plus, I didn't want her to find out what I was doing.

I also didn't know how to tell her it wasn't possible. I told her to pick one day because I had some things I needed to take care of. She wasn't really tryna to hear me though. I wasn't tryna hear her either because one day was all I really had for this weekend. This was perfect timing to ask her why her parents didn't trip about her not coming home Saturday. I also wanted to know how she was going to manage a whole weekend without going home.

So I just outright asked her.

She replied, "I rarely go out, and my parents aren't as strict as you might think. I told them I was going out with you, and they didn't question it."

It sounded crazy to me, but okay, I'd rock with it.

"They're going to want to meet you sooner or later, so be prepared for that."

I knew that was coming since she was spending time with me and always on the phone with me, but was I mentally ready for it? Probably not. Fuck it, though, I had bigger fish to fry. I'd think about that later.

Where was I going to put this money? That was all I could think of on the bus ride to school. This shit might have to go in storage or something, I thought. Sabrina was talking to me, but I was really aloof to the point she started squeezing me and asked me what I was thinking about.

"Nothing. Just tryna figure out where to take you on *the day* you wanna chill."

"Baby, in all honesty, I don't want to do nothing. Your presence is enough for me."

I knew she'd say that, but I still wanted to do something, so I told her I'd figure it out.

Our school was coming up, so I pulled the tab to alert the bus driver to stop at the next bus stop. We got off and stopped by the breakfast cart on the street. I got my regular bagel toasted with butter and jelly and also apple juice. I asked her if she wanted something, and she picked up a juice. I paid for our stuff, and we proceeded to the school entrance.

It was a nice-ass morning outside, and in two weeks, the school year would be over. I honestly didn't really have to go to school anymore. I had finished all my Regents tests and handed in all my projects. Our grades were just about ready to be finalized in a matter of days. At this point, I only came to school because there was nothing to do at home when all your homeboys were in school.

I dropped Sabrina off to class, and I went to find my guys before the bell rang. I had no time at all. Stopping for breakfast held me up this morning. Fuck it, I'd get with them at lunch. Lunch came, and I saw them all standing by the door, waiting for me. I hit them with my long "Yoooooooooo." They responded with the same call back. We dapped each other up and sat in our spot.

Risk started speaking. "Steph, I got your beep this morning. What's up?"

I told him to break this coke shit down scientifically so I wasn't missing anything. He did just that. He broke it down to every gram as I sat there in shock.

Stunned, I asked, "How much will my three Kis bring me back?"

"I broke them down to three for each brick. So that's nine bricks for you, and the estimated total is about $850,000."

At this point, I knew I looked visibly stupefied. I didn't even try to hide it. I exclaimed, "Oh shit! Yo, that's bread, son!"

He waited for me to calm down and then told us them shit was moving fast. Even though he cut them, they were still stronger than any other product on the streets uptown.

"Yo, I watched a feign come back for more like five minutes after one of the workers gave him the work."

Satisfied, I turned to the rest of the crew and asked how everyone else's shit was moving. They all said the same thing. It should be done by Friday or Saturday. We could have Harlem, Brooklyn, and Queens on smash if we worked it properly.

I told them I was going to talk to my workers and have them selling pills and coke. I was sure it wouldn't be a problem since they loved money just as much as I did. Something kept popping into the back of my head though. When you were getting money like this, people would start noticing. We needed to not attract any attention in our direction. This went from living above what would be seen as "within our means" down to having any problems with other crews who were also pumping on the block.

The goal was to put people on and for us to not touch anything I told them. They all agreed. "No matter how much money we get, we will come to school every day and live regular. Nothing flashy to draw attention to yourself. Got it?"

They all nodded in agreement. If we were going to do things like this, we would have to be smarter than the dudes before us. We were hyped as ever now, and all I had was one more question for them.

"Where are we going to put all this money?"

We all started laughing.

"Seriously, though. If I'm bringing in 850K this go-around, I'll tally up to almost a mil. I can't put that in sneaker boxes."

Risk replied, "Son, we might have to rent storage units."

"Funny thing is, I thought the same thing earlier," I told them. I didn't know how secure I would feel with it in a storage unit. I was more hands-on when it came to money. It would have to be a short-term fix for the meantime. I was going to see how much I could get in these sneaker boxes until then.

I told them that further down the line, we would need to start thinking about business opportunities to wash this money. They heard me, but they weren't thinking as far as I was.

The bell rang, and we all headed to class. Risk and I had science together, and we normally just slept in this class. It was boring for us because we already knew a lot of the shit the teacher was teaching. I didn't want to sleep today, however. I wanted to talk to Risk more offline about future arrangements. We were always on the same page; plus I respected his views a little more. Not saying I didn't respect the other guys. It was just that Risk had the same love of money as me and he stayed low key. I told him we needed to really get it and get out. He agreed and started talking businesses.

I laughed because I was thinking to myself, *What seventeen-year-olds have you ever run across that wanted businesses this early?*

We knew what we needed to do, so it was always an interesting topic.

CHAPTER 6

"So you're tryna move coke and pills. son?" G blurted out.

I told my workers about the planned expansion. They were all in because they were all about money. As long as they didn't have to stop selling ecstasy, they were good. That shit was like a gold mine to them. Also, they didn't know much about selling coke, so they wanted to stick to their bread and butter. They knew it would earn them a lot of money though.

The only one who knew about coke was G, and that was because of his uncles. G was a hustler. He was smart but was just as stubborn. He had no cares in the world and had a whatever attitude. This was quite dangerous in our business, but he was still younger than me, so I worked with him. I gave them prices on how much the Kis were. I told them to get their money right and we could start as soon as possible.

Once D-Money heard the price, he instantly became happy. "Thirty-three a key? That's it?" he asked.

They knew street prices were way higher, but I didn't want to get rich off my guys. There was more than enough money around for us to all get paid. I figured the lower the prices and better the product, the more customers would come swarming in. This formula was usually correct. I told them to get their money together because on Friday, after school, we were going to re-up. I gave them the same pep talk I gave my brothers, with heavy reiteration on the "not using" part.

With that, all agreed. I dapped everyone up and headed home. I wondered, *What's for dinner?*

I got home, and I could smell fish being fried. It was exactly what I wanted. I kissed Grandma on her cheek, and I asked her about her day. She proceeded to tell me about hers, and then she asked about mines. We ate and shared a few laughs before we were interrupted by the phone ringing.

"Hello," I said into the receiver. I heard a familiar-sounding chick's voice in response.

"So you have a girlfriend now?"

It was Tiffany from the skating rink. *I knew she would call.*

I laughed and answered, "Yeah, I do. Why?"

She started going on, talking about how she missed me, but I knew it was just game.

In my head, I was thinking, *Fuck outta here. If you really missed me, you could've called the same way you're doing now. My number hasn't changed.*

I went along with it. If I wanted to fuck her again, I could, and I knew this. But that wasn't exciting to me. She only called because she saw I had a girl and she tryna fuck some shit up. I'd keep her on the benches for a rainy day, but I was not fucking with her right now. She looked good, though, and I knew I could control her if I wanted to.

"So when's the next time we're gonna see each other?"

I felt like she was trying to be funny toward Sabrina, so I said, "When I come to your job again with my girl."

I punctuated my statement with a laugh—cold and hollow, lacking any traces of amusement. She knew how I was. It let her know to not say anything like that to me again. I was still going to keep her around because one would never know; plus, she was cool and fun also. We talked for a few more minutes, and then I told her I'd call her back and that she could hit me up whenever.

"Okay. But I still want to see you, and I don't care about your little girlfriend either."

I knew that was coming, and I just chuckled. "Aight. I'll holla at you later." I hung up the phone and headed to my room.

I was lying in my bed, thinking about things, when I got another phone call. However, this time it was Sabrina. She wanted to come over. I told her she could come over and asked her if she was spending the night. She laughed and asked me if I wanted her to.

"Hell yeah!"

I wanted her to meet my grandmother too. I hung up the phone and went into the living room. I started talking to Grandma, and I told her I wanted her to meet my girlfriend. I had never asked my grandmother to meet any girl before, so she knew it was serious. She didn't react too dramatic though.

She just smiled and said, "I would love to meet her."

"Good, because she's on her way over right now."

We both shared a laugh, and she told me, "That was quick."

I called Sabrina back and told her I would come to pick her up. I figured I'd knock out two birds with one stone. I would go meet her parents while I picked her up, and she could meet my grandmother. I got dressed quickly and headed to her block. I knocked on the door, and her father answered the door.

"Hello. I'm here to pick up Sabrina," I said, all while maintaining eye contact. I could tell he was trying to intimidate me during the stare-down, but I wasn't budging at all. He spoke back and invited me inside their home.

I walked into their crib and looked around. I commented to her father that they had a very nice house. Before I could finish my sentence, he cut me off.

"What are your intentions with my daughter?"

I anticipated this question on the walk over here, so I already knew what to say. "Honestly, sir, I'm just trying to make her happy, finish school, and get into St. John's University right now. That's what I'm mainly focused on right now."

I knew from the way I switched it on him that I would gain his respect. Making his little girl and my future important while standing out was the way to do it. He didn't even mention her after I uttered those words to him. He was intrigued by the fact that I stated college was definitely in my future.

"St. John's, eh?" he replied.

"Yes, sir, for business administration," I answered. "I want to own businesses someday, sir. I feel they have all the tools I need to succeed."

He sat in his chair with the look of someone impressed by someone or something. I glanced to the left of me, and I saw Sabrina's mom. I saw exactly where she got her looks and body from. Her mother was bad. The dog in me wanted to flirt with her too. Sabrina looked just like her, just a few shades darker.

I thought to myself, *If I cum in her, she's definitely going to give me pretty babies.*

Her mother came over and hugged me while introducing herself to me. I did the same. My eyes were fixated on her mother. Her mother started speaking in Spanish, telling Sabrina to come here.

She switched back over to English and said, "Sabrina, he's handsome. You have a cutie."

I started smiling, showing dimples with a slight blush. Sabrina came out of her room with her bag and book bag for school in the morning.

My eyes were still fixated on her mother, and Sabrina made her way over to me. As she walked past her father, he slapped her ass, and we made eye contact. He just winked and smirked at me. I started dying laughing on the inside because he probably knew what I was thinking. He wanted to display his dominance in a playful manner. and that was cool with me. I hugged Sabrina and took her bags from her.

She hugged and kissed her parents as I opened the front door. Her father came up to me and shook my hand and asked me if I watched basketball.

"I sure do. A die-hard Knicks fan."

"Yeah, you can date my daughter. Honey, we have a winner here. He's a Knicks fan," he yelled back to his wife. He told me I should come over sometime and watch the games with him. I agreed to it, and he patted me on my back as Sabrina and I exited the door.

We started walking to my crib.

"My dad really likes you, baby. He never talks like that. And I mean *neverrrrr.*"

I just started laughing.

"I don't know what you did, but I've never seen him this excited about a guy before."

"That's cool, but your mom is bad!"

She punched me in my stomach and said, "Don't be looking at my mother, motherfucker." She had a frown that was hiding a hint of amusement.

Laughing, I said, "You look just like her. Just a few shades darker, that's all. If she is bad, then what does that make you?"

She blushed, smiling this time, and told me I had a way with words. Mentally, I gave myself a wink. *Of course, I do*, I thought. *I knew how to switch it at any moment with ease.*

I opened my door and introduced Grandma and Sabrina to each other. She liked her immediately. I could see it in her face. She called her pretty so many times I lost count. Grandma started asking mad questions. I guessed it was because I had never brought any girls to meet her or anything like that. She took full advantage with her questions, so I knew she was all in.

"Grandma, chill. You'll have plenty of time to talk to her in the future. She's not going anywhere. Leave the girl alone with all these questions."

We both started laughing because she knew she was rambling from her being excited.

I took Sabrina to my room and asked if she needed or wanted anything.

"No, you know what I really want!"

I smirked and told her I'd serve her up shortly.

She started to look around my room and noticed how neat and clean it was kept. "You clean your own room, or your grandmother cleans it?"

"I clean it myself. My grandmother doesn't come into my room at all."

She looked impressed and stated she thought all guys' rooms were messy. She looked around more, and under my bed, she saw all my sneaker boxes.

"You have mad sneakers."

"It's a hobby of mine. I love collecting sneakers. Uptowns are probably my first loves."

"How many loves have you had? How many girls have you had over here?"

I already saw where this was going. "I never had a love before you. I fucked a few chicks over here. None have ever slept over, nor have they met my grandmother."

I had nothing to hide, so I gave it to her in the order in which it came. My answer pleased her enough for her to stop asking me irrelevant questions. She came over and kissed me and told me she loved me very much. I hugged her, told her the same, and slapped her ass. I turned the television on to catch Martin and took some undergarments out of my drawer for my shower. I left Sabrina in the room and headed to take a shower with a grin on my face.

She's gonna start leaving shit over here and all, marking her territory. I know it. I can see it now, I thought to myself.

I finished washing my body and rinsed off and hopped out. I dried off and wrapped my lower body in my towel and headed back into my room. When I opened my door, I saw Sabrina naked on her stomach, with her ass sitting high in the air. My dick got rock hard through the towel.

She knew exactly what she was doing. She turned around and told me to come to her. "Papi, I want to please you. Show me how to please you," she said while taking off my towel.

She grabbed my dick and started gently massaging my dick. I've never felt with one as soft. She took my dick and put it in her mouth. I let out a sigh because the warmth from her mouth felt so good. While she was orally pleasing me, she looked at me to see how I liked it. I grabbed her hair to give her guidance on how I liked my dick sucked. She started playing with my balls and took my dick out of her mouth.

"Papi, show me now," she moaned.

Her accent when she called me papi turned me on so much. I put my dick in her mouth and told her to massage the tip of my shit and get nasty and sloppy with it. She put her hair in a bun, all while keeping my dick in her mouth.

I looked down at her like, *Damn, girl! Really, that's how you're gonna do it?*

She started gagging on my shit and doing everything I told her to do. I felt entitled to play with her pussy while she got me off. When I touched it, she was already wet. This had to be turning her on, but I didn't want to cum yet. I picked her up and threw her on the bed. I tried to eat her pussy, but she stopped me.

"Babe, let me please you."

I wanted to let her finish, but I was getting more aroused by the minute. I lay on the bed and told her to sit that pussy on my face. That way, she could continue to suck my dick and please me. She sat her soaking-wet pussy on my face, and I started licking it to the point my whole face was wet as she moaned. I was eating her pussy so good she had stopped sucking my dick because it felt so good to her. She laid her head on my thigh and started moaning more.

"Papi, I'm cumming. I'm cumming. Don't stop."

I could feel the intense pressure as she started shoving her pussy into my face more. I grabbed her small waist, pulling her toward me so I could clean her pussy up real nice. I felt her body start shaking, and I knew it was over for her at that point. Her body was depleted as she clasped onto the side of me, not moving.

She thought it was over, but this was just the beginning. My dick was still hard, so I crawled beside her. I aggressively spread her legs and started slowly stroking her, missionary style.

She started kissing me and dug her nails into my back. I knew that was a sign of how deep and good I was fucking her. I took her off the bed and started fucking her against the wall. She was moaning so much I was almost sure the neighbors could hear her over the music, but I didn't care. I wanted to leave no doubt in her mind that she was mine and no one would ever be able to top me. Our session started getting more and more intense as the positions started to switch. She creamed all over my dick, and the sounds her pussy was making while I fucked her was driving me crazy.

I told her I was going to cum, and she told me to cum inside her. In the next split second, I had to think real fast! Do I want to cum in her? Lord knew it was good, but I was not ready for a child. This nut was sure to bring a child in the world, I could feel it. I pulled out because I didn't want to rush it. That shit covered her whole ass and lower back.

I thought to myself, *Yeah, that was a kid.*

She wiped her ass off with my towel and headed for the shower. She was tired, I could tell, but I was still not finished with her.

CHAPTER 7

Time was moving fast until that Friday hit. I couldn't front. I was craving to see if Risk was right about that money. Money was my motivation, and I had school to back it up. I saw the importance of having both book and street smarts. All the old-timers were street smart, but they didn't fit school in. My crew and I blended in with both. It was necessary. I helped them understand why it was important to do both, and they understood the logic.

What am I going to do with all that money? I thought to myself. A low-key crib out in Jersey would be ill, but I was still young, so that was further down the line. I could cop a car, but that'll draw attention to me that I didn't need.

The only thing I could really think about was businesses. I could probably play the stock market or something too. I wasn't sure what I wanted to own or anything. Nothing was really in clear perspective yet. I just knew it was in the cards. I knew I didn't want to sell drugs in school anymore. It was a huge risk I just didn't want to take anymore. I needed to get with my brothers to figure out more plans.

I snapped back to reality as I realized I hadn't spoken to my guys all day.

What the fuck? I haven't seen Risk all day. Where is he at?

Sure enough, minutes later, I got a beep from an unknown number. It had our code, so I knew it had to be him. The bell was about to ring, signifying the end of the school day. All I was tryna do was get to a pay phone ASAP! I called the number back, and as I thought, it was Risk. He kept it brief and told me to gather up everyone so we could talk. I could tell from his tone that it was done and he had it.

The fellas were just as anxious as me to see the bread. We met at our usual spot, and I saw Risk with gym bags, so I knew it was done. I never really got hyped to the point where it was visible, but this time was different. I was hyped as fuck. How could I not be?

He smiled and dapped me up. "We did it, bro."

I looked in the bag and saw stacks of twenties and fifties. Still in a state of slight shock, I glanced over at Risk. "Yo, it's all here, right?"

He dapped me up again and laughed. "Hell, yeah, nigga. It's all here, B!"

Everyone on the team had at least six figures; we were all eating in a major way. I told them to come with me to the crib so I could put this bread up. We would all then go to meet the connect, as I had promised. We were about to flood the streets, and I knew it. I was going to buy ten keys for my workers and ten for myself.

That's going to run me a cool half a mil, but I know I can make that back with ease, I thought.

I just didn't feel safe holding all that money. So the drop was a must before the spot. My grandmother hadn't seen the guys in a while, so that'll be good too.

I wanted to talk to Risk more because he was the one who handled my work out in Harlem. My ten keys were going with him, and I felt it was time for my other workers to meet my brothers. This way, they'd know whom to speak to when I was not around. It would be a few hours before I returned home that night, and Sabrina was already blowing my pager up. We had to get in and get out. I wasn't sure how many keys the rest of the team was copping, but I knew for sure I was getting twenty to twenty-five bricks of that shit.

My mentality was grinding and eating together. What was family if we didn't all eat? I didn't need jealousy in my team because we'd come from the bottom and deserved it all. I heard Rah, John, and Rock talking about how many keys they were getting.

All I could think was *Damn, we're really doing this shit.*

I had to make sure we were all on the same page. Even though I knew we were, I felt the need to reiterate what I had always preached.

"We can't get complacent or sloppy now. This is the biggest step," I told them.

I hit the pay phone on my corner to call G. I told him I wanted to meet with him, D-Money, and the rest of them in two hours. I hung up the phone, and we walked the rest of the way to my crib. I opened the door and greeted my grandmother. She saw the fellas and greeted them with hugs and kisses. From the looks of things, with these gym bags, it looked like we were about to hoop on this nice Friday afternoon.

We go to my room, and I pulled up the floor panels where I kept work. I emptied out a few more sneaker boxes to put the cash in. Rock and Risk helped me count out 290 thousand and put it in the boxes. We placed the boxes back neatly under the floor. Surprisingly, I had enough room for it, but I knew that was about to change. In the next few weeks, I would need a storage unit to put the money in.

I told Grandma I would be back in a few hours after we finished hooping. We usually hooped on Fridays anyway, so everyone was prepared. I told them all to change and make it look like we were actually going to hoop. That way, when we left the connect's spot, we wouldn't look suspicious in the streets.

"Son, that's smart. I didn't even think of that," Rah stated.

I knew it was smart. *And that's why I'm the captain, and you're the first mate,* I thought jokingly. I didn't say it out loud though. I didn't want it to come out the wrong way, so I just nodded in agreement with him.

We left the crib and headed to the connect's spot. I was feeling a little nervous because of how deep we were and him meeting everyone. My guys were all mature, so the feeling passed real quick. If I felt like they weren't ready, there was no way I'd let them attend the meeting with Jose. The cab ride to the spot was nothing but jokes and laughs. It felt good to see everyone happy and living in good health. The cab stopped at the spot, and we got out.

"This is it. No turning back. Y'all wanted to meet him, right? Aight then, let's go."

We entered the spot, and I saw Jose. He greeted me with his usual banter. "*Que lo que, loco.* You're back already? I see you brought your *panas* too."

I replied yes and started introducing them to him. He shook all their hands and told them he would be honored to do business with them. After that was over, I told him I wanted twenty kilos. I let him know all of my guys individually wanted various numbers of bricks too.

He laughed and said, "Damn, loco, you're not playing at all. That's a hell of an order, but I know you always have the cash to back it."

I gave him my gym bag full of money, along with the money from the half of brick he fronted me. He started talking to Juan, one of his henchmen, who was always there when business was conducted.

"See, this is the type of guy I like. He is never late with money and always comes back to buy more. His word is gold to me."

Juan agrees because he knew I didn't play with the money.

"I assume that I don't have to count this, *verdad?*" he asked more rhetorically than an actual question.

I knew this but answered anyway, "Correct. When have you ever had to count it? I always come correct when I step to you."

He clapped his hands, laughing, and gestured in my direction as he told me how ambitious I was. I turned toward my guys and told them to put in their orders so we could get out of there. They started blurting out numbers. I heard 4, 5, 8, and 6. I could see they weren't playing either. I stood there very proud of them. They paid Jose, and I told them we had to go because we had one more stop to make.

Risk corrected me, saying, "Two more stops."

I was standing there, lost, like I missed something.

"Y'all cutting. Y'all own shit now. I got a spot uptown not too far from the crib with workers that will get it done. But I can't do all this shit by myself."

We all laughed because we missed that step. And what was more, I was for sure about to give him my ten for that purpose alone.

We finished conducting business and hopped in a cab to go meet my workers. We were running a little late, but I knew the guys were there. All my workers were at the spot with their cash, ready to get these keys off. I was sure they were going to step on them, too, and make more money because they were smart as hell.

I introduced everyone and told my workers to get real cool with my brothers. I let them know they were going to be working hand in hand. They were all cool with that. They'd heard me mention my brothers before, so it was kind of nice to finally put faces with the names. I told them I had ten bricks for them and all of them could get two bricks apiece.

Kev blurted out, "Good, because I only bought enough money for two anyway."

I laughed and said, "You're on point then."

They gave me the money one by one. I checked it all and put it in my gym bag. I gave them the beeper numbers of Rah, Rock, John, and Risk. I told them to page them if they needed help or anything. We dapped them up and caught another cab uptown.

I looked over at Risk and said, "Yo, if I have to catch another cab, I'm going to be tight. I'm tired of getting in these damn cabs."

He laughed and said, "Well, get tight then, nigga, because knowing you, you're not going to hop on a train or bus tonight. Definitely not like that." He pointed to my bag. I smiled and flipped him off. He was right. I wasn't doing anything of that sort with all this money on me.

The cab took us to a spot a few blocks from St. Nick Projects. I knew the area well. Risk and I used to sling dimes and nicks on these blocks when we were twelve.

"The fifth floor is where we are going," he said.

I nodded, and we walked into the elevator. We got to the floor, and from the outside, it looked like a regular floor. Once you got inside of apartment 5C, you would immediately notice they knocked two apartment walls down and made it into one big-ass room.

There were a bunch of chicks there, cutting dope up, and it amazed me how they did it. I watched the process a few times as they perfected it. I didn't have time to stay, so I gave Risk the keys, dapped everyone up, and hopped in another cab headed home. I had about $750 thousand, if I did the numbers correct in my head. I was more than happy with the day. My beeper was still going off, and I knew Sabrina was mad I didn't reach out to her yet. I knew I was going to hear it. I finally got home, put the rest of the cash up I told him right off, and started to settle down.

Sabrina had to be clocking me because as soon as I laid down, the house phone rang. I knew exactly who it was. I answered the phone and said hello. Before I could say anything else, Sabrina started yelling and cursing at me in her fast-ass Spanish accent to the point that if you weren't listening hard, you wouldn't understand it.

"Baby, I just got in the house. I was out with the fellas. You can ask my grandmother. We came here first to change into our hooping clothes and left right back out."

Still mad, she said, "So you didn't see a pay phone on the way at all, huh?"

"Yes, I did, but I know how you are. So I waited until I got home to hit you up, so you weren't screaming in my ear in public. I'm a private person, so please don't get mad at me for wanting to get yelled at in private. Sheesh."

"Don't try and make me smile with your charisma," she said while laughing.

I did it so well that I never realized when I did it. I told her it came naturally.

She told me she missed me and wanted to come over. I was tired, so I told her no. I told her I would pick her up in the morning and we'd go shopping. I hoped that would smooth everything over. She really hated that I was good with words and knew how to make her feel better at any time.

"Well, I'm coming over anyway," she said.

"If you do, I'm going to sleep, so there's not gonna be any sexual activity tonight."

She started getting mad, but I knew that would stop her from coming over. Plus, I was truly tired, so much so that I felt like I was about to pass out on the phone. She told me to go to sleep and that she would see me in the morning. I was sure she'd be over early to wake me up. At least she was letting me sleep now. I told her I loved her and then hung up the phone.

CHAPTER 8

I couldn't' front. I slept well last night. I was long overdue for some rest. I rarely ate breakfast, and this morning wouldn't be any different. I was spending the whole day with Sabrina and wanted to start it off by taking her out to eat. I turned my music on and hopped in the shower. While the music was playing, I started thinking about how much money I wanted to bring out to go shopping. I didn't want Sabrina asking questions, nor did I want her family asking questions about me buying her something very lavish.

This was where a job would come in handy. I had no intentions to work for anyone. I was comfortable with being my own boss. I made more money than the people that worked a nine to five. Why would I want to add that stress in my life? It would still be a good cover-up. I decided I was going to bring two grand and leave Grandma some money too. She could use it for the house or however she chose. I did things like that with her often. It was never nothing too extreme, but I liked to see her happy.

I picked out an outfit, but just like every other day, I didn't know what sneakers to wear. I had a thing for Nike, so I went with some Uptowns. I'd probably pick up a few new kicks while we were out there. I went through my stash and took out the two grand, but I didn't grab the fifties. I took the twenties because those were less suspicious. I was real cautious about shit like that. I hated attention or, should I say *unwanted* attention? I took some more money out and put it on the table for Grandma. I didn't smoke or do anything that would have her worrying, so she never really tripped on me.

She knew I loved basketball and would spend hours hooping, so she figured that was where my passion lived.

As I was heading to the door, I let Grandma know I was leaving. "Grandma, I'm spending the day with Sabrina. Not sure when I'll be back. Beep me if you need anything."

She just smiled. "Enjoy her company." She continued with "Look at you, all in love."

I told her to chill out and leave me alone with my addictive laugh following that true statement. She wished me well and to have fun. I kissed her on the cheek and closed the door.

Walking to Sabrina's block, I started thinking about businesses and homes. Shit, I had three-quarters of a million saved up with ease. I felt like I was always aware of my surroundings so I couldn't lose. Sabrina was looking good as hell when she answered her front door. I told her she looked mad sexy and that her mom looked good too.

She pinched me and said, "I told you to stop looking at my mother like that. Next time, you're not coming in."

I laughed and told her, "Okay. I'll just keep my thoughts to myself from now on."

Her mom heard her yelling at me and told her to leave me alone. She said, "Nenita, ya tú sabes que me veo bellísima. Déjale en paz. Solo está diciendo la verdad. [Girl, you know I look good. Leave him alone!]" It was all in Spanish. I was not sure if she knew I understood Spanish.

"That's exactly what I'm saying. I don't mean any disrespect."

She looked at me in shock because she didn't know I knew Spanish. She smiled and winked at me as Sabrina turned away, pulling me toward the door.

I chuckled in my head and thought, *Yep, she wants me.*

Sabrina closed the door and said, "Don't do it again!"

So I comforted her and told her that she was the only one I was crushing on. I gave her a kiss while grabbing her ass to butter her up. I knew how to get in her head, in more than one way, and she hated that. I made her feel good, so she didn't argue much with me after that. She told me she wanted to eat breakfast at this Colombian spot not too far from the neighborhood and we could walk there. I let her know I was for it as well.

The day was nice and sunny, so it would be nice to walk and talk to her. Our conversations were always great, but I wanted to see where her head was, what her plans were after high school. I knew college was in the future for her, but I didn't know where. She explained that she wanted to attend a university but she didn't really know where. She had a bunch of choices, from Penn State to Syracuse University. I honestly wanted to hear the colleges she wanted to go to see how far away they were. I was pleased with her response.

She asked me the same question. I told her that I only wanted to go to St. John's University and that was why I kept my grades up. I was sure I'd ace the SATs and get in without any problems; that was my dream school. She wanted to be close to me, and I wanted her near too. I just didn't think it was very smart of her to base her future off something fairly new. I didn't mention any of that to her though. I didn't want her to feel like I was pressing her or implying I didn't want her near. That wasn't the case at all. I wanted her near. I was just a logical thinker.

We got to the Columbian restaurant, and we were seated. As the waitress handed each of us a menu, I began to look it over. I had no idea what I wanted. Sabrina took my menu and said, "Let me help you, babe. You should get *cayeye* and *huevos pericos*."

I didn't know what they were, but if she suggested them, I was sure they were great. I trusted her judgment. I said, "Okay, I'll take that."

After she ordered, I told her to explain exactly what she suggested for me. It sounded good once she gave me the details. I could visualize it already as my stomach started to growl. The food came, and it looked delicious. I couldn't front; it tasted good too.

I thought to myself, *She makes me happy, and I want niggas to know she's mine.*

So I decided I wanted to buy her an iced-out chain but nothing too crazy. Just a small piece with my name on it. That would be dope. Plus a nice little cross to go with it. I was gonna have to do it on the sneak tip though. I asked her if she wanted to go to downtown Brooklyn, to Fulton or to Jamaica Avenue? She told me that she didn't care. She just wanted to spend time with me and told me to choose.

I knew a few jewelry stores in each spot, so I was good either way. Since it was going to be custom, I could pay when it was done, but I wanted to pay upfront. I needed help right now.

How am I going to do this shit without her knowing? I think I might just have to beep Risk, have him meet me on the low and let me hold some bread until I get home later tonight. Or I could have him pay for it, I thought. However, I wanted to pick the design out, so that was out of the question. I needed a few grand, though, on the fly. *One of those motherfuckers are going to let me hold something.*

I told Sabrina I was going to use the bathroom real quick. That way, I could sneak and make a call. I called Risk because I knew he always had bread on deck and he would make it to me in a timely manner. He told me he had five grand on him, and I was good for it. I told him the address, and he said he'd be there shortly as he was in the area, running through Brooklyn for the day.

I hung up the phone and went back inside to finish my food. I looked at Sabrina, and she looked so beautiful to me. She felt my intense stare and looked up as I was smiling at her.

"What? Stop staring at me eating, babe."

I told her exactly what I thought at the moment. "You're beautiful, baby. That's all. Don't mind me."

She smiled as she finished chewing and thanked me. I leaned in toward the middle of the table, and our lips met for a kiss. A few minutes passed, and I was almost finished with my food. As I took a bite, I looked up in the doorway and saw Risk standing there, trying to get my attention. I didn't want to make it obvious, so I acted like my beeper went off and told Sabrina I needed to call the person back. I kissed Sabrina once more and headed to the doorway.

Risk started laughing and handed me the bread. "You always on a date, nigga. When are you going to take us on a date?"

We both started laughing, and I responded, "When y'all pussy is as good as hers."

He started laughing harder and told me he was coming to my crib tomorrow so he could pick up the money. He wasn't in a rush for the cash, but I appreciated his willingness to get me the bread in such short notice. I wanted to show the same respect, so I told him tomorrow was cool. I then went back into the restaurant. I told the waitress I'd take the check because I was done eating. Sabrina was done too, so this was perfect timing.

I paid the check, and we left the restaurant. Now the question was, Where were we going? I didn't really care where; that wasn't my main focus. I wanted to know what she wanted, so I asked Sabrina where she wanted to go.

"Let's go to a Victoria's Secret, so I can get something to model for you."

"Oh, really?" I replied with my eyes big like a kid in a candy store.

She nodded her head and said, "Yes, papi."

This was a wrench in the plan because I didn't even know where a Victoria's Secret was at. *Damn! Does Queens Center Mall have one?*

I was stuck, but then it occurred to me there may be one in Manhattan. I knew for sure that there would be one in the city on Fifth Avenue or one of those avenues, so the train was our best option.

The train was packed, and I was kind of regretting taking it at this point. All the people here made things really tight. The only good thing was, I could hold Sabrina the whole ride and talk to her, so that made me relax. The ride was surprisingly pleasant. We got to the Victoria's Secret, and she started going crazy, asking me a bunch of questions in excitement. Did I like this? Did I like that? She had the perfect body to me, so it didn't matter what she wore. It would look good. I told her to get whatever she wanted and I'd buy it.

We got to the register, and I reached into my pocket to pay. I already had the money separated because I didn't want to pull out a wad of cash and get asked a million and one questions. I was smart though. I had thought about all this the day before. I paid the bill, and we left. On the next stop, she wanted to get some jeans and a few outfits but not from the city. She said that was too fancy for her. I decided we could go uptown to get her something fly. There was a few spots Risk and I used to shop at, where we used to sell weed. She liked sneakers just as much as I did, so we could knock us both out with one punch. There was also a jewelry spot up there I was very familiar with. I copped my Jesus piece from there, and I knew the owner very well. He was a cool Muslim dude named Ahmad. I was sure he'd give me a good deal on the things I wanted to get.

We got to the store, and I let her shop. I told her I wanted to go next door to speak to my man in the jewelry store. She had no idea what was going on, but I told her I would only be like five to ten minutes to put her at ease. I walked inside the jewelry store, and I saw my man Ahmad. I greeted him and dapped him up, telling him, "Long time no see." I let him know I didn't have much time because shorty was next door. I told him I wanted to surprise her with a name chain and ring to match but I didn't want cheap shit. He knew I didn't want anything cheap and showed me a few plates to help me with my idea.

I found the perfect one and told him to do my name in script. I told him to put diamonds in it for my girl but not too big and not too small. He told me it would take a few days to make, but I already knew that, so I wasn't concerned. I just wanted to know numbers. I let him know I also needed a nice cross or heart locket for her. The first one he picked up drew my attention, and I told him right off the bat I wanted that today.

I asked Ahmed the most important question, "So what's the damage going to be?"

He paused for a second, doing the math in his head. "For you, $3,500."

It should be more, but there was nothing I could do with that. I let him know that it was cool. I paid, and he put the necklace in a box and asked if I wanted a bag. I declined and told him I'd put it in my pocket. I was going to give it to her later on when she least expected it. I also let him know Risk would pick it up when it was done, so I put his number down for the point of contact.

My ten minutes was up, and I knew I had to hurry back before Sabrina came to find me. I walked out the jewelry store, and she was still looking at stuff, being very indecisive about the things she wanted.

"Babe, just get it all if you can't decide."

"Are you sure?" she said with so much excitement in her voice. I nodded yes and started looking around at the sneaker section. I wanted to get some new kicks and a few outfits for myself. I picked a few pair of Uptowns, Airmax 95s, and some Jordans. I knew what I wanted. I was a man of simple tastes.

To keep her happy was my goal. I still couldn't believe her parents let her spend a night over at my house like that though. Maybe it was because I looked like a really nice guy and had things going for me. I knew if it was my daughter, all this would be out of the question. Their trust in her was beyond me and definitely something I'd never seen before. She gathered all the things she wanted and continued to pass them to me, like I was her human-sized shopping cart. I took all the items to the register and paid for them.

This was a long day so far, and I was hungry again, but I didn't want to go to a restaurant. I was craving some White Castle cheeseburgers. I asked her if she liked them, and surprisingly enough, she said yes. That just made me love her even more. On the low, I loved White Castle. They never messed up my stomach like they did everyone else's.

After we ate, we hopped in a cab and headed back to my crib. While in the cab, I was plotting on the right moment to give her this heart locket. I knew the perfect time to do it, and she would love it. We had a good day, but I was so tired of carrying all these bags. I loved this girl, and I wanted to tell her everything, but I didn't want to lose her.

I'd never lied to her at all. She hadn't asked me questions about money or these dates, but I could feel them coming soon. She probably already knew what I did. I mean, she did say I looked like the boss at our first actual encounter. I had many questions with not enough answers.

We got to my house and started watching TV on the living room couch. She snuggled up against me, and I knew this was it. This was the perfect time to take the locket out of my pocket and put it around her neck. I was smooth with it. I told her I had something to show her, and I pulled the black box out of my pocket. She started smiling and asked me what it was.

"Just open it, and see."

And she did just that.

The look on her face was priceless. Then she kissed me along with the biggest hug. In between kisses, she told me I was the best boyfriend ever. I unclasped the locket and pulled her hair up so I could put the necklace around her neck.

She kissed me again in a more seductive manner and whispered in my ear. "Let's go in the room, and I'll thank you properly, papi."

I smirked and followed her as she led me to my room.

CHAPTER 9

I started thinking about what Risk said the previous day. He was right. We really hadn't hung out like we used to because of all the money we were making. It was time to do something with the fellas. Maybe we could go to a theme park or something. Six Flags definitely sounded like the move for today. I knew Risk was coming over shortly for the money he loaned me yesterday. I decided to just call the fellas and have them come through too. I was sure no one was really busy, and if so, they'd cancel everything for a trip like that. We needed wheels to get there though. I knew Rock usually borrowed his mom's truck on the weekends, so I would let him know, and we would be straight.

I called the fellas up, and they all agreed to the trip. Everyone thought it was a dope move, although Risk gave me a little bit of shit.

"I see my little date line from yesterday had you thinking," he said.

Both of us started cracking up, but I couldn't front; he was right.

"Shut the fuck up, and get over here as soon as possible, son."

I showered up while Sabrina still slept after a long night of sex. When I got back to my room, I woke her up to tell her my moves for the day. I told her I was going to be gone with the fellas the whole day. I wanted to come home to her, so I gave her my key to make a copy. I let her know I left her some money to do whatever she wanted but that she better be here when I got home. I kissed her on the forehead and made my way out of the room.

I told Grandma the plans for the day and about Sabrina. She just smiled and nodded her approval. This was a risky move because

I had a lot of money in that room and she could possibly snoop around. I wasn't too worried, though, because the money was so far underneath the real shoes. She wouldn't bother to go that in depth with it. I didn't keep any letters or anything chicks gave me because they never really meant much to me. I had nothing to worry about. I knew I was good. As I approached the door, I saw Rock was in the front of the crib, waiting for me to come out.

"You ready to go to Six Flags, or you still on a date?" He laughed, and the rest of the fellas joined in on the joke.

I shot back, "Oh, y'all got jokes today, I see, huh?"

They'd been fucking with me lately because they'd never seen me so involved with a female before. I never slacked on the business aspect of things, so they knew it was because I cared for her. On the drive to Six Flags, I told them they could hit up the connect whenever. I wasn't trying to be greedy with it. I wanted everyone to eat and get money.

In the past, a lot of people got killed or lost friends because of shit like this. Not trying to let their friends meet the connect put a wedge between them. I truly watched and learned from the older heads. Money would never be an issue between the crew. I felt as though greed ruined a lot of good teams in the past and a lot of good niggas got left because of that fact alone. They were happy, so what more could I ask for? The only person I really had an issue with selling drugs was Rock, because of his skills on the basketball court.

I didn't want to feel responsible for him not excelling to his max potential because of me. I kept him under the wing for that alone. He understood where I was coming from when I mentioned it, but he was still at it. This was his fallback just in case the basketball thing didn't work out. I often wondered how life after high school would be. Where would they go to school? These were my brothers, and I would die for them. I wondered a lot about their futures as well as mine. This game had no love in it. It would chew you up and spit you out in a heartbeat, so you had to be on your toes at all times.

We got to the park, and it was not as packed as we thought it would be, so we were all relieved. I wanted to get on the craziest roller coaster they had, so I bought us all tickets, and we looked for just that. The day was probably one of the best days we'd ever had together, and I was very pleased.

We snapped a few flicks, and I was thinking, *Damn, this is going to be a good memory to tell the families about in the future.*

We had it all, and we were on our way to being richer than most. We lived without a care in the world. I started wondering how Sabrina was doing. Was she looking through my stuff? Did she find the sneaker boxes full of cash?

I was sure all was good because if it wasn't, she'd be blowing up my pager right now. She was probably hanging out or getting her hair done. I was cold toward females. They meant nothing to me. So for me to be thinking about Sabrina like this, it was definitely new to me.

I didn't want to lose focus on my bigger goals right now. Not saying she was not important, but I knew better. Should I be more guarded with her? I didn't know, but whatever she was doing to me, I liked the feeling. I couldn't wait to get home to her. I wondered if she made her key already? Tons of questions were looming through my head, but I was so happy I had her.

CHAPTER 10

The final week of school was here, and I was as hyped as could be. I had made tons of money off these pills and coke. It had been a successful year for the team and myself. I had over a mill stashed in storage spaces, and my team wasn't far behind. We were winning on all levels! Just as that thought entered my mind, I got a beep from Jose. I knew it was Jose because of the code he used.

What could he possibly want from me this early in the morning? I wondered. I decided to take a trip to the pay phone outside of the school to call him back to see what was on his mind.

I hit him up, and it turned out he wanted to see me to discuss business. I couldn't front. I loved to hear things like that, so I left school early. It wasn't like I needed to be there for the final days anyway. I only went because all my homies were still in school. The whole cab ride to the spot, I was trying to think what kind of business he wanted to discuss. I couldn't come up with anything, but fuck it, I'd be there soon enough to find out.

The cab pulled up to the spot, and I gave the cabbie a fifty. I told him to keep the engine running because I knew it wouldn't take long. He agreed to wait. I walked in the spot, feeling a little apprehensive but also excited. Anytime Jose mentioned wanting to discuss business, it meant money and not chump change. Jose embraced me with a handshake and hug.

"Tiguere, I know you're in school. Sorry for the bother."

"It's cool, but what was so important you couldn't wait until after I was finished for the day?"

As soon as the words left my mouth, I kind of regretted the way the statement sounded. It sounded almost confrontational. That was not the intent of my question. Jose either didn't notice or just ignored it.

"You've brought me a lot of customers in the last few weeks," he said. "Your boys are buying kilos every week."

I knew this because they always told me their moves. "Okay, so what's up?"

He chuckled a little bit. "No issues, loco. I want to give you a better price." He stopped and looked at me as if to make clear his next point. "But this price is only for you."

Shit, I can dig that, was all I was thinking.

"How much?"

"Instead of $28,000 a kilo, I'll give it to you for $20,000. This is only for you, because you've been loyal to me for years and I need to move more of this shit faster and I know you can handle it."

Shit, that's eight grand off a great price. I could cop heavier and make so much money off them with or without the cutting. I told him that I'd take the price, and I would be back later to get more work.

I shook his hand, thanked him for the price, and left the spot. I hopped in my cab, so I could head back to school.

All I could think about on the ride back was if I should tell the fellas I got a better price. I didn't want money to be an issue with my team, but I didn't want any friction between Jose and me either. He just looked out for me in a major way. I had to make decisions and make them quick. Fuck, this was going to be hard. How was I going to play it off? I thought about it a little more.

Jose had never counted my money, and he knew the guys would come correct when it was time to cop, so he didn't really check their money either. Besides, if he wanted it to be between me and him, it would be wise of him to not count in front of the fellas.

Fuck it, this can work. I still have $750,000 under my bed in sneaker boxes that I can use. I'm going to have to reach out to my cousin Jay and front him a few bricks to expand the operation. I need work *everywhere. I don't want any droughts. If there's a drought on a block, I want to be able to supply them.*

I still felt bad that I couldn't tell the fellas, especially Risk, but I had to get it. I still kept thinking if this might cause trouble in the future. Or was there a way for it to work for all of us? Would they do the same for me? I loved these dudes, but the only dude that I knew for certain would do the same for me was Risk. I'd been in plenty of situations with him, so I knew it'd work with him.

I told the cab driver to turn around and take me back to the spot that we just came from. I started thinking maybe that was a test from Jose. I couldn't accept that offer without Risk getting the same deal. Shit, he's the one that steps on the keys for me so it's only right he gets the same price.

I walked back into the spot, and Jose looked surprised to see me.

"That deal you just gave me is great and all, but I wouldn't feel right if my man didn't get the same deal, the one I brought to meet you the first time. He's my other half when it comes to this."

Jose replied, "You're a loyal kid. I can see you don't want money to come between your crew. I'll give him the same price I gave you, but that's it—no one else."

I felt 100 percent better. I couldn't wait to tell Risk about this shit. I knew he would be happy as fuck too. I hopped back into the cab to head back to school. I started laughing because I knew this cab driver was like, "I'm getting paid off all these trips."

I got back to school around lunchtime. I knew the homies had questions for me because I wasn't there for the start of lunch. Sabrina was definitely looking for me after second period, and I was nowhere to be found. As soon as I walked into the building and turned the corner, I saw Sabrina. She started talking fast with her Dominican, New York, accent.

"Where the fuck was you at? I haven't seen you in two periods. Where were you?"

I didn't even have an answer for her. I had really just thought about the possibility of me seeing her only a few minutes before the encounter.

"Babe, relax. You're going in for no reason at all. I was talking to Dean Chapman about next year. I wanted to know if he had any good recommendations I could use to get into St. John's after high school."

I knew she wasn't expecting that. That would hold her over for the time being, I thought. Her facial expression reflected my sentiments. I felt bad about lying to her, but I had to cover my tracks.

"Well, you could've told me something. You had me waiting for you, and you never showed. Anyway, I wrote you this letter."

She kissed me while I gave her a tight hug and grabbed her ass at the same time. I let her know I couldn't wait to read her letter and we'd chat after school. The cafeteria was packed today for some reason. I was not too sure why, but it was the end of the school year, so it was to be expected.

I saw Rock and John from a distance as I made my approach to our table. We went to sit down when I saw motion in my peripheral vision. A dude that I'd seen around the school before tried to lay me out with a sucker punch. I never knew the dude had a problem with me, nor did I have a problem with him. I saw him swing a punch, so I dipped it and threw up my hands. My adrenaline was rushing. I hadn't had a fight in a while, so this was new to me.

I did a quick mental check to see if I had drugs or anything on me before I mopped the floor with this dude. I didn't even get my book bag off. There was no chance to give him one up on me.

While creating space between me and him, I wondered what this was over. At this point, it didn't matter to me. It was time to do work.

He swung at me first with a two-piece, missing with the right but connecting with the left. The hit didn't hurt, but I heard the crowd roaring for him as he connected. I knew this fight would have to end soon because school security would be coming shortly. He threw two more shots, missing them both. I dipped them and moved in swiftly, hitting him with a three-piece combo. The uppercut dazed him, and he wobbled backward. I knew I had the upper hand, so I dug in some more. I hit him with a strong right and a rib shot to put him down on his knees.

I had this kid on his knees, and I was just beating his face in to the point where I saw blood. I saw Rock and John moving in, ready to stomp him out, but I waved them off.

"Nah, let that nigga breathe, yo!" I said while grabbing his shirt.

In my head, I didn't want beef with anyone, but I wanted to punish this kid—punish him to the point that when niggas saw him, they would know and understand what I was capable of. He was leaking bad, and if security didn't get here soon, I was going to do more damage to this kid. As the last strike I gave him connected, I saw one of the security guards coming toward me. It was my man Al. I took my left hand, unclenching his shirt full of blood, and let him drop to the floor.

I threw my hands up as Al rushed over and tried to subdue me. Another security guard was coming to help with the scene. I just kept telling myself, "Calm down, you already won, so there will be no more problems with this guy." But who was this dude? It was the only thing playing over and over in my head. I knew I would find out soon. I could see Rock and John holding their hands up. They felt like it was a major victory for us, but they knew how I was.

Al took me to the dean's office, and as we were on the way, he asked me what had happened.

"I don't know at all. Al, I've never even spoken to that dude before. I came in the lunchroom. I'm walking to my table, and he tried to sneak me out of nowhere."

I knew I wouldn't get into trouble because I didn't start the fight, but I did some serious damage to that kid. As soon as those thoughts entered my head, I saw the dude come in the office with the other security guard. I was still trying to figure out what I did to him that was so crazy that he wanted to sneak on me.

Al blurted out, "Donavan, what happened?"

So now I have a name for this kid. All I needed now was to find out what was his issue.

"This nigga stole my girl!!"

I wanted to know who his girl was. I replied, "Who's your girl, dog?"

He replied, "Sabrina."

I chuckled to myself and said, "How's she your girl? I've never heard her speak of you or anything. So you sneak me because of a chick?"

This was insane to me. I thought I had real beef with this dude, but I was sadly mistaken. I wasn't taking it lightly though. She didn't tell me she was talking to anyone at all—not that it really mattered. I never got that heads-up from her at all.

"Were you going with her, or were y'all just talking?'

He said nothing. I knew exactly where to find these answers, so I didn't bother to ask any more questions. I asked Dean Chapman if I could leave because I was just defending myself. He said I could, but he had to call my point of contact to inform them of the situation. I knew Grandma would be worried, but not too worried because I rarely got into trouble.

He called and spoke to her first. When he finished discussing the incident, I asked to speak to her.

She asked if I was okay and if I won. I replied, "I'm good, Grandma. Of course, you know I did. I don't even have a scratch on me." She knew I was okay. I told her I'd see her later tonight and that I loved her.

I hung up the phone and walked past this guy Donovan as I went back to class. I wanted it to be over, so I hit him with a nod. I wanted to let him know and understand I didn't want problems from here on out. However, with dudes like that, one never knew.

I started focusing more and more on my surroundings. If this wasn't a major factor to wake me up, I didn't know what else it would take. This guy messed up my day. I didn't get a chance to talk to Risk or talk to the guys about how their stuff was moving on the streets. I went to the bathroom before returning to class to wash the blood off my hands. My hands were definitely hurting after that fight. I had questions for Sabrina, so all my afterschool shit was going to get pushed back. I had to get to the bottom of this today. I walked inside the classroom, and the class went wild, yelling all crazy. I saw chicks looking at me seductively, like they wanted to get with me too. I knew exactly what it was. It felt good, but I didn't want the attention right now. I saw Risk in the back of the class, and he was smiling, telling me the whole school heard about the fight.

"Where the fuck were you in the midst of all this?" I said to him as we dapped each other up.

He started cheesing crazy hard. "Son, I had a joint I was fucking with during lunch, so I was in the bathroom."

I was dying laughing because that was some shit I would do. I told him we had to chop it up after class, just us two. He was trying to get me to tell him now, but I told him to just wait and that it would be worth it. He understood and dropped it.

All I was thinking was *I really washed that kid up.*

A few minutes passed, and the bell was about to ring. I put my books away and get ready to leave the classroom. As soon as I put the last book away, the bell rang. Risk and I walked out of the classroom, and we started talking about the fight earlier. I told him who the dude was and why he wanted to fight me.

We both laughed as Risk stated, "He really tried to get at you over a chick?" He shook his head. "That's crazy."

I knew it was crazy, too, but I didn't want to get into all that. I wanted to let him know about the price change with the bricks.

"Yo, the connect beeped me earlier today, and I went to see him."

He looked directly at me and replied, "Okay, so what's the issue or news?"

My response was short. "He gave us, as I pointed to us two, a better price. Twenty a key is what we are getting, but you can't tell the rest of them. I picked you because you're my right hand. You break the shit down so we can make more, so it was only right. He only wanted me to get that price, but I couldn't leave you in the wind."

A huge smile crept over his face, and he replied, "Son, that's dirt cheap even if we don't cut it. We could still make mad bread off them."

I shook my head in agreement with him because I knew it was true. He thanked me and told me he would hold it down as usual. This was a come-up for us, and we had to take it. We talked about expanding. I had Canarsie and Coney Island on lock, but I wanted to move into East New York, the Stuy, and Crown Heights. He had Harlem locked down from St. Nick Projects and further down. We needed Queens and the BX, and we would have the city on lock.

I told him I had a few people that could move shit. Only thing was, I would have to front them a few bricks in order to get them on their feet first. I knew I still had to call Jay and meet with him. I also had a few more good dudes that would be down for getting money. I told Risk to give me a week and it'd be worked out. We were going to have to find other spots to chop up these blocks because we didn't want to make the spot hot. Everything needed to be worked out, and I knew just how to do it. I just needed time. Cocaine and pills were all we needed. The weed wasn't major to me. That was for beginners to us. I sold weed uptown when I was twelve on Risk's old block with him. It was a good product, but I didn't see major money from it.

The day seemed to move really fast after the fight in the lunchroom. Everything was boiling down to the point where I was going to see Sabrina again. The wait was over, and as soon as the bell rang, she actually came to find me with the look of concern on her face. She had no idea that I was just hotheaded with no kind of patience whatsoever.

The first words she uttered to me were "Really? You're fighting now? The whole school has been telling me about how bad you beat up Donovan."

I decided to chime in.

"Yeah and who the fuck is Donovan? Why is he saying you're his girl and I took you away from him? Why did he try to sneak me? What is it that you're not telling me?"

"Yeah, I have questions, too, and I want answers now."

She looked at me with sort of a shocked and confused stare.

"Donovan is my ex-boyfriend that I stopped talking to way before we got together. We aren't together. He has been stalking me for some time now."

It was adding up. When I came into the school after seeing the connect, I definitely peeped him. He wasn't too far from the lockers where Sabrina stood, but I dismissed it. I figured he was waiting for someone. He must have seen the kiss, hug, and slight grope I gave to her right before entering the cafeteria and couldn't take it anymore.

"So now you're telling me I have to watch my back from dudes you used to mess with? Let me know who they are right now, so I can protect myself."

I knew there wouldn't really be any problems with this anymore, but I still wanted to hear answers. Sabrina was in tears because of the situation, but I had no intentions of calming her at that moment. All I wanted to know was where this kid lived so I could go check him—one, to make sure it was dead and, two, for her safety. I didn't want anyone stalking my girl.

I asked Sabrina where he lived. She told me he was from Brooklyn and that he lived in Crown Heights, on Crown Street. I knew the area, so I had plans to find this man and talk to him. I didn't want beef. I just wanted peace. When someone knew they could be touched with ease, people tended to relax. I could have dudes camped out in front of his crib and leave him right there.

I was livid with Sabrina, although it wasn't her fault. It was still her fault in my mind. I still gave her a kiss to comfort her before I went to handle that situation. It would be dope if I brought her with us to let her know it was real. Then again, that was risky because that was an uncharted town for us, so we might need a hammer for this function. I wanted to get to his block and not really shut it down, but I wanted to talk to him and let him know my intentions. It was time to gather up the team, but we needed a hammer for this outing. I knew Rock had one, so I told him to bring it and meet me at my crib. He was about that action. He hung up the horn and was at the crib within minutes. I didn't think we would be needing the hammer, but you never knew with some people. Hopefully, I could talk sense into this dude, or it could get real ugly quick.

I see Rah, John, and Risk approaching my block. I knew it was about to get crazy. I planned on waiting all day till he went to his crib. I could've had more people with me, but there was no need. I didn't want beef, and Rock had the hammer. He wasn't scared to pull it either. We started heading to Donovan's crib, and it was nothing but jokes and laughs.

"When he connected with that first punch, I thought I was gonna have to jump in, son," Rock blurted out, followed by a laugh. I started laughing because I knew the joke would come up, but I also knew the ending of this story.

"I had it, son. Even great fighters get hit sometimes," I replied.

The train ride to Donavan's crib was full of excitement. It felt like we haven't had that much fun on the train in ages. We finally arrived on his block, and I couldn't front; I was feeling nervous. In the same breath, I was feeling untouchable because I was with my homies. I also really wanted to see the dude's face because the swelling didn't kick in when I saw him. We knew the block he lived on, but we had no actual address to knock on doors with.

John started asking people that went in and out of buildings and houses if they had seen Donovan or knew where he lived. We sent John to do the dirty work because he had a friendly face. It would've looked crazy if I were to ask people that. Surprisingly enough, John found out exactly where the dude lived and all. John checked to see if he was home and didn't get an answer, so we knew no one was home. We waited for about an hour before I saw him walking up to his crib.

I saw him first as we locked eyes. He was *dolo*, and I had my guys with me. To be honest, I expected him to run, but he didn't. He had heart, and I could see that at that moment. His face was really beaten up from the fight. I couldn't lie. I felt accomplished at that moment, like I did something with that fight. Donovan picked up his pace, walking rapidly in our direction, as if he were ready to take on all of us. I respected his heart for that moment.

He made his way to me and shouted, "What's up?"

He was in defense mode, but I didn't want the trouble. I just wanted to talk to the man. That was all. He didn't even peep. I had Rock off to a distance with the hammer. I had him afar, so he could blend in with the block. But if it got shady, I could give him the look and have him do him in.

I responded, "Chill, son, I'm not here for that. I don't want beef or trouble. I came to talk to you." His face showed visible signs of relief that I was not there to continue today's fight. He agreed to talk to me.

"Sabrina told me you were stalking her, and she didn't like it. I don't like it either. So it would be wise of you to stay away from her because she's already spoken for."

This was a little jab thrown out there to see if he would take the bait. I really didn't want problems because I didn't know this guy. I had no idea what he was capable of, but I wanted to get my point across.

He replied, "That bitch is lying. Ain't nobody stalking her."

Now at this moment, I could erupt and beat his ass again because of the disrespect, but I replied in the calmest voice ever, "Watch your mouth, son. She's no bitch, and I don't appreciate you using those words or language toward her."

All this while still remaining calm. He respected it and didn't use any more derogatory words about her. I knew I had his attention, and I made it clear I wasn't playing. Plus, I knew exactly where his head rested. He was in no position to try to challenge.

We shook hands, and we went on our way. Risk and Rah started joking as we walked away, saying, "Shit, when he called her a bitch, we were going to rush him, but you responded with a good clean up to that mess."

We laughed. It was a good day. We didn't have to use any guns or any more violence. Plus, Risk and I also got a better price for the keys, so we were winning.

Oh shit! I forgot Sabrina wrote me a note. I suddenly remembered our exchange earlier. I looked down at my swollen and sore hands and said to myself, *I'll read that shit later.*

I just wanted to ice my hands and lie down because I was tired as hell after the long day.

CHAPTER 11

Weeks had gone by, and surprisingly, I had stacked up close to $2 million in cash. The product was moving, and I had plans of extending the business further than expected. I started thinking heavily about moving the pills Down South. More so because of the climate always being warm and the crazy nightlife, I could make a killing. I could take over cities like Miami, but I had to get down there and find the right people. It was summertime, so the trip shouldn't be hard to do with the team. Finding the right people to move it down there was the issue. I'd cross that avenue when I decided to move that way.

The summer was panning out to be dope, and Sabrina was looking so good with her fine self. We hadn't had any problems since that fight in school a few weeks ago. I thought that it was time I did something to show her I really cared. I actually forgot about the name chain my man Ahmad made for her. Risk probably picked it up and had it sitting on his dresser or something. I hit him up to see if my assumption was correct.

I called Risk, and his little brother answered the phone.

"What's up, little man? Where's Risk at?"

He replied, "Right here. Hold on."

I could hear him yelling for his brother in the background and Risk asking him who was on the phone for him. Little Man told him it was me. Risk must have thought it was important from the urgency I sensed in his voice when he answered.

"I just wanted to know if you went to get that chain for me, son?"

"Oh, shit, yeah. I had it. I forgot to give it to you a while back. My fault. You want me to run it your way?"

Relief audibly flooded his voice.

"Yeah," I replied.

He told me he'd be over in an hour or so to drop it off and hung up the horn.

I felt like hooping today but wasn't too sure if I wanted to waste a bunch of energy. The truth was, I could really play basketball on another level. I just didn't want to play on the team due to long practices and things like that. I did it just for fun and the love of the game. There was money to be made, and that NBA life wasn't a sure shot thing for me. I knew a spot in Queens that was low key. I could get up some shots and work up a little sweat for a few hours. I'd head that way after Risk came through, and he should be here any minute.

No sooner did the words enter my head than the bell rang, and I knew who it was. I didn't bother to even ask. Risk came inside my crib and dapped me up while handing the necklace over to me. He started apologizing for not getting it to me weeks ago. I wasn't mad at all. Shit, I even forgot, so it was cool to me. Risk then entered the kitchen where Grandma was cooking and listening to her music. He greeted her with a kiss on the cheek and asked how she was doing. My guys were like brothers to me, and Grandma treated them as such. There was never any bad blood in the crew, surprisingly. I guessed we didn't let money ruin our bond. You couldn't put a price on loyalty and friendship with great people.

I asked Risk if he wanted to hoop with me in Queens. He started talking about how he didn't have anything with him, which meant nothing in all honesty. He knew we could go to any store and pick something up, so that wasn't an issue. He was probably more focused on getting money or future goals. I knew him well. I told him I had extra shorts and a tee and we would pick him some sneakers up on the way there. Plus, we could talk business as well. He liked talking business, so I knew that would work on him.

We left the crib and started walking toward the end of the block.

"You trying to sell drugs forever or what?" I suddenly blurt out.

It wasn't supposed to come out that way, but the question had to be asked. He looked at me a little perplexed as to my line of questioning and replied, "Nah, son, you know I have bigger shoes to fill."

"So what do you want to do?"

The conversation became interesting at that point because Risk started talking about different businesses, how he wanted to be the first person to bring a business to NYC that was mainly a Down South attraction. I was intrigued; I couldn't front. I wanted parts in it too.

We had years to go before we could make it happen and go legit. We just had to move accordingly and not get sloppy along the way. I wanted a bunch of businesses to make me a lot of money I knew for sure. I didn't want to sell drugs for the rest of my life. This drug money shit was so fast and easy; it worked for us right now. I started thinking if it was possible to make the money that I was making now go legit. Or was it just something I made up in my head? From the sounds of it, Risk was on to something, and I liked the lane we were in. It was very fitting and promising.

I knew the other guys had similar plans, but they weren't thinking that much toward the future like we were. We all still pretty much had the same vision. Most importantly, I didn't want Sabrina to find out this side of me. She was so ill, and I felt like I would let her down if she found out. I wondered if she knew already but was waiting for me to tell her. I had no clue, but I wasn't going to come forward and tell her I moved heavy weight. If she wanted to know, she'd ask. I was just not ready for that day yet.

"Ayo, Steph! We should gather up everyone and go get a few games in," Risk said.

I told him it was a good idea, and we could get something to eat afterward. We both agreed and took a trip to Rock's crib to scoop him up. We could use his mom's truck to pick everyone else up. It would be good to get everyone together and kick it and play a few games of ball. As we walked up to Rock's house, we saw him sitting on the stoop. It looked like he was waiting for someone, but then again that was typical for NYC in the summertime. No feeling was greater than hanging with your boys with no school or projects due the next day.

As we approached Rock, we saw he already had a ball. It was like he knew we were coming his way. We dapped each other up as we told Rock what we had planned for the day. Rock was with anything that involved money or basketball. Basketball was his life, and he took it seriously. He was ranked as one of the best guards in the city, so he was nice for real. We could all hoop, but he took that shit way more seriously than we did. I respected him for that.

"Ay yo, Rock? You think your mom will let us use the whip to pick Rah and John up and head to the courts?"

"I'm sure she wouldn't mind as long as we put gas in it and don't get into any accidents."

At that moment, I thought we needed a car or truck of our own to drive around in. It would be kind of dope for us to have a car every day for senior year. It was kind of funny that I had a few million stacked up, and I didn't even own a car.

"She said yeah!" Rock said as he came out of the house with the keys in his hand.

We hopped in the car and drove off to pick up the rest of the guys. I almost forgot about the sneakers and shorts for Risk. He wasn't thinking about it either though. He was zoned out, listening to music with his eyes closed. His head was nodding as if he were decoding the lyrics as they were being spat out. He let out a "Mmmmm" while nodding his head, feeling the beat knocking. I didn't even bother trying to reach him. He was in his zone, and I understood that.

As John and Rah hopped in the truck, I told Rock to make the quick stop so Risk could get his sneakers and shorts. When we got to the park, it was kind of crowded—not only with hoopers and spectators but also pretty chicks on the benches watching whoever was playing.

"I'm about to kill today," I told the crew. They shook their heads in agreement, with the intentions on doing the same thing. It was time to show off, and there were girls there, so that was an extra incentive to kill on the court. We called next as we started warming up.

I knew one of the dudes already playing. He was nice, but he wasn't a team player. Plus, it looked like his chemistry was off with the other four guys he was running with. From the looks of it, it looked like he'd never played with these dudes before. I knew we had the advantage because we'd been playing together for years. We were actually a great team. I could run the one or the two. Risk played the two or the three. Rah played the four and John the five. Rock could play the same positions as me, so we were really good.

We get on the court, and it was just as I expected. We were going to twenty-one by ones and twos. I let Rock push the ball up and orchestrate the offense. It was natural to him, so he started running plays for us. I got the rock and dumped it down low to John for the post up, and it was looking like easy work. Next play, it was the same thing. But I gave it to Rah for the midrange jumper, and he connected. The team we were playing was good. They hit a few shots and tied the game up. However, I knew I hadn't even shot the ball nor had Rock. So I told Rock that I was going to push it up this time. I wanted to go at a faster pace and potentially draw the double team. I'd then kick it out to Rock to see if he could catch an alley-oop then shoot it or pass to Risk for the open three.

I drove to the basket after I hit one of the dudes with a mean in-and-out crossover. I dished it to Risk for the open three on the elbow. Risk hit the shot and started talking shit to the dude that was supposed to be guarding him.

"You should put your hand up or something, son, or else I'll be hitting that all day."

I laughed and pointed to him as we trotted back down the court the other way.

"Oh yeah, got 'em!" I yelled out as I caught a bad pass for the steal.

"We're going the other way, Rock. Let's go. I got you on this one," I yelled to him.

I started pushing the ball even faster across the court and make eye contact with Rock, and he knew the alley-oop was coming. I saw him take off as I threw the ball in the air for him to catch it and freak it with the jam. Rock caught the ball and windmilled it. The crowd went crazy.

I couldn't front; I got hyped at that moment. I smelled blood from our opponents, and I wasn't going to let up. I started playing tighter defense after the jam. I wanted to keep the intensity up to the highest level that I could and, at the same time, involve the crowd with as many oohs and aahs as possible to keep the other team out of it. I didn't think the other team realized that I could shoot from anywhere on the court and bring it inside if I wanted. I just hadn't so far because I was trying to get everyone involved.

I told the team to clear it out, and I was ready to make my defender dance with the dribble I had packed for him. I started dribbling, drove, and hit him with a mean bow tie, which left him still. Then I drove to the rack for the layup. I already made up my mind that I wanted the next basket too. It was going to be a sham god crossover with a jumper this time. I saw the prey trying to tighten up the defense as I was coming down the court, just as I expected. I wanted him to do just that.

I baited him until I got him to the three-point line, and I initiated the crossover move. The move hit him so hard he fell, and I just threw up the jumper as the crowd went wild. I didn't care if I made the shot or shot the ball anymore for the rest of the game. After I made the dude fall, my mission for the rest of the game was done. The shot went around the rim like a Draino shot before finally dropping. My team went wild as I stood there with a smirk on my face as I hit them with the MJ shrug.

It was over now. The other team tried to make a run, but they weren't as confident as they were earlier. I got my guys a few more easy shots to get ready to wrap up the game. I wanted Rock to get the last point to end it. I brought the ball inbounds and passed it to Rock and told him to finish it. He was the secret weapon, the one with scholarships and all, so I wanted everyone to see what he was made of. I knew he was going to go for the dunk, but the type of dunk he was going to do I wasn't sure of.

So I wanted to sit and watch like it was a movie. Once Rock drove, I saw the lane part like the Red Sea, and he took off with a crazy-ass dunk that I had never seen him do. Rock went in between his legs with it, as he adjusted himself in the air to avoid the block for what looked like a Dominique Wilkins pump followed by a rattle rim-shaking dunk. The whole park went crazy.

I started smiling and told him he didn't have to do that man like that. We ran a few more games till we were tired and couldn't go anymore. Being out on the court like that made me want to take basketball seriously, but I had no intentions on practicing and drilling every day. My discipline wasn't anywhere to be found when it came to that. Still, it was a great thought. I needed to get home and shower up. I also needed to see Sabrina. She hit me a few times on the hip, which led me to believe she probably wanted to see me too. I was starving, and a nice meal from Grandma would definitely do the trick.

Walking down my block, I saw a chick that resembled Sabrina. I was a distance away, so I wasn't too sure if it was her. As I approached, the figure became more and more visible, and I saw it was, in fact, Sabrina. I started walking to her. I knew she was probably going to curse me out because I didn't beep her back.

Before I could say anything, she started yelling. "Where the fuck you been all day?"

I smiled and pointed to my sweaty body and wet T-shirt. "You see where I was, so don't come at me like that."

She replied, "So they don't have any telephones out there?"

I shook my head in disbelief and said, "Baby, are you serious right now? I'm not checking my pager while I'm playing basketball."

She looked at me with her deep brown eyes and responded "You should have" with the most innocent face ever.

"Yeah, you missed me. Come here and give me a hug and kiss," I said as I pulled her toward me.

"Ewwwww, stop, you're all sweaty and stuff. Get off me."

I started laughing and said, "So you mean to tell me I can't hug you or kiss you because now I'm sweaty? You wanted attention, so now you're getting it."

I squeezed her tighter and let her indulge in my sweat. I thought it was funny, but she didn't think so. She pushed me away once more and said she would have to shower again because of me.

"When has that ever been a problem?"

I like when she's fresh out the shower anyway. She smiled and leaned in to accept my kisses. She knew it was going down in a few hours and I didn't have to say anymore.

"Are you hungry?" I asked her.

She chuckled and replied, "I'm always hungry, babe."

I told her I would get Grandma to cook us something to eat. While she was cooking, we could shower and watch a movie until the food was done. Knowing Grandma, she probably had something cooking or already cooked, waiting for me to come in. I knew I wanted to sex Sabrina up that night. She knew how to get me in my feelings. No other chick had ever done that before, and I loved that feeling. She knew she had me in her web and how to bring things out of me that others weren't able to. I was rocking with it because it felt good.

As I opened the door to my crib, I could smell the food in the air, and it smelled marvelous. I thought she was making lasagna or spaghetti from the aroma I caught as soon as I opened the door. Grandma came out of the kitchen with a smile. I assumed she heard me walk through the door.

"Hey, Grandma. I would hug you, but I'm still sweaty from playing basketball all day. You're gonna have to settle for just this kiss."

She accepted my offer and smiled as I kissed her cheek. Sabrina gave her a big hug and kissed her too.

She loved Sabrina and could tell I cared about her a great deal from her being around so much. I let them talk as I went and showered and got myself together. I was tired, but fucking around with Sabrina, I'd be up all night, trying to make love to her sexy ass. I started thinking maybe I needed to distance myself from her before I was in a world of hurt. I wasn't supposed to feel the way that I did about her at all. She made me feel alive, and I felt like I should better myself in all situations because of her. So why would I want to get rid of that?

I couldn't distance myself from her. The only person that would be hurting would be me. And being completely honest, I didn't want that feeling at all.

She wasn't tryna hear that anyway, I thought while laughing.

There would be no not talking to her at all. Her crazy ass would show up at my crib, asking all kinds of crazy questions, tryna figure out how and why we had a problem. Whatever the case was, I knew what it was, and I was stuck. As I put my hands on the shower knobs, my body was met by a strong gust of wind from someone opening or closing the bathroom door.

Sabrina stood in front of me, butt naked, with her perfect complexioned body and nice curly hair. Smiling, she joined me in the shower. My body was weak from playing basketball all day. However, as soon as I saw her walk slowly toward me, I instantly found strength from within. I grabbed her by the throat and listened to her body exhale slowly. Her body was tense as though it knew exactly what I was about to do to it. I began kissing her with my hand still around her throat, applying pressure but not too much. I wanted her to feel good and enjoy every moment of what I was about to do to her. I started kissing on her neck as she grabbed and clutched me closer. I didn't want to just fuck her. I wanted to eat her pussy and taste her juices.

I grabbed her leg with one hand still upon her throat and pushed her against the shower wall. I slowly lifted her onto my shoulders. I began to lick her clitoris in the most aggressive manner she had ever experienced with me. Her sighs turned into deep moans as she held my head in place. She was looking down at me, biting her bottom lip in enjoyment. She started moaning and calling for God in pleasure. I knew at any moment she would cum, so I gave her long, slow tongue licks to help her reach her climax.

Her body started shaking, and I knew it was time for me to give her some dick. She felt obligated to give me head, but this wasn't the time for that. I wanted to please and destroy her in the best way possible. I gently put her down on the shower floor as I kissed her and let her taste her own juices. As she kissed me, I grabbed both of her legs and inserted myself into her. I was ready in full form to dish out punishment to her body. I began to stroke her slowly to find a good rhythm. I started hitting her spots, and her pussy started getting wetter and wetter.

I put her down and turned her around, ready to give her back shots. She bent over and looked back, ready to take everything I was going to give her. I became the aggressor and started to press her. Her ass was so fat—this was all I could think of as I started to stroke her. I started hitting her spot, and her body responded with a gush of wetness.

"Papi, I fuckin' love you. This shit feels so fuckin' good!" she said, looking back at me as I worked her pussy with long, hard strokes.

I grabbed her hair and wrapped it around my fist and pulled her head back. As I kissed her, I told her I loved her and that her pussy was mine.

Out of nowhere, she started throwing her ass back and doing tricks with her pussy. It caught me off guard. She told me she wanted me to cum with her. She didn't want to keep cumming alone, and that shit turned me on. She knew backing it up on my dick was going to do things to me, but it wouldn't finish me off. She started speaking in Spanish, repeating everything she just said, and I couldn't hold it anymore.

I yelled out, "Oh, shit, baby, I'm about to cum. Oh shit." She started cumming right along with me.

I pulled my dick out of her and came all over her backside. "Fuckkkk!"

She smiled, looked back, and leaned in for a kiss. I couldn't help but kiss her back. The sex was so good, and her body was so appealing. It wasn't hard for me to get back up to full form. Her kisses aroused me so much that we had to go for another round.

CHAPTER 12

As I lay in my bed, I couldn't help but think and miss my father. He was a good dude, tried to stay out of harm's way. I was not sure this would be the life he wanted for me. The school part was a go, but these streets were very dangerous. They claimed lives. They claimed a lot of good and smart people's lives before me. Hell, they'd keep claiming them after I was long gone too. The streets were crazy, and in a way, they claimed my father's life.

I still thought back to the day I found out the news. He was killed over a drug deal that went wrong. I was twelve when I found out the news. It hurt me to see him go in that manner. The newspaper read, "Drug Dealer Slain." Maybe it was a setup from the beginning, which in turn was the reason I was so cautious now. What type of person would leave a child out in this world fatherless over something so avoidable? The sad part about the situation was, they didn't even rob him. He was scooping up bricks in Southside Jamaica, Queens, and they popped him right in his helmet, left his jewels and the work right there with his dead body.

This led me to believe he was getting too much money for whoever's liking and they had to get rid of him. Was it an inside job? Maybe it was someone close to him. Five years later, his killer was still on the streets at large. We had nothing but good times before his passing. Funny thing was, he never showed me he was a drug dealer—or should I say we never talked about what he did for a living. It was sort of an unwritten/unseen silence, but I always knew.

My fascination with the drug game was due to my pops. He was smooth with his shit and never caught a case. I looked up to him, and he showed me unconditional love, no matter the situation. Our summers were always crazy. He would take me to theme parks, and we would just flat out have a ball, with no cares in the world.

After his passing was when I decided to get off the benches. I was ready to start moving whatever I could get my hands on. Weed was my first move, out in Harlem with Risk. It was a good move. It taught me a lot about the game and the rules that went along with it. I felt like since my pops was gone, I was in charge of the house. It was my job to provide for whoever lived in it. What was I supposed to do? Starve and go without? Nah, I had big dreams, and I wanted all that I lost and everything else that was coming to me.

To be honest, I still felt really angry that my father left me in this world alone with no guidance. However, he gave me the tools to succeed in life no matter what route I went. I respected him for that. Sometimes I just wanted to chat with him and get advice on certain situations going on in my life. Fuck it though. I was a man now. He might not have liked the route that I took, but I had to take care of business.

As I looked at our picture beside my bed, I thought of what life could've been if he were still here. Would he help me knock off the work, or would he change my thought process? I saw why they said it was important to have your father in your life at all times. Only men could raise men. My mother was very sweet and kind to everyone, but God took her from me at a very young age. Like my father, the streets claimed her life as well. I hadn't seen her since. I thought about her often. Would I ever see her again? Did she think about me? How could she leave me in this world without a word or something? Shit, anything would suffice—anything that would help alleviate the pain caused by her not being around.

All these thoughts still lingered in my head. Still, to this day, my heart was as cold as a day in February in certain situations. I missed them dearly. I couldn't deny that. I was glad I had Grandma though. She kept me grounded and sane at times. I was always one of her favorite grandchildren. With all the shit I was doing, I still tried to maintain my grades in school and make her proud. No one saw this coming at all. For me to have high grades and continue to strive was kind of shocking for the family. They all figured I would go into a vault and lock away my feelings and stop caring about life.

That wasn't the case for me. I needed the bad energy and words from others to help me want to do better. In my eyes, I was the man for real. I was well-known, and I never had to front. I showed respect, and people showed much respect in return. I was living royalty around these parts, but I still remained humble. Staying low key helped avoid the big eyes from looking at me. I still sat and reminisced over things my parents taught me. Those core values were held supreme above the rest.

I started thinking about the future, a bit further than expected. I wanted to give myself a glimpse of what could be when the time was right. As funny as this sounded, drug dealing wasn't even high on my list of things I wanted to accomplish. College was high on my list. For some strange reason, I knew I would do well in it. This was a gift for me; plus, I was very street savvy, so I had the best of both worlds. I just had to figure out different ways to make this money clean. It was very hard at this level to maintain and stay the same. I actually had a few million stacked up in storage, and I was only seventeen. Could you imagine the frontin' I could do to people my age or even the ones older than me?

I wanted the nice cars and homes, but the timing had to be right. If the timing was off, it wouldn't work at all. I was more concerned about having eyes on me because of the luxurious things I had acquired than having luxurious things to front on people with. Attention wasn't my thing. This was why I tucked my chain when I wore it. Not that I was scared of anyone. I was just cautious at all times.

This summer was starting off nicely, and I couldn't really complain. I knew what I wanted to do for the summer, and I wasn't going to be stopped. I had a lot of things on my mind, things that I needed to break down, get over, or keep hidden. For instance, I told my cousin Jay I was going to hit him up about that business proposal the night I took Sabrina out. I also needed to get these pills to Miami so we could have more spots than just the city.

Jay would work perfectly for the Bronx, and I knew a few good people out in Staten Island. I could front them some bricks to help build their blocks up with my product. I didn't know what made me think about business at this point, but I was ready and more focused on things right now. I decided to give Jay that call and tell him to meet me somewhere for lunch. I wanted to talk to him about the keys I wanted him to move in the Bronx.

The Miami move could wait. I knew Rock was thinking about college in Florida, but it still wasn't a sure thing. I needed that move. Even if he wasn't looking at something in Miami, some school in Florida close to Miami would do. Just him being close enough to keep an eye on that market would be good enough. The amount of potential out there was mind-blowing.

As was very obvious, I loved money. It was what made the world go around. But besides making money, I loved music. Hip-hop was my thing. I listened to oldies a lot because of my grandmother. Her love for some classic groups like the Temptations, the Miracles, and all the groups from the sixties and seventies grew on me. It took some time because I hated it when I was much younger.

I threw on Busta Rhymes's "Put Your Hands Where My Eyes Could See" to start off my day. The beat was crazy, and it had the city going bananas. You couldn't walk around anywhere in New York without hearing it bumpin' in someone's car this summer. It definitely set the city on fire when it came on. That was just the first song I had on tape though. I thought I had some Mase and Puffy on here too.

Hip-hop was going through some things. This year, we lost Biggie and Tupac in less than six months—two of the biggest stars in music gone over some bullshit. Shit was crazy, but good music was still coming out through all the mourning. I took my shower and headed out the house to the spot I told Jay to meet me at.

CHAPTER 13

The spot I met Jay at was dope. It was in a secluded location in the city with great food. Before the food came, I started to break it down to Jay. I let him know I had some shit I wanted him to move. I continued to give him the rundown on how I figured he could help me set up shop in the Bronx. Jay was in his midtwenties and was always about money. It was kind of funny to me he was taking orders from his little cousin. I just saw it as me having the voice or vision to further dreams, and most of the time, everyone ran with it.

People and family didn't look at me as a teenager. They looked at me as a grown man because of my mind-set and how well I spoke around people. Nevertheless, it was always funny to me when I was giving guys older than me orders. They never argued or tried to challenge anything I said. They knew it would benefit both of us if it was done my way. They always knew my plans were well thought out.

After I told Jay the moves that I wanted him to make, he was amped. All he wanted to know was when he could start moving the stuff. I told him to set his crew up and give me three days to get the work he needed to succeed. I gave him the prices of the keys and asked him how many he wanted to get. I told him if it was really serious, I would give him some bricks on consignment. I had enough money and work to hit him off with my bricks and let him get where he needed to be.

I normally never hit anyone off with bricks but he was family. He knew how I moved, so I didn't feel it was any real trouble. We finished our food and I told him I would hit him on the hip with the drop to pick everything up. Daps were exchanged and I knew it was only a matter of time before the city was on lock. All I really needed was SI and we could flood the city with keys.

I needed to talk to Risk to see if he knew someone trustworthy enough to set up shop in Florida, specifically the Miami location. I decided to catch a cab and head to his crib since it was on my mind at the moment. I figured he'd be somewhere around his block if he wasn't in his crib.

I went to Risk for a lot of things, not just drug-related things. He knew a lot and was probably the most loyal out of the bunch. Not that the rest wasn't. It was just I didn't have to say or explain much to him. He just always understood with little words spoken.

The cab pulled up to Risk's block, and I hopped out and began to walk to his building. I knew a bunch of people around his way, and they showed me major love. It was something that was unheard of in most cases, but for me, it worked out perfectly. I showed them the same love they showed me, if not more. I didn't believe in trying to act tough on someone else's block with no army with me. I was usually dolo when I came through, and they liked that too. I was just respectful and didn't create many enemies.

Before I could enter the building, I see someone signaling me from a distance. From the looks of it, the person looked like Risk. I wasn't sure but I began to walk in the direction the person was signaling me from. As I got closer I realized it wasn't Risk, it was his little brother.

"Shorty, what's up?" I said, greeting him with a smile. His eyes met mine and lit up as we dapped each other up.

"You know me, son. I'm out here chillin', looking for the bitches. I'm tryna be like you."

Rel was a few years younger than Risk and me. That was my dude. He was too young to really do what we were doing in our minds, but he always wanted to be down.

"Ayyy, yo, Steph, when are you going to put me on, son?"

He knew a lot, but I didn't want him in the streets like that.

"Son, you know I'm not gonna have you out in these streets like that. I need you in school, trying to become a lawyer, doctor, or something. You could play basketball, son. You're nice in that too. It's no reason for you to hit these streets. You know your brother and I got you if you need or want anything. Keep your grades up, and you already know what it is."

He smirked with a look that sort of resembled disappointment but also a hint of understanding crossing his face. He knew everything that I just told him was true, and I had nothing but love for him.

He replied, "But…"

However, before he could finish the sentence, I chimed in. "No buts, son. School is what matters, kid, and that's all. Bitches want the drug dealers and shit now. But when they get out of that phase, they're coming for the ones who have shit going for themselves. Believe me on that. I've seen it happen so many times before."

I gave him the truth right from out of a sinner's mouth. The message I was teaching was true, but I didn't follow my own scriptures. I knew he understood, but I wanted to make him feel better about doing the right thing. I continued the conversation in a slightly different direction.

"Yo, Risk told me your grades are looking really good and you're trying to play varsity next year. Is that right?"

He smiled and replied, "Yeah, I'm doing my thing in school and working on my game."

"So why would you want to be in the streets if you're doing so well? You need to be on those courts, working on your game."

I spit it to him in a way that let him know I was proud of him and not scolding him.

I knew he didn't have an answer, but he looked up to us. He saw us making money and moves, so he wanted a part of the action. I knew this was what ran through his brain at that moment. He didn't even have to say such. I told him to go upstairs and get his report card and let me see it. I let him know if things looked right, I would talk to Risk and have a gift for him later on. A spark of excitement crossed his face. He knew it would be something dope if the story added up.

He began to run toward the building entrance. I yelled toward his direction and asked him where Risk was.

"He went to the corner store to get a sandwich. He should be on his way back now." I nodded my head and sat to wait for them to come back. A few minutes later, Risk approached the park bench, where he expected to find his younger brother waiting. He was shocked to see me instead.

"Yo, son, what you doing here?" he yelled to me as he approached.

When he got closer, we shook hands. I quickly filled him in on his little brother wanting to be down with us and how I had sent him upstairs for his report card. I let him know I wanted us to buy him something to take his mind off that street life.

"What you have in mind to get for him?"

"I was thinking of a dirt bike or four-wheeler. I figured it would be dope for him and unexpected. You're going half on it though," I said quickly with a laugh.

"Oh, shit. Hold up. Hold up. Just like that, you're gonna volunteer me to help with your idea?" he asked, laughing.

"Yeah," I replied, laughing as well.

I told him I had five stacks on me and the dirt bike would cost at least seven. We would split it down the middle.

"Stop fronting like you don't have the bread, son. We're neck and neck with cash, so don't front. You don't want your brother in the streets, and neither do I. This will definitely take his mind of that fast life. Plus, I got some stuff I need to talk to you about on the way to pick it up."

"Damn, we're getting it now?" he asked.

I nodded my head in affirmation. I let him know I was just waiting for Rel to come back down with the report card then we would make that move.

Shortly after, Rel came downstairs with a big smile on his face as he handed me the report card.

"Damn, kid, you have all As on this motherfucker."

I pulled him closer and wrapped my arm around his neck as a form of love. I told him I was proud of him and to get on the court to practice.

"We'll be back in an hour or so to drop off your gift."

As we departed, I told shorty to be safe and take it easy. I knew a good spot to cop the bike or four-wheeler from. I told Risk we should move quickly to the spot and I'd brief him on what I wanted to talk about.

It was a nice day out, so we decided to walk and talk for a little bit. Risk asked what I had on my mind. I explained to him I already set the takeover for the Bronx in motion with my cousin Jay. I continued telling him how I was really thinking about moving these pills down south, in Miami. I wanted someone who could be trusted with that much work and who knew how to move it, someone who could get things done without us having to go down there and doing it for them.

We were focusing so heavy on this coke for the last few months that we forgot about the easy money we made off the pills. It was a safer investment with less work, in my opinion. Risk nodded his head in agreement but didn't say much until I was done talking. I figured once we set the pills up, we could import the cocaine down there also. I wasn't trying to step on toes, but I wanted to try expanding down in Miami. It was a very long shot, but it could be done. I went to Risk because he always knew someone. If not him, his pops did. They had connects to make sure shit got done in the proper way.

"Yo, I don't even know anyone that could really hold that much weight in such a short period of time. I mean, I know a few old heads down there that could set up shop, but in order for that to work, it'll take time."

"You know you don't trust a soul that you haven't known since you were little, so I would have to work it until you felt comfortable. I think you and I should go down there and check the club scene out, hit the beaches up and see what it looks like. You could bring Sabrina and I'll bring my joint Kendra and make it look like a weekend getaway but it would be strictly business."

"If you want, we could bring the whole team and just do it like that. Rent a bus and a driver and have them take us down there. I have a person that can get a package shipped with some of both products to try since I know you don't want to travel with anything."

I thought about it for a second and responded, "Yo that's a good idea Son, I've never been there so let's do it. We can bring the team and have fun with it."

This really worked for me, and I wasn't even thinking on that level. I was happy about the decision we just made. This was why I always went to Risk above the rest for insight on things like this.

Now it was time to get this dirt bike! I had made it up in my head that I wanted to get him a dirt bike instead of the four-wheeler. I had five stacks on me, and I knew how to talk people down with shit like that. When you had cash, it was kind of hard for people to say no to you, and I knew that.

"Risk, how much you got on you? I have five racks."

"I have about the same on me," he replied.

"Okay, cool. We're gonna do the bike today and the four-wheeler before school starts back if he acts right. Cool with that?"

He nodded and said, "Yeah."

We got to the spot after a long walk followed by a bus ride. A few bikes drew my attention upon arrival at the shop. The red one they had in the walkway was dope, and it looked fast. Risk must have thought the same because before I could utter the words to him, he began gravitating toward it, trying to test it out.

"This is the one, Steph. He's going to like this joint."

I told him I thought the same thing. "Get the helmet for it, and let's talk numbers with the sales rep." The sales representative came over immediately after she saw Risk on the dirt bike.

She asked if she could help us with anything. Shorty was bad so I began to flirt with her. I wanted to see if I could get the numbers down a bit.

"Yes, ma'am, you can. We would like to buy one of these dirt bikes, specifically this one right here." I point to the bike we agreed on.

The price sticker read $7,500, just like I expected, but we had no intentions on paying that price at all. I didn't really want to punch anything over $6,500, but any discount would help out.

"We're trying to buy our little brother this dirt bike. He's getting good grades and doing well altogether. We saved up just enough to get him a gift he would love, especially in the summertime with all this nice weather."

I noticed her face changed as though her heart had melted from the story I had given her. I found the soft spot, and Risk knew exactly what to do to bring it home.

"Yes, ma'am. He's a great kid and deserves this, but we don't want to spend all our money on just the bike. We want to get him some gear and a nice helmet to wear also. You know safety is paramount, so is there anything you could possibly do for us?"

The look on her face said yes without any words. Her response was rather amazing as she began to talk.

"Since it's for a great kid, I'll make sure you get it for a great price. How does $6,500 sound? That's with no tax, and I'll include gear and a nice helmet."

"That sounds great, ma'am!"

Risk and I spoke the same words at the same time.

"Okay, great, gentlemen! Right this way please," the sales agent said as we followed her.

We followed her to the register. Since that was in the bag, I started thinking about us getting back to his block. I wasn't catching a bus, nor was I walking anymore. We had some extra cash, so I figured it would be dope if we bought a moped. One of us could keep it and come back for more for everyone else later that week. I told Risk the exact thoughts in my mind, and he started laughing.

"Yo, it's funny you mentioned that. I just thought about which one of us would ride this joint home. I wasn't getting on the back with you, and I'm sure you weren't going to get on the back with me."

We both began to laugh because this was the truth. The mopeds were cheaper than I thought, and we could actually buy one for $1,200 easy. I told Risk that the moped was on him. The rest of the cash I was going to slide to shorty for the tip, and I'd give Rel a grand to play with. Risk agreed to the terms. It didn't really matter to us. This was little pocket money we were throwing away. I just wanted to put the bike in the air. It had been a while since I'd been on one of these things. This would be fun.

The sales rep came back and handed us the key as she wrote up the paperwork. We told her about the order for the moped because we didn't want to ride it together back home. She laughed and added it the paperwork.

"Your total is going to be $7,700, gentlemen, and how would you like to pay this?"

Risk smiled and answered, "Cash. And he'll take your number and name too." He pointed at me to set me up. That got her to blush, and I knew the number was sure to follow.

We paid the bill, and she really slid me her number as she walked us out the door. I reached in my right pocket and felt the money that was already separated. I gave her the tip as an equal exchange. The more I examined the paper, the more I could see it had a few numbers on it as well as her name.

"So Tavia it is, huh? Okay, was a pleasure to meet and do business with you."

Still blushing, she responded, "The pleasure was mine. I gave you my beeper, home, and work number. You should use it sometime. Maybe we could get up." I nodded in agreement.

I left the walkway to catch up to Risk, and he had a smile on his face. "Yoooooo, I didn't think that would work at all. You need to hit that, son. She was on you from the door."

I smirked and told him I was chilling. I'd save it for a rainy day or something. He knew I would do just that. That was too easy. Shorty was bad. I couldn't front but, I had Sabrina. I told him that I should've let him have her though. We laughed it off and got on our vehicles and decided to race back to the block. I knew I would beat him, so I let him get a head start while I got myself situated. I started doing wheelies for blocks at a time. Yeah, I definitely needed one of these for myself for the summer. I was having too much fun on this shit.

I began to catch up to Risk on the moped, and I could see his building was only a few blocks away. We pulled up to the block and parked the machines by the park benches. I could see the look on Rel's face when he saw the dirt bike. His eyes were fixated on it in sort of a fascinated way. He ran up to us and started hugging both of us.

"Yoooo! Is this mine for real?"

Risk responded, "Yeah it is, but you have to promise me you won't let your grades slip and you'll still maintain your skills on the court. Most importantly of all, stay out of these streets. You got it?"

His response was short and to the point. "Yes, I got it."

That was good enough for me. I handed the helmet over to him and took my hand out my pocket. I placed the grand in his hand I promised Risk I would give him.

"Listen to me, son. You'll always be good fuckin' with us. Just follow the rules, and everything will be smooth. Aight?"

He understood and hugged me once more as I moved out the way. I told him to go ride and not to be out there, pulling wheelies, like Alpo, for blocks at a time. He laughed and told me he'd try not to.

As he got on the dirt bike, all the kids from the park started surrounding him, admiring his new gift. I told Risk to let the little kids have the moped for the time and have it go up with Rel later on whenever he came upstairs.

"Yo, we're gonna get some more dirt bikes tomorrow. It'll beat taking cabs or the train when I want to come out here to check you."

Risk was with it without a doubt. He told his brother the moped was his too and he could let his people use it if he wanted.

"I hope your mom doesn't trip over the gifts, son."

"Nah, she won't. She and my pops know how we are, and she'll understand the logic behind the gifts. She won't trip. Trust me."

"That'll work. Let's go get something to eat from that Jamaican spot not too far from here."

Risk agreed with me. We were both starving, and some beef patties and coco bread sounded like it would hit the spot.

Without a doubt, the spot was a good place to eat. After we finished eating, I went for a walk around my block. I really just wanted to enjoy the evening and see what was going on in the neighborhood. You could see everything in the hood, if you really paid attention. The pumpers were out heavy, trying not to miss a sale. The chicks were playing the stoops, and the kids were just enjoying life with no cares or homework to complete.

This was the typical NYC summer day. You might catch the little kids opening the fire hydrant, trying to charge the cars that passed for a wash. These were the true hustlers to me. I didn't know what it was, but being born and raised in New York City put some sort of drive, ambition, hustle in you. It was like we were born in fucked-up situations, but we managed to stay afloat. We found any way we could to hustle, legal or illegal.

The odds were never in our favor, coming from these hoods and project buildings. The key to making it out was looking past the pissy hallways, elevators, and project windows and seeing the big picture. I was halfway there, but I did a lot of my dirt in these same streets that I was trying to get out of.

I loved the view I was seeing. The neighborhood looked peaceful and full of life. The old heads were playing cards at one table and dominos at the other. My wandering around led me over to Sabrina's block, where it seemed that I knew everyone. I started getting love as I walked down the street. Before I could cross the street to the next block, I could see Sabrina outside with her girlfriends sitting on one of their stoops.

I knew she would have a problem with me walking through her block and not stopping to speak. Honestly, I didn't want to. I just wanted to take a good walk, breathe a little bit, and think. She started her approach toward me, and I began to meet her halfway.

"You were just going to walk past my house and not speak?"

I knew that would be the exact words to come out of her mouth.

"Yes, I was just walking and thinking. I wandered down this street without thinking too much about the location. I was just looking around and seeing how everyone was doing."

I should've taken the last part out of my sentence because I knew she wouldn't like that part. It was already too late but like many other times before, I dismissed it.

"So you think that's okay to just check on everyone except me?" she asked incredulously.

This was exactly why I knew I should've taken the last part of that sentence out. I knew there'd be backlash from it. I had to clean it up quick before she got completely irate, so I spoke to her in a calm tone.

"No, I don't think it's okay, but I wasn't thinking. Now I'm here. You see me. Now what? I get it. You feel a certain way, but I'm not trying to argue with you at all. I just want to continue my walk with you, if you aren't too busy, and that's it."

I flipped it on her, and she knew it. But she couldn't argue because I just gave her an open invitation to walk and talk with me so we could enjoy the scenery.

"Why do you always do that shit?"

"Do what?" I knew exactly what she was talking about, but I knew how to clip the conversation short too. "Are you walking, or are we going to sit here and waste this beautiful evening, talking about something that doesn't matter?" My impatience was slightly showing through my otherwise calm demeanor. That made her move and think quick on her feet.

"I really hate you sometimes. You get on my nerves with your slick-ass mouth. Let me tell my friends I'll be back shortly."

"I love you, too, darling," I replied. Then I smacked her ass, kissed her, and watched her as she walked away.

It was crazy how she was always in the right spot at the right time, even when I didn't want to be bothered. Her company was always welcomed. I liked it no matter what mood I was in.

Walking with her was comforting and relaxing. Having her under my arm was a good look. I wondered if she would be down for the lifestyle I'd been hiding. Would she accept it, or would she leave in the wind? I didn't have the answers yet, but I knew I would have to eventually tell her. If she really loved me like she said she did, she would understand and either make me change for the better or adapt to the circumstances. I figured the odds were in my favor if she were to find out, but the questions still lingered on.

"What are you thinking about, baby? You're quiet."

"I'm not thinking about much, baby, just life and a few goals of mine. I'm always quiet. I'm enjoying the view with the prettiest girl in the world in my eyes. That's all."

She smiled as she clutched my arm and leaned in for a kiss for a sense of closure. I wanted her mind off the fact that I tried to walk past her house and not speak. It was working. I was sure she felt a certain way about it but wouldn't bring it back up unless I did. I told her I was sorry for walking past her house without stopping. I really just wasn't thinking at all. She pinched me and told me to never let it happen again. She was crazy, and I liked that side of her.

Her next statement was even better than the first. She said she didn't care what I was going through or not going through; we'd get through everything together. I admired her for that. I started telling her about the Miami trip Risk and I had planned earlier that day. She seemed intrigued by it. I wasn't sure if she had been to Miami before, but I knew that move needed to be made.

CHAPTER 14

B efore our trip to Miami, I wanted to see the boss and let him know my plans. I decided to take a trip to see him for a sit-down before we left. The trip was a few hours away, so I had time to make the meeting and get back to get ready. I just needed to pack some stuff and cash for the trip. I called a cab and headed to the spot.

As my cab pulled closer to the connects spot, I saw something that blew my mind. Sabrina's father was coming out of the spot with Jose. I was shocked. So many things started going through my mind at the moment. Did he know about me? Had he always known about me? Did Sabrina know about me? Was he setting me up? What was he doing there? How did he know Jose?

So many questions ran through my mind, but I had to think quick because the cab was slowing down to let me out. I told the cab driver to circle the block as I slid more toward the middle of the back seat to avoid being seen.

Fuck! I needed to get my mental together before I stepped into the spot. I felt like my brain was going through a test and at any moment, it could go into overdrive.

As my cab pulled back up, I wondered if Sabrina's father was in a car nearby or scoping me out from a distance. Shit, I was not the average teenager right now, and this was looking crazy. I wanted answers, but that had to wait until after this meeting.

As I walked into the door, I saw Juan.

He smiled and greeted me in Spanish. "Como estas? Todo bien?"

I gave him a handshake and returned a salutation.

Jose was sitting down, listening to music, sipping a drink. "What's going on, tiguere? I haven't seen you in weeks. You always send Mr. Risk to pick up your drugs for you now. Is everything good?"

"Yes, everything is good. I let him pick up the shipments to get to know you a little better. That's my man. He always does right by me, so I send him if I'm busy. Is that cool with you, boss?"

"Sure, that's fine, manito. I was just curious." He assured me all was good and waved me over so we could talk.

I nodded to confirm what was said. "I wanted to talk to you about this move I'm trying to make with this X in Miami. I think it's money to be made with the nightlife out there, and I wanted to test it. If all works out, I'll be moving it out there, too, along with the cocaine."

"Good. I have plenty of work for you. Also, I have good friends down there that can get you set up with good spots if you're trying to really get established. I'll call my men and let them know you're coming and to watch out over you. You and your guys are my gold mines, and I can't afford to lose you. You're taking your friends, I presume. Correct?"

"Yes, I am. They're coming too."

I took out $200,000 for the re-up while I was gone. Just in case things went well and I'd ended up staying a few extra days, I wanted my workers to be straight. I didn't want anything drying up while I was gone. I'd take the twenty kilograms and keep it moving. The equal exchange happened, and I was ready to hop back in my cab and make the drop-offs before I packed my bags.

I call D-Money and all my workers for pickup and gave them the time for the drop. The drop was made, and I had to figure out what I was going to do with all this cash I had on me. How much money would I need in Miami? I was still trying to hide who I was from a girl who might very well know who I was. Why hadn't she asked me about the expensive necklace or shopping sprees? Did she know and didn't care, or was she waiting for me to tell her the truth?

I was so confused at this point, and I really wanted answers more than anything.

I made up my mind that I would bring $25,000 with me to Miami. I didn't think I would need anything else. After I made my drop, I went home to finally pack my bags. I told Grandma I was going out of town with the guys, Sabrina, and their ladies for a road trip. She smiled and told me to enjoy it because these were the best times of my life and I wouldn't get another chance like this while in high school. I left her some money in an envelope on the table. I kissed her on the cheek and departed the house.

I jumped in my cab and headed to Sabrina's house to pick her up. As I walked to her doorstep, all the questions I had in my mind earlier popped up again. Just as the thoughts entered my mind, her father opened the door and greeted me with a smile.

"Hey, Stephen. How's it going? You're here to pick up Sabrina, right?"

It didn't seem as though he knew anything, but I couldn't tell. Was he living a secret life too? Their crib was decked out but still low key. I'd find out more about him when I got on this bus. I'd interrogate Sabrina without her knowing.

"Yes, sir, I am. How are you today?"

"I'm great. When basketball season starts back up, we're going to catch some games. I'm sure you'll love the Garden and seeing Ewing, Sprewell, and Houston play. I would love to spend some time with you and catch up on things. It'll be fun."

Was this an open invitation to the business I was already in? Or was this really just a chance for him to get to know me better? I didn't know at all, or was I supposed to read in between the lines? Did he see me when I came on the block in the cab, or had he really known about me from day one?

"That will work, sir. I'm with it. You know how I feel about the Knicks. I'm all in."

"Please call me Tony. We're family now."

I was trying to analyze everything he was saying to help me make sense of it all.

"Nah. No, thank you, sir. I'd rather remain respectful with my elders. I'll leave the first-name basis for your really close friends and family."

I could tell he liked me, but I still had a bunch of unanswered questions. He smiled and finished his beer. He told me he really liked me and that I had heart and courage, among other things that he admired.

Soon after he uttered those words, Sabrina's mother came from one of the rooms, and she looked good. I mean her ass was nice, round, and looked very soft. From the way she walked, I could tell it was. If she wasn't Sabrina's mom, I would've definitely tried to hit on her pretty ass.

"Hey, *mijito*, you look good," she said as she came over and hugged and kissed me on the cheek.

I didn't know whether to hug her back or just stand there. Her husband was standing a few feet away from me and staring. I wasn't sure if Sabrina's mom was a flirt or if she was flirting with me, but one thing was for sure. She could get it any day of the week. As I stood there motionless, receiving the hug, I saw Sabrina coming our way.

"Ma, get off him. He probably likes you anyway. No more hugs for him." Her tone was sort of playful but had a tinge of jealousy in it.

I began to blush and shrugged my shoulders. I also smirked to let them know it might have some truth to it. I still tried to remain bashful at the same time. Her mother smiled and winked at me as she walked away. I was the only one that caught it, so I knew she was definitely flirting with me.

What kind of family is this? I thought in my head.

Her mother looked like she could pass for her early to midtwenties. I knew if I tried it, I could very well have a piece of that action with no effort. I figured Sabrina's mother had the same taste as her, and this was why she was flirting with me. I didn't let my side thoughts distract me from the real questions that were still lingering in my head.

Sabrina's father probably slung weight back in the day and settled down when he had Sabrina. Maybe he still was in the game. I had never seen Jose outside in the open, talking to anyone before, and I'd known him for years. This let me know her father wasn't a threat and had to be a good friend of Jose. He was way too careful with movements and being seen doing anything that would put his business in jeopardy.

Jose also didn't talk about business to anyone. Maybe they were catching up on old times, and he told him about the kids that were taking over the city. This was dangerous ground to be leveling off, now that I thought about it. I knew I wasn't in any grave danger, but I wanted to know what he knew about me and who he was. What made Jose embrace this man so much that he felt he wasn't a target in the streets?

As Sabrina and I walked out her front door, her father grabbed me and pulled me to the side.

"Do you need any money or anything for this trip that you and your friends are going on?"

Was this a test? I wasn't sure. Should I be testing him to see how much money he would give in situations like this?

"No, sir, we'll be fine," I replied.

He smiled and said, "My man Stephen, taking care of things. The boss."

I was freaking the fuck out at this moment but still managed to remain calm and keep the same facial expression. I didn't like that line at all! It made me feel as though he knew it all without saying much.

"You don't have to be ashamed of taking money from me. I told you once you started dating my daughter, you were family."

I began to calm down just a bit more because that let me know he didn't know who I was.

"No, sir, I'm sure we'll be okay. If anything, I wouldn't be afraid to ask since you put it like that."

He smiled again and told me I was an all right kid. He patted me on the shoulders as I walked toward the cab to Sabrina.

I was no longer nervous about shit at all. Maybe he did know who I really was. Maybe he didn't care. All I knew was, I was way too smart to play mind games with or to be caught in between some crazy shit. Sabrina kissed me as I sat down in the cab. She told me she had invited two of her friends to come with us to Miami. I told her

I didn't have a problem with it, although she could've told me earlier and not the day of. I would make it work though.

"As long as they make it to the bus on time, we shouldn't have any problems," I said, trying to hide my slight annoyance.

"I already told them the location and the time to be there. You know Latonya and Ashley, right?"

"Yes, I know them both. They're pretty, too, so I'm sure one of my homeboys will be flirting with them."

This was about to be a wild trip!

I told the cab driver to make a U-turn and head back to my house. I told Sabrina I forgot to pack something, and I'd be quick. I wanted to get more money because of the extra invites. I wanted to make sure they were comfortable too.

I ran into the house and told Grandma I'd forgotten something. I ran to my room and grabbed another $25,000 just to make sure everyone was good. I hurried and put the cash in my bag and locked my room door behind me. I kissed Grandma once more and hopped back into the cab. We headed uptown to where we would be boarding the tour bus. I was excited to go down to Miami and be with my friends and the girl I loved. This trip was going to be one for the ages.

CHAPTER 15

"Yooooo, this trip is ill!" John shouted to me as the bass pumped from the tour bus speaker.

We were living like music artists on tour with this bus. The bus was really decked out with everything you could think of—from TVs to PlayStation's. Everyone wanted to party and have fun. I liked every moment of it. We managed to get some liquor on the bus for the long ride ahead of us.

I didn't really care for the alcohol at all, to be completely honest. Plus, I was still thinking about Sabrina's father, but this wasn't the time nor the place to ask her about him. I had to put it in the back of my head for now and revisit the situation at a later time. I definitely had to tell the fellas about this. I was sure they wouldn't believe it at all and would probably become skeptical about everything.

The girls were all dancing with one another, having fun. I really couldn't have asked for more on this trip. I made sure there were no drugs or any weapons on our bus. The liquor was the only thing, and that was minor when you knew how to talk to people. No one could see into our bus, and the walls were soundproof, so we were good on all levels. I asked Rah how much money he brought with him on the trip. He told me that he had $15,000. He didn't think he needed more. I thought that was a decent amount of money to bring for the trip, but I wasn't sure, so extra cash flow was needed.

Sabrina came over to me with a drink in her hand, looking like she was nice and maybe a little tipsy. "Hey, baby, what are y'all talking about? Why aren't you drinking with me?" she yelled.

I knew she was trying to get me on the same level as she was. The look in her eyes was telling me that she wanted some nasty, passionate sex, and I was up to it too. I slapped her on the ass and told her I was talking about money and I'd have some drinks with her soon.

"You don't need money to get me, baby," she said, looking a little too happy, and I knew for sure she was tipsy.

I told Rock to pour me some Henny straight. I was gonna have a drink with Sabrina like she wanted me to. I told her that eventually one day I would marry her. That was if she continued to make me happy like this. Then I would open up more to her and tell her things she didn't know about me. The sober truth was starting to come out, but I had it all under control. I wouldn't tell her everything, but I would lure her in more. Who knew that she would be open to drinking or sipping like this? I didn't think she would be. She was such a good girl, and it was different seeing her like this. I couldn't front; it was very assuring.

This tour bus had rooms. Well, they were sort of like rooms. Now that I think about it, this bus is kind of flashy. I was glad we caught the bus in the city rather than in the middle of the projects. That would have had people on us heavy. The bus drivers were moving, taking shifts to get us to our destination in a timely manner. From the city to Miami, it would take, like, a good day to get us down there. I didn't really care about the time. My only concern was the team being good and everyone enjoying themselves.

Sabrina's friends fit right in too. They seemed to be the life of the party. Bad chicks too, some of the baddest in the town around our age. I was glad this was a smooth transaction with everyone. I wondered why Sabrina didn't ask me where her friends would be staying. Did she know about me? No matter how hard I tried, I couldn't help but think about her father at the connect's spot. I really felt like she knew everything about me and didn't care or had a different motive.

Trips like this weren't cheap, and she'd never questioned me about affairs that involved money. She might be used to it and didn't say much about it. As Sabrina approached me, the look in her eyes was rather ravishing and unique. She was telling me she wanted me without even speaking a word. The slow strut gave me all the information I needed to know. My eyes became fixated on her beautiful face and lovely body. It was time for me to deliver, and I wanted her more and more now.

She began to pull me toward the little room on the tour bus. I palmed her ass and made my way past the crowd into the room. She knew how to control me with something as simple as a touch or a slight nibble on my earlobe. As the door closed, she pushed me onto the bed and began to seduce me unlike she'd ever done before.

The liquor must be kicking in on another level because I'd never seen this side of her. I couldn't front; it was very appealing to me. Everything she did was seductive and held plenty of passion behind it. She began to suck on my neck, and if my dick wasn't hard from the seduction leading up to this, it was ready now.

Sabrina took complete control, something I wasn't really used to giving up. She started working her warm, wet tongue up and down my chest, all while maintaining eye contact. She had that look in her eyes that asked me if she was pleasing me, all without words. I'd like to call it the look of love. I loved her, and I made it known. Her voluminous, warm lips were driving me crazy as she ran her tongue against my chest once more.

In one swift motion, she started to lower my pants. I helped her undo my belt so it was an easy transition. She pulled out my dick and started sucking it with aggression, like she had a point to prove. The alcohol made her horny beyond measure, and her mouth was warm and wet as she began to spit on my dick.

"Damn, baby, that's how you feel? You're just trying to get nasty with it, huh?"

She said nothing but shook her head in agreement while keeping my dick in her mouth. I liked this side of Sabrina. The aggressiveness turned me on as I replayed what I was seeing over in my head.

She began trying to deep-throat my dick, choosing my pleasure over her own oxygen. That thought alone made me made want to please her more than anything in the world. I didn't want to cum from head, so I pushed her off me. I grabbed her hair and put her on the bed, showing her my aggressive side. I held her by the throat as I pulled off her shorts and panties in one motion. Her breathing had grown from shallow to a rapid, upbeat tempo.

I wanted to show her everything she just showered me with and then some. I began to devour her pussy, pulling her closer to me, as though I was trying to find my way inside her vagina. The licking from my tongue was making her body tremble, as if it were acknowledging some sort of defeat.

She started moaning loudly as she climaxed. I won this battle, but the war had just begun. As I lifted my face, covered with her juices, she began to kiss and lick my face, which made me hornier.

Sabrina grabbed my organ, checking the stiffness as she played with it on her vagina lips. I was more than ready and didn't want to be teased anymore. I forcefully stuffed my dick in her as she sighed with pleasure, and I got more comfortable with my size inside of her.

My powerful love strokes began to take over as I kissed and bit her neck. As she received my pleasure, her hands and nails started digging deeper in my back with every stroke. She moaned and spoke occasional Spanish to me, letting me know exactly how she felt. I could hear her pussy talking to me with every inward and outward thrust from her pelvic area. I was very in tune with her body, and I showed no sign of weakness.

I wanted her in every position I could think of at the moment, so I switched her and turned her over on her stomach. I started to slowly stroke her from the back as I talked in her ear. I had the upper hand now. She couldn't take me talking real nasty in her ears for long before she would explode.

"You like this shit, don't you? Yeah, you love this shit. Whose pussy is this?"

She was trying to get a response out, but I kept asking questions as she covered my dick with her juices. I was ready to win the war. She started doing shit that I had never felt from her pussy from that position. Sabrina was working the pussy from the bottom, and it felt amazing.

"Papi, is it mine? Tell me it's mine! You love this shit, don't you? You're going to give me a family one day, you know that?" She was right. I would.

"Yes, baby, you know it's yours. I'm going to make you my wife one of these days."

Sabrina had me. Just when I thought I had control of this round, she took over and switched the roles on me.

As I continued to stroke her, she told me she was about to cum and she wanted me to cum with her. She started increasing her tempo and winding motions in order to make both of us have an orgasm at the same time.

"Oh shit, I'm about to cum, baby. Oh shit!" I said as I felt myself reach the edge.

She started winding and grinding harder. "I'm cummin', too, baby. Don't stop!" she yelled.

Seconds later, I pulled my dick out from her milky pussy and came all over her cheeks. She lay there with her body shaking from the strong orgasm. she hated me for not cumming in her, but the orgasm I just gave her left her depleted on another level. She began talking to me in Spanish, telling me how much she loved me and how she wished we could just lie like this forever. We were on top of the world at that moment, and the party was still going on outside of our little love room. I couldn't ask for much more.

CHAPTER 16

"Aight, when we go in here, let me set everything up, and I'll introduce you to my father's friend," Risk stated.

It was his show, and I had no intentions on trying to run this. I just wanted someone to hold this city down, someone trustworthy.

"You got it, son," I replied back to Risk.

"What's good, Jason? How's everything?"

Risk began to speak to the unfamiliar man as I stood in silence. Jason was from the Caribbean, and he had a strong accent, but he spoke very well. He stood about 5'8" to 5'9" tall with dark skin. I was analyzing everything about him as they spoke in a friendly manner. His crib was decked out and looked as though he retired well-off.

"Brethren, me haven't seen ya since ya little. Big man now." Jason continued to converse with Risk. "These ya friends?" He pointed over to myself and the rest of the guys.

"Yeah, he's the one I told you about," Risk replied as he pointed at me.

I stood there motionless for a minute, just staring into this man's face. I wanted to see if he was the right person to deal with. He points to me and asks me to come over to him. I began my stroll to where he was standing.

"You're the man with all the power, I hear. That's you, correct?"

His English was no longer broken when he spoke. I was thrown off for a moment but quickly recovered.

"Yes, sir, I am the man you speak of," I shot back, establishing full control of the situation at this point.

He smiled and said, "Good." He continued talking, saying he'd heard good things about me. His friendly face was inviting as I walked over to discuss business with him. Miami was looking really nice. It had everything there, and I started to envision more for the city than I initially demanded.

"I hear you want to move ecstasy around here on the club scene. Correct?" Jason replied in my moment of deep thoughts.

"Yes, sir, I do. I have the product, but I don't have the team to move it down here as you would." I wanted to give him a sense of hope in letting him know I needed him for the job.

"You know it's going to come with a fee if I do this for you, right?" Jason replied once more.

"I'm sure it will, but I wanted to talk about that too."

As I spoke the words, his face suddenly changed. It was as if he was waiting for a better deal to see what I had to offer.

"I noticed this city looks really good—good enough to manage more than one type of product. I have good coke or should I say great coke that I would love to get off if you want in."

Something told me he knew about the cocaine already and was waiting for me to offer that.

"Yes, I heard you are well connected on that end too. Chris told me."

I knew Risk had put him on to what I was trying to do. It was so weird for me to hear someone use Risk's real name.

"So what can you offer me, Stephen?" he asked as he chimed into my thoughts again.

"I can get you whatever you want. What do you need?"

"I heard your coke is really good. Can cut it different ways, and it still smokes or snorts the same. Is that true?" he said as he sat down on his couch.

"Yeah, that's the word on the streets, boss. We haven't had any complaints. Only issue is, that's more of a risk to get down here from up top. I'm sure you've already thought about that."

He nodded his head in agreement with what I said. "I'll give you a good price for the cocaine, and I won't tax you on the delivery, but you'll have to wave the fee for the ecstasy. We're taking on more of the risk. Sounds good to you?" He chuckled and smirked as he looked at me from a distance.

He continued, "You remind me of your father. Oh, you think I didn't remember you? I knew who you were when you entered my home. You probably don't remember me, or maybe you were too young, but your father and Chris's father did a lot of business together. I haven't seen you in years, kid. You speak like your old man, but you're smarter than he was. Shit, I've never seen kids like you and your friends before. You're definitely smarter than we were at your age. Y'all still in school, I'm assuming. Correct?"

Jason's words had drawn me in more. I began to look really deep into his face. I was trying to remember something from the past that would connect the two. I looked over at Risk, and he was smiling because he'd known all this the whole time.

"Oh shit, you're the dude that used to have that 850 BMW."

It was coming back to me. He was fly from the time I remembered him.

It's funny how life works out, I thought to myself.

Jason smiled and leaned in to dap me up. "Damn, kid, you have the memory of an elephant. Yeah, that was me. Sorry about your pops. The last time I saw you was at his funeral. You was a shorty then."

"Yeah, I'm trying to stay afloat with school and now this. You look like you retired well."

He laughed and answered, "Yeah, I'm retired, but you're trying to bring me back in with this deal."

I really was trying to give him a good deal because I needed him if this was going to work.

"Your father did a lot of solids for me back in the day. I'll take the deal. We will work the numbers later. I want to show you something."

He took us to a room and pulled out a photo album. He flipped through some pages and then stopped. He stopped on a page with my father and Risk's father back in the eighties with heavy jewels on. They looked so young, but from the picture, you could tell they were getting it back then.

"Damn, that's crazy. It's a small world too!" I said.

"How'd y'all get down here? Y'all have wheels?" he said as he looked at my crew.

"We rented out a tour bus for us and our girls."

"So none of you guys have cars?"

"Nah, we like expensive cars, and we don't need the attention. So we play the normal role in order to keep a low profile."

He smiled and shook his head. "Yeah, y'all are smarter than us. We would've had cars galore and jewelry."

We were smart, and our time would come to be flashy—within reason, of course.

"Aight, son, since you're here, I will take care of y'all. No need to spend your own money when you're out here. I will show y'all around the city and get y'all right. We need to do something about the wheels though. For your senior year in high school, y'all need cars. I'll make it happen, but nothing too flashy. And I'll pay for them."

That sounded like a good deal, but I was still cautious about the attention we would get.

"Just look at it as a graduation gift from an uncle," he said as he watched my facial expressions struggle to agree with the before terms.

"Okay, cool. I'll agree with this one."

Before I could crack a smile, John, Rah, Rocky, and Risk started celebrating.

"Shit, it's about time! I was getting tired of cabs, buses, and trains," Rock said while laughing.

I knew they wanted cars, but I just didn't feel like it was the right time to do so before. Jason pulled me in with a warm embrace. Senior year was going to be *ill!* I just knew it. I started to think about the situation that just arose and how it was the perfect cover. Jason just offered to show us a good time out in Miami, so this could look as though he funded the trip. It made perfect sense. Now all I had to do was introduce my long-lost unofficial uncle to my girl, and everything should go smoothly.

This was big for me, mainly because if Sabrina knew who I really was, this would throw her for a loop. Sabrina never asked how or why, so for all I knew, she didn't know. Maybe she didn't care who I was, and she just wanted to be happy. She definitely found that happiness with me, so nothing else mattered. I loved this girl, but me seeing her father with my connect, I wasn't sure if she was to be trusted at this point in time. My wild thoughts had taken over my mind, and I thought about the worst before the best. Maybe she was an innocent bystander in this situation. I just didn't know, and for the first time in my life, I was kind of scared.

"Do y'all have money on y'all?" Jason asked as he looked at each of us.

"Of course!" We all spoke at once with distant laughter in the background.

"Well, save it. I got y'all while you're here. Everything is on me. I mean everything. Your money is no good around here."

Jason had a strong pitch in his voice as he finished the sentence off. He didn't know how many people we brought with us, which led me to believe he was really holding dough for real. As he took us downstairs to his garage to show off his toys, I saw he had new joints with crazy horsepower. Off in the cut, I saw the all-white BMW 850ci coupé fully loaded, just like I remembered.

"Yeah, you see it. I knew you'd remember it from the last time you saw it. That's my baby. I don't take her out much now, but she still damn near new. I'll keep her forever."

Jason's car collection was ill. I couldn't even front. I wanted some nice cars like this in the future.

"I know you want one of these things, Steph. I can see it in your eyes. You and your crew are so used to being low that you forgot to live a bit. So I'll tell you what. The cars I get you guys for school will be dope and fast. You can't get in trouble for it because I bought them. I know you guys are smart enough not to have dumb shit like guns and drugs in your cars that you drive daily. Correct?" Jason said.

"Yeah, you're right. That's not in us at all," I replied back.

"Aight, cool. So in the next two weeks, I'll have the cars sent to your spots. That'll be my gift to you guys for staying in school and putting me back in the game."

I was cool with that 100 percent, but I had a few rules for the guys before anything.

"Listen, y'all, no drops in the cars, no crazy flashing, no pistols in the cars unless you have a stash box built in for it. No smoking weed in the cars either. I don't want any hiccups with what we got going on. I can't afford to lose none of you guys, so let's do it right if we are going to do it. Take a cab or the bus if you're going to re-up. Nothing has changed, and let's continue to get this money."

I had to let them know because I knew how crazy a nice car could get in any hood. Chicks would be on us even more, and more eyes would be out now, so the routine had to stay the same.

"Damn, Steph, I wish we had someone like you in our set growing up. We would've been rich a lot faster. You and your boys are as smart as some of the smartest people I know. What I've just witnessed is somewhat unheard of from someone your age. You'll go a long way in this business that way. I respect those moves."

"I'm just making sure we don't mess up the operation by doing something dumb or crazy in the process."

I knew the guys were thinking something along those lines, but I needed them to see and understand the big picture. This money and school would get us far if we continued to keep it smart and low key.

"So where to?" I asked Jason.

"First, we'll get the ladies, and then the fun shall begin."

"Okay, cool. I'm with that."

I felt good inside knowing I had a backup, just in case Sabrina did know about me. Not to mention I didn't have to buy a car and my uncle was going to look out for the team. I knew he had taste, so it wouldn't be a cheap car. I was expecting something along the lines of a BMW or Benz. My team wouldn't expect anything less than what I'd receive, so we were all in good hands.

Shortly after we pulled up to the hotel, Sabrina and her friends were sitting poolside soaking up the sun rays. Boy, were they all looking good as ever.

"Hey, baby, how was your day?" she asked me while leaning in to kiss me.

"Good. In fact, it was very good. I brought my uncle over here for you to meet. He sponsored this trip, so I wanted y'all to meet him."

Jason smiled and shook hands with the ladies as they thanked him simultaneously.

"So where to now?" I asked after everyone had formally met.

"Let's do the food first, sightsee, and we will do the club scene tonight. I'll make sure y'all get in," Jason replied.

The plan for the day was in effect, and I couldn't complain. I was down for it, and I let everyone know that was the move for the day.

CHAPTER 17

A few weeks passed, and everything was moving smoothly. I stacked up a few million, and the Miami move was a great one. Those pills were moving like crazy out there. I had no complaints about how things had been going. I still couldn't get my mind off seeing Sabrina's father at the connect's spot. I wanted to know the answers to the questions I had, so I decided to go with a bold gut move. I planned on asking Jose who was the man he was talking to outside of the spot a few weeks ago.

I had to know how he knew Sabrina's father. It was time for me to re-up again, so I'd probably ask him once I made the drop. I knew he'd tell me, too, because I'd shown nothing but loyalty to him and his product. I came correct with every drop, never a dollar short. That meant even if I was short in the past with the re-up money, I made sure he had his portion.

As I pulled up to the spot, I got a weird feeling about everything that had been going down. I knew I had to do it though. I couldn't wait any longer. Things weren't going bad, but I wanted to ease the situation so I could move forward and figure out how I was going to play it. I'd always wondered how long Jose had been in the game. I was sure he was worth millions on top of millions. What made him stay in the game so long? Why did he outlast the rest? What were his keys to success in this game? These were the questions I began to ask myself. Meanwhile, there I stood in front of Jose with a head full of questions, hoping to get answers.

"Jose, I have a question for you. A few weeks ago, I saw you standing outside with a man. I've never seen you in public before, so I know he had to be someone you respected—respected highly enough for you to get out your element or comfort zone a bit."

Jose responded immediately as though he knew exactly whom I was talking about.

"Tony? Yes, I've known Tony for many years, papi, but why does that concern you?"

"My concern is, I'm dating his daughter. I had no intentions on ever seeing him here, but we just had a casual conversation, as though he had no cares in the world."

"Ah, Mr. Steph, I see now. You may think you're in a bit of trouble, but you aren't. This is good for both of us. You see, Tony was one of my henchmen and sold drugs for me nearly fifteen years ago. He is retired, but something tells me you already knew that. Maybe he was looking to get back in the business that day. I can't be too sure, but what I can tell you is, your secret is safe with me. He knows nothing about you, and I won't mention you to him. All should be well, *tiguere*, if you continue to move the way you have been for all these years."

"Here's the only issue you might run into. We talked, and he asked how was business going. I let him know I had some young teenagers that ran the city far better than anyone I've ever run across in all my years in this business. Don't let it trace back to you or your friends. Move accordingly, loco."

"Shit, he might have the drop on me, but he really likes me. I'll take heed to what was just said and continue to move in the right direction. Thanks for looking out for real."

I was the cash cow of the whole operation, so I knew I was good. Nothing would happen to me from Sabrina's father's end even if he found out I was living a double life. I was happy with the results I had received from Jose also.

"Okay, now back to business. I brought the cash with me for a re-up, but I'm not taking anything with me this go around. I'll be taking this route from now on. I feel it's safer for me this way. I'll hit you with the location later on today, and I'll have my guys make the drop and keep it pushing. I need re-ups for both products, equal shares too. That Miami move a good move for us.

My guys will be ready shortly. Just beep me when you have the shipment ready."

As I explained how I wanted things to go, I saw Jose getting excited. I knew he loved money, and today I brought a lot with me to keep shit flowing.

"Okay, papi, that sounds like a plan. I know you always come with all my cash, never been a penny short. I respect that. I'll send Juan and some of my other guys to make the drop to your location when it's ready. Just let me know when you're ready. Okay?"

We shook hands, and I told him I should be back around within the next two weeks. I'd come around the same time to do the same thing. He nodded with a smile and agreement. We shook hands once again, and I went on about my business. I had to make more moves before I got the location I wanted my people to pick up the work.

I was moving a little differently due to something feeling a bit unusual, but I knew how to maneuver around it all. I felt a bit at ease knowing that Sabrina's father knew nothing about me. I feared the unknown. Jose said that was one of his henchmen, so I knew he moved on dudes with the cruelest intentions. I might want to rethink my outlook on the situation with his daughter so I wouldn't be on any list of his. My mind was finally clear minus the shit I just thought about. I wanted to meet up with the team to discuss the changes I'd made with drops and pick-ups.

On my way to meet the team, I got a call from Jason telling me he had something for me. He said I should get the surprise delivered to me in a few hours. I instantly grew happy because I knew it was the car or something he'd promised me. I let him know I had some things about to fly in and he'd be happy sooner than later. Immediately after I hung up the horn, I got a call from Risk telling me to stop everything I was doing. He needed to see me ASAP. As per the tone in his voice, I couldn't tell if this was good or bad. I did know something happened, so I gave him my coordinates. I posted up on the block until I noticed him.

Twenty minutes later, I saw him pull up with a mean black Benz with smoke-gray tints. I knew at that moment why he made me stop what I was doing. He wanted to stunt on me for a little bit.

"Steph, you see me, son? Yo, Jason looked out with this joint. It's fully loaded."

Just as soon as he said that, I saw the rest of the team pull up in cars equally similar to the joint Risk was driving. Rah, John, and Rock all had a kitted-up Lexus SC 400 triple blacked out. Them joints were tough. I couldn't front at all. When they came to a rest, all of them popped out their sunroofs and started fronting hard. I saw the smiles on everyone's face, and at that moment, I knew we were living.

John screamed out, "Yo, we're living, son! You see this shit? We're about to have all the hoes, son. No lie."

I smiled and nodded because I knew it would be on. This just made senior year a little bit more appealing to me. Risk began to ask me all these questions about the cars.

"Yo, where's yours at, son?"

"I haven't been home in a little while, so it could be waiting. Jason called me not too long ago, telling me about a surprise, so I'm sure it's there I just haven't made that move yet."

"Bet, let's head over to your crib and see what you got. I want you to ride shorty with me while I really test this joint out too."

I laughed and got into the passenger side of his Benz. We weren't the average teenagers anymore. We just came up in a major way. From the looks on our faces, we were living good.

There was one thing on my mind though. If I could see the changes, people who knew us would see the changes as well. We needed to follow the rules I gave the team back in Miami a few weeks ago. But I couldn't help to think we'd be a target for all cops. I would be sure to remind my brothers of the dangers ahead of us.

As I was doing all this thinking, I realized how smooth this Benz rode. Risk had a crazy grin on his face as he drove me to my crib. He was bopping his head to Hot 97 like he didn't have a care in the world.

"Yo, son, this whip is ill and all that, but we can't be flossing crazy with them."

"What do you mean?" I replied.

"You and I both know we are targets in cars like this, and the fact that we are still teenagers is a problem. Grown men in the hood seen riding this hard, son. I mean, think about it. Right?"

We shared the same sentiments on that matter.

"Son, I thought the exact same thing. Like I said before, no work or anything in the cars. If you need a hammer, you need to have a stash box for it. But there can absolutely, never be any work in the cars at all. Never." I knew Risk would understand, but I wasn't too sure everyone else would understand how serious I was. All they saw was stunting, money, and pussy, which was cool. But the stakes were higher than before now. As we pulled up to my block, I saw Jason sitting on a red car with a bow on it.

"Yoooooo, what are you doing here? I thought you were in Miami when you called earlier. That's me?" I pointed at the car. I couldn't help but express my feelings of joy with the car I was given.

"You know it is, kid! I figured you like this joint. You looked like a BMW guy, and Chris helped me choose the color. I think this car was the easiest to pick out. You seemed to like my old 850, so I went and got you the upgrade. It has all the specs and modifications you would need with it."

This car was fire for real, and it was sure to turn plenty heads in any hood. I was extremely grateful for the cars for the team and myself. They were just sitting on their cars, posing mad hard with nothing but smiles on their faces.

"Oh, I forgot to tell y'all, all these cars have stash boxes in them just in case. It might be hot outside, and you don't want it on you. Y'all don't need those problems. A few buttons, and it opens up," Jason said, and he showed us how to use them in my car.

It was like he read my mind with this stash box shit. I was definitely going to get one installed, if it didn't come with one.

As I looked around, I could see people on my block looking at the gang of cars and giving us nods, telling us them shit were tough. I had to take the shit for a ride with the windows down—you know, live a little bit. I felt like I needed to have my big jewelry on, untucked, fronting hard on everyone. Yeah, I needed to go out, shop a little bit, and pull up on a few blocks with the team.

I went upstairs to grab some cash and tell Grandma about the gift I received from my father's close friend. I had the perfect cover for it all because Jason's record was clean and he owned legit businesses. I knew Sabrina would really love this car too. I couldn't wait for her to see it and sit in the passenger seat. I opened the door and greeted Grandma with a kiss followed by a tight hug.

"Grandma, guess what! My pop's close friend just brought me and my brothers cars. You should see it. I'm talking about fly for real."

She didn't really understand why he would do such a thing, so I explained to her that we met up with him in Miami and Risk reconnected us on the trip. He took us under his wing and promised to look out for us. She understood everything after I explained it to her. I then let her know she was welcome to meet him since he personally delivered and he was downstairs. She decided to take a trip downstairs and see what I was so excited about. I ran to my room real quick and took some cash out to splurge a little on myself and Sabrina. I closed my door while simultaneously locking it behind me, and I made my way down to the car.

"Grandma, you like it? It's ill, right? Yeah, I see your face! You like it!"

I knew she liked it a lot. She didn't have to say anything; her facial expressions told everything.

"It's too much, baby. It's nice, but it's really fancy, baby. I just don't know. But if you're happy, and I know you are, then I'm happy. Just be careful out here, son."

I shook my head to agree with what she said and then hopped in my car. I yelled to the fellas out the window, asking them what was the move. I wanted to head Uptown and cop some gear and new jewels. This wasn't who I intended to be, but it was happening, and I couldn't control it.

I told Risk I was going to swing by shorty's crib and see if she wanted to roll and then head Uptown. I told him he should probably do the same thing. He agreed to follow along with the rest of the team, and we would make the move together. We pulled up to Sabrina's crib, and I hit her on the horn. I told her I was out front and to come outside. When she came outside, she looked shocked as she walked up to my new car.

"Hey, papi, whose car is this?"

"Mine, boo. My uncle you met in Miami a few weeks ago came through with cars for all of us. This joint is dope, right?"

She smiled and said she loved it. "But where are we heading to?" she asked.

I told her, "Hop in. Let's cruise the city and see where it takes us."

This car had some power behind that engine, for real. It might have been the fastest of all the cars we received that day. I wanted to open her up on the Brooklyn Bridge on our way to the FDR, so I started speeding a little bit, and the crew followed. In and out of traffic we went, laughing as we glanced at each other.

I was so hyped about the car I almost forgot about the drop that was supposed to be made later that day. What I didn't forget was to give the rules out again so it was fresh in their minds. I knew they were feeling themselves, but one slip could compromise the whole operation, and we didn't need that. When we got to the next stop, I would hit a pay phone and let Jose know where to deliver the work.

As I looked over, I saw Sabrina staring at me, smiling. "What's up? You aight? Why are you looking at me like that?" I asked.

She leaned over and kissed me and said, "I love you, papi. You're so sexy, and I missed you."

She knew just how to get me, talking all seductive and shit. That shit made me drive a little faster. I was guessing she caught a buzz from the thrill of going faster. Moments later, we were shopping and enjoying life. I copped a bigger chain, one that mimicked Biggie's Jesus piece. Now the decision was to tuck it or let it hang for the most part of the day. I still wanted to remain low, but this car might be changing me into something else. All the fellas felt the need to do the same. I guessed they saw the boss moving this way, and it became cool.

Whatever move I make at this moment will affect them regardless, I thought to myself.

Sabrina didn't even ask me about the large amount of money I had on me. Maybe it was because of the car I received; she thought it might have come with the gift. Either way, I was happy with not being questioned. Risk walked up to me and pulled me aside to ask me a few questions. Before I stepped away, I gave Sabrina a few grand to go shopping with the rest of the girls. She took the extended offer as she kissed me slowly. I walked over to Risk to see what the deal was.

"Yo, son, what should I get shorty? What would you get your shorty?" he asked.

"Jewelry is a must for starters, if you really fuck with her. It doesn't have to be wild crazy, but the thought should be where the gift comes from. Then I give them money to go shopping, while I pick up little shit on the side, like perfume or something. You determine her worth, son."

He agreed as Rah and the rest of the crew approached us to catch up on things.

"Yo, Steph, what you wanted to holla with us about?" Rock asked.

"The rules of the game and a few changes I made to this little thing of ours. Y'all know how we have to do this shit. Nothing changes, because we have nice whips now. Oh yeah, I made a few changes to drops. Now we won't be handling the work anymore. You send your workers to handle the drops. It's risky out here now with more products on these streets, and I don't want any of y'all taking risks like that. I'm about to set the location up for the drops. Make sure your workers are in place once I give the word. Yo, come with me to this pay phone so I can make this call to Jose," I told the crew. I hit the connect and told him a nice chill spot in Queens in a secluded location. I let him know my people would pick it up from the location and distribute it throughout the city.

"Now that business is all set up, let's tend to the ladies and get this money."

CHAPTER 18

The first day of school was here, and I was happy to be starting this school year. It was my senior year, and I planned to go out with a bang. Everything was looking like a good move on all levels. I got out my bed, turned my music off, and got my stuff ready for the shower. I felt like this day had happened before, sort of like déjà vu.

Either way, it feels like a good day, I thought as I turned the water on to shower.

Once I got out of the shower, I looked over to the clothes I had taken out the night before. I had my whole outfit laid out down to the fresh socks. I felt like doing the Uptowns with the bubble checks today. The red, black, and white joints I'd been on for a while. I threw on my black Guess jeans, a Polo shirt, and the matching Durag to match. I couldn't front; I was feeling myself this morning, and I knew why.

I didn't have time for breakfast this morning, but I couldn't resist the fresh bread Grandma was making. I took a few slices and stole some kisses from the lovely lady that prepared it for me. With the bread in one hand and an apple juice in the other, I made my way outside to my freshly detailed car. I was in full-front mode, and I knew I looked good.

I couldn't wait to see what everyone else wore for the first day of school. I was especially excited to see what Sabrina had on. As I pulled up to Sabrina's block, like clockwork, I saw her coming out of her house. She must have felt my presence or something. She looked sexy as fuck with her hair swinging and her jeans fitting just right. I couldn't wait to get her out of them once school was over. My eyes didn't shy away from the fact I was thinking just that.

"Damn, baby, I look that good that you're staring like that?"

I didn't even try to deny it. I smiled while biting my bottom lip, agreeing with her. She opened the door and leaned over to the driver seat. She hugged and kissed me like she missed me more than ever. Our bond had grown tremendously over the past few months, and I was loving it. I couldn't help but want to get closer to her as the days grew longer. I needed her in my corner, but most of all, I needed her to understand and accept me for who I really was.

At some point, I knew I would eventually have to open up to her and let her know the truth. It would be one of the hardest things I ever had to do. I tried my best to avoid it at all cost, but the day was approaching soon, and I could feel it. With all that on my mind, Sabrina interrupted my thoughts. She started playing with my dick as I pulled off.

"Let's start the year off right, Daddy. I hope this is a great year for the both of us," she said as she pulled my man out of my jeans.

"Damn, baby, shit! You doing it like that this early in the morning?"

As she began to deep-throat my dick, my moans got more and more intense. I could feel her warm saliva dripping down my shaft. Head on the way to school behind smoke gray tints. This was probably the best way to start any day, for real. As soon the thought entered my mind, I started to feel a tingling sensation. I began to push Sabrina's face down as the urges grew stronger. My moans, along with my aggression, made her go harder to try to please me. I couldn't take it anymore, and I let an intense orgasm go off in her mouth. She swallowed it and kept sucking my dick, almost causing me to crash the whip.

As I pulled up to the front of the school, I could see my team parked up, getting mad attention. I saw smiles on all their faces as all the pretty chicks started talking to them. All I could do was chuckle because I predicted this weeks ago. The attention was crazy, but it was real.

Out of nowhere, I heard John say "This guy..." in his most sarcastic voice.

I pulled into the parking spot, and it felt like a movie. I was the main attraction, and my supporting cast was there to help set the stage.

I pulled in slower as I gave everyone a head nod and a smile to go with it. Everyone was looking at us like we were doing it major, and we had no problem with it. We were targets for all the tough guys and fake tough guys out there in our school. Although we didn't have many problems with anyone, people always seemed to have issues when you were doing better than them. I was prepared for this, and I made damn sure the team was on the same page as well.

I decided not to sell in school this year. My workers would be pumping for me in my school as well as theirs. I felt like I had graduated from the school of hand to hand, so I moved on to bigger and better things—let the pawns run up, and do the dirt. If they ever got caught, it would be hard to trace things back to me or anyone from the team. I built this team to withstand any obstacles and storms, as long as they understood and followed the rules.

As I stepped out my car, I could swear it felt like a movie. All eyes were on Sabrina and me as we made our entrance.

Risk approached me with a dap and a grin on his face. "Son, we're fly out here. You see the looks we're getting? It's going to be a good year."

"Son, I already feel it, too, but I don't want to get too hyped. You know?"

He nodded because he understood exactly where I was coming from. We headed to our homerooms to find out our schedules for the school year. We all ended up with the same homeroom, so it was about to be nothing but jokes and pure laughs. I couldn't front; we had some bad-ass chicks in our homeroom this year too. I saw a few familiar faces I'd seen throughout my four years in this school. I gave them all the same downward nod with a "What up?" to go along with it. The chicks were staring at us hard as we made our way to the back of the class. As I sat down, I could feel someone staring me down, trying to grab my attention. I knew shorty, but she'd never spoken a word to me before. She would just look like she wanted to speak but never had the heart to say something. Today was definitely different.

"Yo, what's up, Tyesha? Something on your mind? You want to tell me something?" I asked while she stared at me.

I knew I shouldn't have said anything to her, but I couldn't help it. She was pretty as hell, with a nice smile and big innocent-looking eyes. Not to mention the nice skin tone, banging body, and nice hair. As I waited for her response, she got up and started walking over to me. I didn't know what got her attention today, but she was going for it. Maybe it was the big Cuban link chain tucked under my Polo shirt or the same smirk that got Sabrina's ass. Either way, she was moving closer toward me, and I had to think quick about how I was going to play this.

"Yeah, I have a lot to say but not right here. I know you got a girl, so I won't say much right now. I don't want you to get into any trouble for talking to another girl. But here, take this. Read it, and use it," she said as she sat down in the empty seat in front of me.

She slid me a note with a number written on the outside of it. She then walked away and returned to her seat, walking like she knew all eyes were on her. I didn't say anything, but I looked at Risk and John, and they started laughing.

"Damn, you got it like that, son. This guy!" said John.

"I guess so, son." I tucked the note into my pocket.

"He got them all, and I'm still here trying to bag Melissa's ass up there in the front of the classroom, but she keeps on fronting on me," Rock said.

The whole class started laughing, and Melissa's face turned red from all the attention she was receiving.

After the initial embarrassment wore off, Melissa finally responded, "If you really wanted my attention, all you had to do was come to me correct, and we wouldn't have a problem. So what are you gonna do, Rock?"

I looked at him with the "You better go get that before someone else does" eyes.

"Shit. Since all of y'all are bagging chicks or getting bagged on the first day, let me find my new girl in here too," Rah said. He moved forward to his next victim's desk. The class started laughing again, and I couldn't help but join in. This shit was looking like a love triangle or something. I could swear it seemed unreal.

Risk leaned over to whisper in my ear, "Son, this is wild. It's only the first day. Shit, it's the first period of the day. You know it's going to be a wild year if it's happening this early in the game. Really? The first day?"

I knew exactly what he meant, so I just shrugged my shoulders, letting him know that. "Why are there so many bad chicks in this homeroom anyway?" I asked him.

He hit me with the same shrug I just gave him. I didn't know what the letter entailed, but I was going to read it sooner than later. I felt like I was changing in such a short period of time. Before, I wouldn't have given shorty the time of day. But now I felt like I was flirting with death. I felt like the old me was back in full effect, and it really felt like I needed that me back at this exact moment. The sad part in all this was, I didn't feel bad or take Sabrina's feelings into any consideration at the time. Maybe I wasn't going to call shorty or open the letter. I didn't really have the answers at that point, but time would tell all.

As the bell rang and I headed for the exit with the team, Tyesha grabbed me and whispered in my ear, "Use the number. I'll be waiting to hear from you." She had the craziest grin.

I'd never seen a grin so devilish on a female before. Once I walked through the door, I saw Sabrina coming toward me with her usual smile. I knew it was a matter of time before the news got back to her. With all the shit that happened in homeroom, she would have questions.

Why the fuck did I even entertain that dumb shit? This was the wrong girl to fuck with at this point. After all that I had found out about her father, it was like I was creating my own death sentence. Sabrina knew my past, so this shouldn't bother her much. I didn't do anything crazy to be caught off course in any circumstance.

If she asked me for the note, I'd tell her I threw it away. I would just give Risk a pound with the note in hand and slide it to him with ease. He'd know to hold on to it until later. I'd tell her I didn't want to embarrass shorty in front of all those people. If she asked why I would care about that, I'd just respond something cool like "Relax, babe, it's the first day of school." Hopefully, that with my smile would be sure to get me out of trouble. Or into it, depending on her mood.

Sabrina was a firecracker with shit like that. It was cool because I knew how to put that fire out with a look or a few words. If I decided to move on shorty, I would have to be extremely strategic in my motives to do so.

"What classes do you have, baby? Any of them with me?" Sabrina asked.

I took her schedule from her hands to compare it to mine. I looked closely at her schedule and saw that we had nothing together. That was definitely a relief to me. It was not because I didn't want her around, but I was trying to focus on my grades. With her in the same class or classes with me, that would only be a distraction. I wasn't letting my grades slip, not this late in the game. I still had goals I wanted to accomplish this year.

"Nah, that's a good thing, baby. We wouldn't get any work done if we had classes together, and you know that. I do see a few teachers we have but not the same periods. I'll be done by lunch anyway, so no worries," I reassured her.

She fixed her frown to some sort of a smile as she reluctantly agreed with me. She knew deep down it was best for the both of us. I walked her to her first period to cheer her up a bit more.

CHAPTER 19

Just as I thought, I was in the clear, and I wouldn't hear a peep about the shit from homeroom, I saw a teary-eyed Sabrina coming in my direction. From her facial expression and eyes, I knew she knew what happened with Tyesha. Damn, who the fuck told her that shit so quick? I was mentally prepared for everything she was gonna throw at me though.

My face showed genuine concern as she approached me. "What's wrong, baby? Who's fuckin' with you?"

Before I could get the finish my sentence, she started swinging. So you know the God had to dip that.

"What the fuck is wrong with you, girl?" I asked while restraining her from attempting to hit me.

"You think you're slick? I'm not these other bitches out here. Why are you playing with me? I heard you was in your homeroom, talking to Tyesha, and she gave you a letter telling you to call her."

"I saw you right after that and you failed to mention that. I seen you after that period, and you failed to mention this to me. So I'm supposed to trust you, and you're probably laughing and joking all in these bitches' faces. Now she's probably laughing at me. Let's go! We 'bout to go find her and set this straight right now," Sabrina said. From the passion in her voice, she was dead serious about the ordeal, but she wasn't ready for what I had to say back to her.

"Okay, yeah, she was in my homeroom class. She gave me a fucking note, and I threw that shit in the garbage. Since everyone wants to tell you shit and wants to be all in our shit, tell them to tell the whole story. One, I didn't smile in anyone's face or anything of the sort, so kill that noise right there. Two, look how you're acting right now. Do you see yourself? Now everyone is staring at us, all in our shit because you can't control yourself. This is why I didn't tell you from the jump, because I knew exactly how you'd react. Three, if I really wanted that chick, I'd be with her, so please stop coming at me with that bullshit. I'm with you, and that's all that matters right now. Right? Tell them jealous bum bitches to get out your ears and get a life and a man of their own. We got bigger fish to fry, so let's keep moving. Aight?"

My response was spot on, and from the look in her face, it did the trick. But to add insult to injury, I added, "If you really feel that way about it, we can go and get the letter out the trash and approach her." I wanted to make her feel crazy as fuck for lashing out at me over another bitch. I knew she wouldn't want to do anything of the sort, and by now, she probably felt stupid for coming at me sideways in front of all these people.

She was embarrassed, and her face kind of shared a red undertone under her brown skin. Who was she to think I would move anything but the right way? I'd given her no reason to think such. All the rumors she heard about me, none of them were visible on her front, so who did she really think she was to yell at me in front of all these people? I wasn't done with her. I wanted to give her a glimpse of how cold I could be, so I caught an attitude and walked off because she knew I didn't do attention and she just caused this big scene.

I didn't even do anything wrong. I figured this could go one or two ways. She would either follow me, asking me to forgive her, or her friends who had hyped her head up would go in and consult her and try to make her feel better. The second option was the one that was chosen. I walked away while the crowd parted for me like I was Moses at the Red Sea. I paid no attention to anyone at that time. I just felt like getting away from the scene right then. She would come around later, and we would have some words about it, I was sure.

I had second thoughts about that letter and number now because if this little shit got out, imagine what else could happen if I fucked her? I thought to myself.

I would sleep on it and decide whether or not to make my move afterward. I really tried to hide that side of me from her, but that was sort of provoked. While I started my journey to my next class, John came running over with a smile on his face that only I could see.

"You're a ill nigga, son. Ha ha! I peeped you dish the note off at the door to Risk and kept it moving. But how you just cleaned that up was dope, and you made her feel like shit. You ain't shit for that," he said as he chuckled some more after finally getting his words out.

I knew I was all the way wrong in this situation, but it didn't faze me at all. I was the man, and I felt like it. I wasn't even focusing on that. I was checking to see if I had seen my pumpers out here, moving work throughout the hallways. Since the last school year, we came up a lot. I was rich as fuck on the low, but I wanted more and more because there was so much money to be made. I had boroughs on lock with the amount of shit I was moving, and I still moved as though I was still a regular dude out here.

Just as the bell rang, I found my seat in this AP chemistry class I really had no connection with. All of a sudden, it all started to settle in, and I began to feel bad for making Sabrina feel like shit. At this point, all I wanted to do was sit and wait for this bell to ring so I could go and find her and smooth things over after the hurricane had hit home base.

The first day of this class was just as I expected: boring with a mixture of the course syllabus and what type of expectations we might have down the line in this chemistry class. Same ole bullshit. But the class was drawing to an end, and I had to figure out how to get to my girl because if I ignored her while she was mad, it was going to give her time to get even madder and I'd have to make up for that too. Maybe I did overdo it just a tad bit. The bell rang, and as soon as I stepped out the classroom, Sabrina was there waiting for me.

She had a guilty, apologetic face on as she spoke "Baby, I'm sorry for wildin' out on you in front of all those people earlier. You know how I can get, so I apologize for making clowns out of both of us. I just can't imagine you with another chick. Let alone fucking her the way you fuck me."

I couldn't lie, I wanted to fuck Tyesha, so I figured I'd try to throw a sly remark in here to see what she would say. "Babe, if I wanted to fuck her, I would make sure you were there so we could fuck her together," I said.

She smiled and hit me in the arm and said, "You better not. That's even if I let you fuck her." I was shocked by the response, and I showed it with my facial expression.

"Oh, really, babe? You're about that action, huh?" I replied.

She dug her face into my arm, looking embarrassed, and said, "Leave me alone."

I figured she was curious, and the sight of seeing me fuck another chick while doing whatever with her would be arousing to her. I got the response I wanted, so there was no need to even creep. I still wanted to read what shorty wrote in the letter though.

I have one more class before my day is over with, I thought to myself. I might fuck with lunch with the crew to see what the move was for later. Plus I was sure Sabrina was going to want me to wait for her to finish her classes after lunch.

As soon as I stepped in the lunchroom, I saw the sections in which the cafeteria was broken up. You had the smart nerdy kids in the cut to your left, pretty girls were to the far right, the graffiti artists were all the way in the back. You could tell who was nice with the pen because everything was tagged up, from the book bags to the notebooks. The Jansport book bags were heavy with the strings; people wore these like a badge of honor. The more strings you had, the higher your status, but you had to look out because there was always someone trying to get you for the strings to the point you had to burn your tips and keep your book bag on at all times. Finally, you had the cool kids or kids that everyone fucked with in the center as though they knew they were the main attraction and people wanted to be like them. I drifted over to that crowd occasionally, but I normally sat a little way apart off in my own world. Rock came over and sat with me as I grabbed my apple juice and my regular soft pretzel with no salt and sat down.

"Yo, son, I heard about that shit with Sabrina earlier. John said you climbed out of it without a mark." He laughed as he said it.

144

"You know me, son. I maneuver well under pressure. It's one of my strong suits. But I'll have to move better in the future if I decide to make any moves on shorty. Yooooooooooo, check this. I threw the bait out there with Sabrina about me wanting to fuck Tyesha, and she got a bit crazy. But she was like, it would have to be done together and only if she allowed it."

"Stopppppppppp playing, son! You lying, son! For real? She didn't say that!" Rock replied.

"Nah, son, I'm so serious. I wanted to see what she was about on that level, and she responded the way I wanted her to, so there's no reason to even creep because she's about that life right now. We shall see though. I really can't call it right now, but she is saying all the right things," I replied. I had plans to test her later on that day, but I didn't want to take it too far where she would think something of it.

I also had to get some cash and re-up up with Jose before the end of the week, so my schedule worked perfect for me with the early dismal. I would slide out park my whip up somewhere, get the cash, and get in a taxi to do the exchange. Nothing was going to change on my end, so I had no worries. Rock and I talked a little bit more before I slid off to go find Sabrina.

CHAPTER 20

A ll I hear was my phone ringing at 2:00 a.m. as I lay in bed with Sabrina. I thought, *Who would call my cell this late?*

I answered the phone, and all I heard was Risk yelling, "Son, get dressed! I'll be over to your crib in ten minutes. Rock got shot, like, an hour ago!"

Instantly, my adrenaline started pumping like never before. I had questions I wanted answered, but I would wait for Risk to pull up to let me know what happened. I didn't want to startle Sabrina, but she could peep my sudden discomfort, so I told her the situation and that I was going to check him and see what had happened.

I threw on all black, just in case it was going to be that type of night. I kissed Sabrina and told her I would be back soon but not to wait up for me. I said I would be careful so she wouldn't worry. She was already worried and begged to come with me, but I told her not to. She didn't argue much because the expression on my face was telling her I just wanted answers. I didn't even know how bad the shot was or if he even got shot more than once. It just seemed to be like a whole lot to take in at one time, so I guessed she got my drift.

I left the crib and grabbed my strap out my car from inside the stash box. I didn't want to take the one in the floor panels inside my room because that would've led to more questions, and I didn't have the time for that right now. Risk pulled up dressed in similar attire, like he already knew what the deal was.

"Yo, son, what the fuck happened? Is he all right? Where did this shit happen? How did it happen? Does he know who did this shit?" I asked.

"I don't know how it happened. He just said he was going to make drop with one of the dudes who works for him. He said he saw someone in the cut as he looked at his man's eyes. He seen someone come out the cut and clapped him and his man up and took the work and the cash. He's good though. He took two, and the bullets went in and out one in the leg and one in the shoulder. He said he recognized the voice, but he wasn't too sure yet. He was out there in Jamaica Queens, not too far from the Ave. You know, he had his ball and gym bag with him, so the cops were looking at it like mugging against an innocent kid. His man got hit in the chest, but it's looking like he's going to pull through," Risk responded quickly.

"Where do they have him at? I'm going to grab some shirts out the car real quick since it's not looking like that kind of night. I don't want to go in the hospital dressed in all black and draw attention to us when you just told me it's looking like an innocent mugging," I said as I hoped out the car.

I took my Roscoe with me and put it back in the stash box for use at a later time. Shit was about to get ugly, and I knew it. This just fucked up a lot of shit on his end and my end. We couldn't afford to get robbed like that and not respond, but I already had a plan in the works in my mind. It would work, too, but we would have to lie low and strike when the time was right. We couldn't move off pure emotion, but I knew something was going to happen real soon. I could feel it. We pulled up to Jamaica hospital within minutes. Rah and John were in the lobby, trying to find out the room where Rock was located.

"Yo, son, this is wild right now. Who did this? Something's got to give, son, and the payback has to be brutal."

But before John could finish his statement, I stopped him and told him that this wasn't the time nor the place to talk about that but that it would be handled. We got the room information from the help desk and proceeded to Rock's room.

Something about the whole situation and this hospital didn't sit right with me, but I couldn't put my finger on it Something was off, though. Walking through the hallway, I felt as though we were being followed, which had my antennas on alert.

We got to Rock's room, and I could hear him tell his mom, "Ma, I'm good. I'm just trying to pull through in time for basketball season to start."

I started chuckling as I entered the doorway and said, "This kid gets shot, and all he's thinking about is getting back on that court. One thing for sure is, you can't question his passion." I laughed a bit more to lighten the mood up in the room and to soften his mother's tears. I gave her a hug and told her everything was going to be okay and that he'd be fine. He had a purpose out here.

She smiled and wiped the tears from her eyes and said, "You always know the right things to say, Stephen. Thank you all for being here for my son. I appreciate it all. This shows me how deep you guys' bond really is." She knew every person in this room was family to us, and it didn't matter if we were related by blood or ghetto Kool-Aid. Family was family, and that was all that mattered to us.

I responded with a smile followed by an "I already know, Ma. We all know." I then turned to Rock and started cursing him out, "What's wrong with you? So you couldn't call anyone else, and you decided to hoop by yourself? You trying to get nice without us?" I didn't really curse him out. I was poking fun at the situation to cheer him up.

"I figured y'all was asleep and didn't want to wake anyone. I was working on my left hand a little bit. You know me. I eat, sleep, and breathe basketball, bro," he replied. "You still could've called us, but it's cool. We'll be there next time, working on our left hand too since you're trying to be ambidextrous with it," I replied with my sarcastic laugh to follow. Rock knew what I was saying as well as the rest of them team.

"I'm just happy you're alive, to be honest. I don't want to ask a bunch of questions now, but I will once they let you out of here," John said.

I nudged him. "Chill out. Let the boy breathe some. He should be getting discharged any moment now since it went through and they stitched him up already. Right?" I stated and asked him the question at the same time.

He nodded. "Yeah, I should be good to go."

"Bet get him some tea. Everything would be okay," Risk replied.

I laughed and said, "Damn, is tea the remedy to everything for black people?"

"Yo, my mom thinks so, so yep, I'm rocking with it. Tea with some honey should do the trick," he replied. Everyone started laughing, including Rock's mother.

"Ma, if everything is cool with you, once he gets up out of here, we are going to sleep over at Chris's house and make sure he's okay," I said. She wiped her eyes once more and agreed to the terms of the deal. I then turned to Risk and said, "Yep, I just volunteered your crib for the night. You got the most room, and Sabrina was at my house."

"Damn, he didn't even ask me or talk to me about this at all on the ride over here, but I'm with it. It's been a while since we had a sleepover anyway," he responded, laughing.

As soon as Risk responded, the nurse walked in the room and told Rock he was clear to go but to take it easy for the next few weeks till he was fully healed. Rock stood up and tried to walk as though he hadn't gotten shot hours ago. To be honest, I was quite surprised to see him do such a thing. I thought it was the determination and drive he had in him to not be seen knocked down.

I told him, "Aye, son, I know you're a tough guy now after taking those two, but you're going to get in this wheelchair and get these crutches and let us help you out." I knew his pride was heavy, but he really wasn't supposed to be walking like he was.

He didn't argue. He just smiled and mumbled "Great. Now this guy is my pops now too" under his breath.

I also told him I wouldn't be able to play basketball unless he got healthy again. I knew that would make him listen and focus up even more. Basketball was his life besides hustling. He took that very seriously.

"We need to talk about this situation ASAP," I said as he sat down in the wheelchair.

He nodded as I pushed him toward the elevator doors. His mom kissed him and went around and hugged and kissed each and every one of us before telling us to take care of her son. Everyone agreed to do such as we entered the elevator.

Once we got to the lobby, Risk pulled up his whip, and Rah and John did the same exact thing. I was standing in the middle of the lobby, waiting for everyone to come back with Rock, and I felt as though someone was watching us. Just as soon as I got the feeling, I looked over my shoulder to my right, and I saw someone standing in the cut, observing everything. He didn't look like a cop or a DT, but his body language read thug or shooter. I didn't like how the situation was starting to feel. His stare was growing more and more intense as the seconds grew longer.

Unable to take my eyes off this man, I started to think about my gun I had left in my car. This felt like a rap song or something to me. The burner was never supposed to be too far from situations like this. How did he have the drop on us? I didn't want to make Rock nervous, so I didn't tell him what was going on. I wanted to wait till we got in the car to tell him, but the way it was looking, I might need to reevaluate this whole situation.

As I turned and looked at the door, I saw Risk opening the passenger door to help Rock get in. I guessed the look on my face had told a story to the point that Risk had to ask me what was wrong. It was then I told him we were being watched by dude in the corner and I couldn't tell homeboy's intentions. I didn't have my roscoe on me, so I couldn't move at all. I knew Risk had his burner on him, but I didn't want him to make a scene and start blasting in this hospital, because it wouldn't be a good look for either party.

Risk looked to his left and my right and observed who I was talking about. The guy wasn't staring as hard. He started to read a paper he had in his hand, trying not to make it obvious. Rock's adrenaline must have been on full once more because at this point, he had gotten out of the wheelchair and focused on the next move. I guessed he figured if some shit was going to go down, he wasn't going to be sitting in the crossfire or he'd rather die or get shot again on his own terms. We had been talking as though Rock wasn't there, so he wasn't taking chances.

Risk clutched his waistband, waiting for me to call the next move. But I could see the guy in the corner wasn't paying us attention anymore, so I told him to leave it alone and we should just get the fuck out of this hospital. We sped up our walk as he headed to the car out front. If the dude was someone to fear, we had him made, so I wasn't worried. We could find him if we needed to.

I sat in the back seat as Risk and Rock sat up front. Risk sped off quickly, and John and Rah followed. I began to ask Rock all the questions I wanted to ask in the hospital but couldn't because of the location and people who were around.

"Son, how the fuck did you get shot? Why didn't you have the burner on you? You said you think you knew who did it. You recognized the voice? How's your worker doing? How are you feeling? You know we have to switch everything up now, right? Protection is needed for real now. This can never happen again," I said all at once.

Rock began answering my questions just as quickly as I was asking them. "I don't even know how I got shot, but the funny part is that I'm always cautious about every move I make but tonight I wasn't thinking about that. I'm normally packing toast, but tonight I wasn't. I know the voice I heard. I seen this dude around before, but I don't know his name off the bat. Sean is good. They didn't ask him much. He looked like an innocent bystander, so the cops were just happy he pulled through.

"His story is the same as mine. We was hooping and was walking to the bus station when it happened. But I'm good for real. That shit burned a lot, but I felt like since it went in and out, I'll be good to go in no time. But my question is, when are we going to get this dude back? This can't go unfinished. I'm not the one to let something like this slide. This nigga could've killed me for real. To rob me is one thing, but to shoot me is even crazier. So what's the move, Steph?"

My mind had been racing for a while, but I had it planned out in my head, so I spoke up. "Yo, give it a while to die down to let them think you're a pussy, and then we will strike like a cobra. I promise we will lay him down and everything in sight to let niggas know what it is. If he has a crew, they have to get it, too, but the timing has to be right. Heal up. Switch the moves around, and we will get it all back.

It wasn't that big a loss, but it was still a loss. I'm plotting right now, son. Believe me. I'm going to make a few calls to Jason and Jose to see about protection. But till then, just lie low. We gonna get it back, I promise!"

Everyone in the car nodded like they knew what the outcome was going to be. I just had to fill Rah and John in on the details when we got to Risk's crib. It was about to go down, but I wanted to do it right with no leaks. Right now, I needed Rock to heal first and foremost, and I would do the thinking for the rest of us.

CHAPTER 21

"Yo, you got the gat on you?" I asked Risk, Rock, John, and Rah as I looked at each one of them. They all nodded. "Hit the lights. Put the ski mask and shades on once we start squeezing at the dude who shot you and his crew. We don't need any leaks. After this is done, burn the clothes and toss the burners. Y'all understand?"

"Son, we been over this shit over a dozen times. How many times are we going to do this?" Rah asked.

"As many times as it takes you niggas to get it. I'm not going down for no dumb shit. Yo, Rock, you sure this is where he's been laying his head lately? The other day, I tailed him in a cab, and he went to a different spot."

I didn't want any mistakes. The worst thing that could happen would be to hit the wrong spot and let them know we were looking for them.

"Yeah, I've been on it like clockwork after I healed up," he replied.

"As soon as he pulls up, we're going to shoot everything in sight, on life, kid," I told them.

I was nervous deep down, but my face said I was ready. Taking a life wasn't what I wanted to do or had any plans to do, but this motherfucker crossed the line. He had to go.

"Yo, that's him right there, but he's with two other people. How do you want to approach it, Steph?" Risk asked.

"You and John take the nigga on the left side. Rah, you clap the dude on the right. Rock and I will handle him. Remember, no words, no names. Just spray the nigga up," I told everyone.

I pulled my ski mask down and put the shades over my eyes, and they followed suit. We opened the car doors slowly and crept up on them as they continued to walk. It felt too easy at the moment, but my adrenaline was pumping on blast. I was finally ready. Just as soon as the thought entered my head, one of the dudes turned around.

"Oh, shit! They're trying to creep!" he let out.

Risk clapped him twice as he tried to dodge behind a parked car. The other dude let out a yell and tried to run, but it was too late. Rah and John was blazing the heat at him to the point I thought he got hit with a full magazine. With all those shots that went into his body, there was no way he would survive. The dude that robbed Rock reached for the gun on his waist, but to no avail. He didn't have time to take it off safety because Rock started squeezing at him. Rock hit him in the chest and the leg so he couldn't run. He fell flat on his face, moaning in pain.

I ran up to him and turned him over. "You robbed the wrong one, motherfucker. Now you'll meet your maker!" I shouted as I squeezed two more into his chest.

Everyone took a shot in different parts of his body. Then I told Rock to finish him. Before I could finish my sentence, Rock had popped him in his helmet. As I looked up, I saw a face that I'd seen before. The dude from the hospital was coming at us, holding a Mac-10. The crazy part was, he wasn't spraying it. Who was this nigga?

I pointed my gun at him and was about to squeeze, but he yelled out, "Yo, I don't want beef! Your uncle sent me to watch over y'all after your man got hit. That's why I'm here. I came to lay the strip down, but y'all beat me to the punch. You can call your uncle if you don't believe me."

From the sincerity in his voice, I knew he was who he said he was.

Why didn't he say that before? I thought to myself. Now wasn't the time to ask questions. We had to get off this block ASAP!

John had already run to get the car, so it was time to get to moving. I told the newcomer he almost got killed in the hospital, but I didn't want that kind of a scene. He agreed it was a dangerous moment for the both of us and that was why he stopped staring. He didn't know how we'd react, especially with our man just getting shot. He didn't want to inadvertently create a situation, which almost backfired.

I told him that I would get up with him at a later time as I hopped in the whip. I was sure going to ask Jason about this dude and why he didn't tell us about the protection. However, the only thing that mattered right now was getting out of these clothes and having John torch this car.

We got to the spot where we stored our cars and hopped out. I reiterated the mission to John once more. I then huddled with rest of the fellas, giving last-minute instructions. My adrenaline was still pumping. I had never killed a man before, and this just gave me a boost under my belt. I felt like anyone who ever tried this line would have the same results.

I felt like an animal that was just released from its cage. No one could stop me now. I started thinking about what just occurred and how my friends just clapped up these dudes with no remorse. Risk looked like a real shooter. I thought one shot put the kid down. As crazy as the shit was, I felt safe now, and our business wouldn't be compromised any further.

CHAPTER 22

It's been a few weeks since we put in that work and handled that problem. I must say everything went smoothly as planned. The police still had no suspects, so we were good. At this point, it was the least of my worries. I was really starting to change. I was having trouble sleeping some nights, and Sabrina was noticing my sudden discomfort. She didn't know anything about the situation at all. All she knew was that Rock got shot a few months ago coming from the park. Sabrina was grateful he was alive and was glad it wasn't me in those shoes. We didn't talk much about that night. I guessed she figured it was a touchy subject for me. Either way, I had no problem not being questioned about the details of what happened.

Some days were better than others, but I had my team. We were stronger than ever now. Because of the incident, we had to start moving differently to avoid a repeat of that night. We couldn't afford to keep getting ambushed. Nor could we go around, stacking up bodies. To the naked eye, it looked as though we were still moving the same and had no protection. That was where anyone who was watching would've been wrong.

I had people camped out in whips on each block, on both corners. That way, if anything was to go down, the offending party wouldn't make it off the block alive. The only people who knew about this were my brothers. I didn't trust the rest of the dudes copping from us enough to share that with them. For me, I still feel like Rock getting shot was an inside job. I felt like the dude that got shot was the person who was trying to come up even more.

I was cautious now, and I didn't hide that fact. I often found myself circling the block more before I parked my whip. Some would say I was crazy, but I cared about my well-being far too much. I couldn't get caught in a situation like Rock did. My planning was spot on at this level. It had to be. I didn't know who was watching or lurking in the dark, trying to predict our next move. I had too much to worry about in such a short span of time. Work couldn't slow up, and school couldn't take the back burner to these streets. I had to avoid the law at all times to make all my dreams lateral. So far so good, but one slip could change things forever.

All I could think about was how we laid the murder game down on that kid and his crew. But what if he was working for someone else, and they still had eyes on us? My mind was in full-time thought mode. I felt like I needed to change things up a bit and expand a few spots. I needed to take over another building. That way, I could have my workers cutting and bagging up in different spots. Just in case someone really had the drop on us, I'd be one step ahead. I decided I would talk to Risk about the move first. Before I made the decision to shift part of the operation elsewhere, I wanted to hear his take on it. I was sure he had a few spots that we could use.

I hit Risk up for a quick meeting so we could hash out the details. I kind of felt bad that I didn't include the rest of the team in my gatherings with Risk. I just felt they had too much going on and weren't as level minded as us when it came to this shit. I didn't really blame them at all. We were still kids and had a little bit more growing to do. Although they were very mature for their age, they still lacked something that I saw in Risk.

I didn't feel totally bad for them though. They were getting to the money, a lot of it too. So it was a win-win for all of us, even if I excluded them from this minor step.

"Yo, Steph! What's up, baby?" Risk asked.

"You know me, son. I'm just trying to make it out here."

We exchanged handshakes, and then we began walking down the street, distancing ourselves from normal city commotion. It was crazy because the older heads knew us well and showed respect. They knew we were getting to the money, but they didn't know the depth of it. We were often embraced by others throughout the streets, but it was still weird to see the older dudes embracing us younger guys. I guessed it was all part of the game. Risk and I walked a few more blocks before I began to let him know what was in my mind.

"Son, we need to expand out here. We need to switch up spots. Well, not really switch them up… We need to add a new one, along with the shit in your projects. Just for safety, son. I'm more paranoid these days, and we can't afford to lose money or get robbed. So we need a new spot, just to put my mind at ease. Any ideas?"

Risk chuckled as though I had said something funny. "Son, how'd I know you were going to call me with some shit like that? The funny thing is, I already started looking at spots because I was thinking the same thing. I think Rock getting shot was an eye opener for all of us, son."

I nodded in agreement with him.

"We all have that paranoid feeling buried inside, even if it's not displayed much to the public or among each other. I got two locations mapped out though. Both are good locations and should be a breeze in and out," he continued.

"I think we should have these people that work for us on shifts, more like parents or teenagers coming home from work or school. Once they enter the spot to work, everything comes off. I feel like it's safer this way and less obvious. That's just a suggestion, though, if you're up to it."

I was intrigued by what Risk was saying, and my face said it all. "Go on. This sounds good," I told him.

"The spots I was telling you about, it's one on the Eastside of Harlem, and the other is out in Brownsville. I figured both are close enough, so either one of us or the guys could check in if needed."

That was what I loved about Risk. He was always on the same page even when I didn't speak it. It was like we were twins separated at birth. The suggestions were tempting, but I had to check them out first before I made a decision.

Suddenly, I had an even better idea. We were going to do both spots just the way Risk explained. That meant more products had to come and go for it to be successful. I wasn't fond of going to the spot to check in on anything though. I let Risk know that, and that he wouldn't be going anymore either.

"We're gonna have someone else do the checkups on the spots. That way, it's not a face to anything, if one of them gets bagged."

I wanted to protect us at all cost. I felt as though everyone else was expendable. I knew Risk wasn't feeling not being able to check on things the way he liked, but he saw the bigger picture I presented to him. He agreed, and we made our way to the new spots to check everything out.

CHAPTER 23

B usiness was moving, and it seemed everything was back to the norm. I no longer felt stressed or like I had to look over my shoulders. I didn't let my guard down, but I no longer felt it needed to be on code red. The thoughts of still lying to Sabrina never stopped lingering in my head. I was honest and a liar at the same time. What was a man to do? Should I really tell her about all the things I was into?

I didn't want to break her heart, and I honestly felt she deserved more. I started to think about it a bit deeper. She'd never had someone be completely honest with her. Her father sold drugs and killed people for Jose. I was sure she knew nothing about that, so I felt bad to an extent. If he could keep that secret up for all those years, I could too. I just had to play my cards right and remain sneaky.

Was it wrong? Sure, it was. However, I felt as though I didn't owe her complete honesty. Well, not yet at least. I wanted to spend time with her because I'd been so distant since Rock had gotten shot. I didn't want her to think I didn't care for her anymore, so time alone with her was needed. I beeped her with my code to let her know I needed to speak to her. Shortly after, I got a call from her, and I started asking her questions. I wanted to know what she had planned for the day and if I could interrupt with some plans of my own.

My words were always so smooth when they rolled off my tongue. I could sense her smile and warm glow over the phone. It didn't matter what she had planned for the day. The moment I told her I wanted to spend time with her, all those other plans ceased to exist. I had her heart, and I knew no matter what I did, she would be forgiving and open.

"Babe, so what are you trying to do today?" I asked her.

"Honestly, it doesn't matter. As long as I'm with you, I'll have fun."

I wanted to do something different with her. I was hungry, so I asked her if she wanted to cook for me. I had never asked her to cook for me, and I didn't know if she could handle that task. I did know her mother was a damn good cook, so I figured the apple didn't fall far from the tree. Still, it was a shot in the dark, but I went for it anyway. I knew my way around the kitchen if she needed help. Growing up, I watched my grandmother cooking, so I knew I could hold it down. My request didn't seem to faze her at all.

"What do you want? I've been waiting for you ask me to cook for a while. I guess you thought I couldn't cook, huh? Well, you're wrong!"

I guessed I underestimated her skills a little bit, but I was ready to put her skills to the test.

"Give me your best meal, baby," I replied with a chuckle.

"I'll surprise you. You won't be disappointed!"

We chatted a bit more before we got off the phone. I started to make my way back home to shower and get ready for my planned meal. It was still early in the day, so I had time to get a few things done, maybe even get a surprise gift for Sabrina. I didn't know what to get her though. Ever since she'd been my girl, I had surprised her with almost everything under the sun. I was truly stuck and out of ideas. Maybe I'd just take her shopping tomorrow. What woman didn't like to go shopping? None that I could think of. That would give us even more time to spend with each other and reconnect. I started to think, Was that my form of connecting with people? Buying them gifts? Spoiling them to show I cared? I didn't know, but I knew that seemed to be my go-to when I wanted to get close to Sabrina. Maybe I felt she deserved everything and more.

After a few hours, Sabrina arrived at my house, ready to hit the kitchen. "Come on, baby, we have to make a store run go before I start cooking."

She had all this time to get everything, and now I had to wait even longer to eat. I was sure my facial expression didn't hide my thoughts because she looked at me and started talking again.

"You didn't think I was going to walk to your house with a bunch of stuff and you weren't going to help with the meal, did you?"

"Yeah, I did. I already waited two hours for you to get over here, and that was cool. Now you're talking about more waiting time. I'm starving now!" I replied sharply, perhaps a little sharper than I intended.

I became another person when I was hungry. I became mean. At this point, I no long wanted a home-cooked meal. I'd rather just go out to eat and save the cooking for another day, when I wasn't annoyed. I could see in Sabrina's face she really wanted to cook for me, but I no longer cared to wait for the food. I had no idea what she was going to make or how long it was going to take. Either way, I wasn't having it, and I didn't care if she felt a way. Before I could utter a word, Sabrina tried to guilt-trip me. It was like she knew exactly what was on my mind.

"So you're mad that I want to cook right now and you don't want to wait. So you'd rather go out to eat because you're so fuckin' hungry right now, huh?" she asked in Spanish. The words were coming out fast and rolling off her tongue like water on a duck's back.

The funny thing was, she was always so cute and sexy when she got an attitude with me. I couldn't help but chuckle every time. She might have me this time, but I wouldn't give her the joy of knowing just yet.

I argued back with her just keep me entertained for a while. "I'm serious. I'm not waiting for you to cook now! I really am starving. I skipped breakfast and had nothing for lunch, so yeah, I'm hungry. I'm sure you can understand that. You'd feel the same way if you hadn't eaten all day long."

She nodded her head and agreed, but quickly responded, "Okay, so you want to go out to eat, right? It's going to take time to get there, right? You aren't taking traffic into consideration at all. That's more time, right? Now we get to the restaurant, and you have to order the food and wait for them to cook it. More time, right? With all that time wasted, your ass could just sit here and shut the fuck up while I cooked. It's going to be that long anyway. I know what I'm doing. This isn't my first time doing this, you know."

I couldn't even argue with her at this point. She brought up some valid points that I didn't take into consideration during my hunger outburst. I felt defeated at this point but wouldn't show it through my facial expressions. Sabrina had one on the scorecard for the day, and I had zero.

Before I could respond, she was back at my neck again. "So just sit your ass down, wait for me to make the food, and shut up."

I couldn't front. Her aggressive nature was turning me on just as fast as the words were coming out of her mouth. I was hungry, but I also wanted to fuck her pretty ass for putting me in my place. I didn't know what it was. It was just something about her that always turned me on. I grabbed her by her neck midsentence and pulled her closer to me. I grabbed her ass and started kissing her with the thought of hunger far from my mind. They were overcome with thoughts of us passionately having sex.

I could feel Sabrina's heart beating faster, as if she knew exactly what was about to happen next. I just knew I was about to substitute that meal I was craving, momentarily, with her pussy right in the middle of this kitchen. As I started taking off her clothes, I made my way down to her panties. I could feel the wetness from her pussy leaking. She was ready for me to do whatever to her body.

She didn't fight with me as I pulled her panties down. I started licking her pussy with different motions, searching to find that one spot that would drive her crazy. I was gonna show her how hungry I was—for her pussy. In no time, I found her spot and kept licking it. She grabbed my head and forcefully pushed me into her pussy while putting her legs around my shoulders. She started moaning softly and telling me not to stop. I complied with every word she whispered to me. She was the boss of me, and I was there to fulfill her every desire.

We were really wildin' in the kitchen, knowing at any moment my grandmother could come through the door. I didn't care. I unbuttoned my pants and proceeded to pull them down. Sabrina attempted to go down on me, but I stopped her in her tracks. I grabbed her by the throat as I thrust myself into her voluptuousness. I wanted to find that exact spot that would have her moaning for dear life.

She started grabbing my shoulders and putting her arm around my neck as I found the spot that made her cringe. The faces she made during our escapade were a sight to see. I noticed that by this time, her body was sliding down and she was starting to look depleted as the sweat glistened off her forehead. I knew what was about to happen next. As soon as the thought entered my head, she started screaming.

"Papi, don't stop. I'm about to cum!"

I immediately increased my pace, biting her neck and clutching her waist as I stroked her. I felt her body shaking as she yelled out she was cummin'. I suddenly got the same urge in my body to do the same. It felt as though her pussy went into another form as it slid back and forth on my dick.

I knew the outcome would be lovely. I didn't fight it. I pulled out and came all over her chest. Before I could even catch my breath, I started talking shit.

"Now you can cook for me, babe," I said, laughing.

"Okay, Papi," she replied, laughing, but not before rolling her eyes and sucking her teeth.

CHAPTER 24

Somehow, I managed to get Knicks tickets, and I thought it would be a good idea to take Sabrina's father to the game. I figured it would be a great bonding experience between the both of us. I had the perfect game. The Knicks were playing the Miami Heat on a Friday night at the Garden. The house was bound to be packed, and it would definitely be a great game. I knew Sabrina's father wouldn't have anything to do. He was low key and chilled in the crib for the most part. He lived like a retired person who worked a few jobs. He gave off good vibes and good energy every time we were around each other. This was always a pleasant feeling for me.

Although I knew he was cool, I still had to protect myself. I didn't take anything for granted when I was in his presence. That was still my girl's dad, and I was still a drug dealer. There was no way around that. I had to make some moves before the game, so I checked Rock to make sure he was good. I checked on the rest of the fellas as well. Their operation was running smoothly, so that meant mine was too.

I went to Jamaica Avenue to pull off a quick outfit for the night. I wasn't sure if I wanted to go with some Uptowns or some AirMax 95s. I knew what I had in mind. I just wasn't sure if I could do it. Plus, I didn't have a lot of time to start shopping, so I had to think quick. The avenue was packed with a bunch of chicks from damn near every part of the city. The crazy part was, it was like this every day. The energy out here was crazy, and it was some bad chicks on the scene as well.

A familiar face out of the crowd started walking toward me, and her eyes gave it away. I knew exactly who she was. How could I not?

She was my crush on the low. I knew I'd see her again outside of our usual setting.

"I see you didn't use the number I gave to you in homeroom that first day of school," Tyesha said in a crazy sort of tone.

"Yeah, I know. You almost got me killed with that little escapade you pulled. My girl wasn't feeling that at all," I replied while laughing.

Tyesha was sexy as hell and aggressive. She let it be known she was on me, and that alone was sexy to me. I couldn't front like I wasn't attracted to her because my actions displayed something different. I wanted to fuck with her, but I wasn't sure how to maneuver with her. She wasn't side chick material at all, and if I wasn't with Sabrina, I would've definitely fucked with her hard. I wanted her, but my approach was going to be way too aggressive for this setting. There were way too many eyes out here. Shorty was cocky with it too. She knew she was ill, and that was another notch on her belt.

"I wasn't worried about that at all. You shouldn't have been neither. I wanted you, and I could've had you years ago, but you weren't ready for me. So I feel cheated because you were supposed to be mine, but you got away."

Before she could finish, I stopped her. The crush she might have had before had evolved into something far greater than she could ever imagine.

"You just gave me all those words for what? You know I fuck with you and all, but your timing is off. I got Sabrina now, and I'm good. What you want from me? You know I can't move the way I would've moved before I got with shorty."

Her rebuttal was just as crazy as mine, if not better. "Look, you know what it is. Stop frontin' like you don't want me all to yourself too. I'm not a side, so don't treat me as one," she said, looking me directly in the eyes. Damn, shorty was bold. She knew how to get what she wanted. "You'd be mad if you saw me out with another nigga, knowing you could've had me but didn't take the chance you wanted to take. And don't front like I'm not telling the truth," she continued.

I couldn't front. I wanted her, and I had wanted her for years. I was too busy getting money that I didn't have time to check her like I wanted to. This was a crazy position the man upstairs had put me in. Even crazier thing about this ordeal was, she was with her friends, and they all looked good too. I was so focused on her that I didn't even peep at them lingering around. I responded as I should've.

"So what you want to do? Because I see you aren't taking no for an answer. I respect that, but what do you want from me?" I countered, trying to maneuver out of the dangerous territory I was in.

Her next move was even bolder, and I couldn't avoid it. She leaned in, grabbed my dick, and kissed me all in the same motion. Her lips where soft as fuck! I couldn't front. For that moment, it felt right. Everything that was happening felt good and a bit surprising.

After she let go, she whispered in my ear, "I want you, as if that wasn't clear enough. Now give me your number because I'm not playing around with you this time. I know you still have my number too. I saw you pass it to your homeboy before she came around."

Damn! I was caught. No wonder she was so sure of herself.

"I knew right then it was a matter of time before I'd catch you again. If you didn't feel the same, you wouldn't have taken that risk to keep the note with my number on it."

Tyesha was absolutely right. She had me cornered, and she knew it. I wanted her but was still trying to be a good dude at the same time. I felt like I had to give her my math. I told her I'd hit her on the jack later on after I finished up for the day. She kissed me again as her friends giggled in the background, and they went about their day.

Now here I was, scraping back to my normal self. I needed to finish shopping and get ready, all while trying to make this game on time. I lost focus for a little while but quickly regained it.

While I started walking, all I could think was, that was a bad move I just pulled. However, I wasn't the same guy I was before. So much had happened to me in a short amount of time. I felt like the pieces of this "man puzzle" were coming together, and I had to be ready for it. I finally found everything I wanted to wear for the game tonight. I had just enough time to get dressed and pick Sabrina's father up before the game.

I pressed my clothes, laced my kicks up, and proceeded out the door. I had no intentions on driving to the city, so I walked to Sabrina's house. I figured we could get a cab from there to the game. As I knocked on the door, Sabrina answered as if she was standing guard of the door.

"Hey, baby! I missed you. What's up?"

"Nothing, babe. I came to take your father to the Knicks game with me tonight."

Before I could ask if he was available, I heard his voice out of nowhere. "Someone said Knicks? I'm there if we're talking Knicks."

I smiled and sort of laughed at his response.

"Give me ten minutes, and we can get out of here, Stephen. I want to change into my Knicks gear real quick," he said as he got up from his spot on the couch.

He looked impressed and excited all at the same time. I figured he would like that since he mentioned it last playoff time, about us catching up on games. As soon as he disappeared into one of the rooms, Sabrina's mother surfaced. Damn, she really looked good as fuck!

Her mom greeted me with her usual hug and kiss on the cheek. I couldn't help but think she was flirting with me every time I came around. I bet she had some good pussy too. I didn't know if she would act differently if it was ever just us two in the room. Sometimes I felt like she was testing me, like she really wanted to see what I was made of on the low. I liked the energy, and the animal in me would've done it, but it was way too risky.

However, this time, I knew she was flirting for real. She brushed her ass against my hand after the hug and looked back at me, smiling. Her mom was wild for that, but her ass was soft as hell. I could feel my cheeks becoming real rosy after the incident.

Soon after, Sabrina resurfaced, holding a drink, asking me if I was thirsty. How ironic. I couldn't say no, but the blush on my face said something.

"Stop looking at my mother, nasty," Sabrina said, laughing.

I started laughing as well. "It was written all over my face, like Rude Boyz and Gerald LeVert, huh?"

She smacked my shoulder and pinched me all while nodding. I knew it did, but I was so calm that it didn't seem to bother her much. It was more like she expected that from me by now.

I joked back with her. "You better act right, or I'll holla at her."

I said this all in a low voice because I didn't want her father to hear me at all. I didn't want those problems, even if it was said in a joking manner. I knew he was about that action, and I wasn't fuckin' with it. A few minutes had gone by before her father, Tony, resurfaced dressed in his Knicks gear with some fresh Shelltop Adidas. I laughed 'cause I thought it was real old school of him to do the shells, but he was fresh though. I couldn't front.

"Let's rock, Stephen. My main man, Stephen," he said, patting me on the shoulders.

I smiled and kissed Sabrina on the cheek. Then we walked out of the door. She was shocked I kissed her in the cheek, but again I didn't want the problems with her pops. Our cab ride to the Garden was smooth, and we were meshing really well with each other. We shared tons of laughs over things we both loved, one being the Knicks. He seemed hurt when we started discussing Patrick Ewing missing that layup a few years ago. I was hurt, too, but we were in a great place with this team we had right now. I knew we'd have a great time at the game.

I could feel the energy throughout the cab ride, and his vibes were good. I purchased the perfect seats for the game, not too far from Spike Lee. I didn't want that we would draw that much attention. This was my first time at the Garden, and I was amazed by how small the court really was. It looked so big on TV, but in actuality, it wasn't that big at all. I felt like a kid in a candy store, seeing all these guys I praised on the court, growing up. To finally see them in person was such a great feeling. We sat down in our seats as the game started.

"How many games have you been to before, Mr. Tony?" I asked.

"A few, but I've never been this close to the court, so this is amazing. I appreciate you taking time out your week to spend with me. This is truly a blessing," he said as he smiled in my direction.

I was pleased and humbled by the remark. Then out of nowhere, he said something that brought chills through my body.

"I've kept my eyes on you for some time now. I know who you are."

I sat there with a confused look on my face. I didn't know whether to be scared or shocked. Or both!

"What are you talking about, Mr. Tony?"

He responded just as quick as the words could leave my mouth. "Yes, I know who you are. Don't be alarmed. I mean no harm to you. You're a good kid, and you're dating my daughter. You probably have big plans for the both of you guys in the future, correct? It took me some time to figure you out, but I got you."

I was still stuck because I didn't know what he was getting at. At that very moment, I felt scared. I tried to play slow once again.

Then he leaned over and whispered into my ear, "I know your homeboy got shot a few months ago, but I wanted to know why him. So I had my guy follow you and clock your moves. You didn't move differently. You ran the same shift pretty much every day until one night."

At his words, I caught a lump in my throat.

Then he continued, "You're a killer. You and your friends killed those men who shot your homeboy. I know this because the person that was at the scene was one of my guys. I didn't want to startle you, so I told him to say he worked for your uncle in Miami. Yes, I know your uncle too. The funny thing about my line of work is, it's a small business and people seem to need my set of skills often."

I felt that lump getting bigger in my throat. I knew he said to not be alarmed, but the amount of info he knew about me was beyond alarming. It was a fuckin' DEFCON 1 crisis.

He continued talking in a low voice so only I could hear. "I told him to say he was working for your uncle so you wouldn't figure out who I really was. You were so stuck on the help you had forgotten to even ask your uncle about the person you had met in the alley. That wasn't like you, so that was your first mistake."

I couldn't even describe the feelings I had as he broke all that down to me. I had never in my life been so careless as to not check up on something I said I would. That was a huge mistake on my part, and I knew it. I felt my heart drop, and I was sure my face probably showed it at that time.

Tony continued, "I'm not upset with you. I understand why you did it. You didn't want your friend to feel him getting shot went unnoticed, so you had to do what you had to do. I like you and admire you. You're way smarter and more organized than me. I know if something were to happen to my daughter, it wouldn't be a question on what you would do. I see how you look at her, so I know you're for real about her. Don't worry. This will be our little secret, Steph. That's what they call you, right?" He patted my knee.

I was still in a state of shock because it all happened too quick for me to process. The one good thing was, he didn't say anything to me about Jose. I was so relieved by that alone. I figured he couldn't really track me on that. I hadn't handled drops or pick-ups as much since the incident happened. I didn't have my guys doing much handling either.

The part I didn't like was me being followed and I'd had no idea. That made me start feeling deeply paranoid. I thought I was secure, and I always had people watching out for me. Maybe I was tripping. I didn't know whether to agree or deny everything he was saying.

He seemed as though he knew how I felt, so he talked some more. "I know I just laid it on thick, young blood, but you're dating my princess, and I had to take precautions. You're good though. I know you can handle yourself. I won't have him following you anymore. But if you ever need a hand or get caught in a jam, I want you to know I got your back."

I kind of just nodded my head and agreed but a bunch of thoughts had entered my head. How'd he know the hospital that Rock was in? How'd he send his guy there so quickly? I figured Sabrina told her parents when she had gone home that night that Rock had gotten shot. There was no way it could've happened any other way.

He spoke one last time before we started watching the game again. "Now you know what I did for a living. Ask your uncle about me. He'll tell you how I got down."

I couldn't believe Jason knew him. I would be sure to ask him a bunch of questions in the morning—after I slept this off. Honestly,

I was not sure I'd even be able to sleep after all this. I felt safe, but I was slightly guarded. I had dealt with enough in recent months, and I felt blindsided. I had to tell the fellas about this shit in the morning; it would be wrong not to. This could be a big problem in the future, if I really thought about it.

I didn't think he would go to the extreme of offing me if I hurt his daughter. I thought he would only hurt her more with me out of the picture. I didn't like the fact that he had one up on me. He knew how I was moving without me even knowing. Thank God I didn't take any meetings like that after Rock got shot. I was paranoid before, and now with this bomb he dropped, it made my paranoia seem more real by the second.

Tony was a killer, and he knew killers. He also knew a lot of people I was cool with. This could potentially be a good thing and a bad thing. Who knew he was well connected like that? I knew he was ill and that his murder game had to be crazy. It had to be on point if he survived working for Jose all those years and he was still here. That was remarkable alone. Things just got a little bit trickier with all this new information. I didn't want to seem like I was overthinking it, so I actually put it in the back of my mind. I focused on the game for the rest of the night. I would handle business tomorrow and talk to everybody I needed to in the morning.

CHAPTER 25

I had trouble sleeping from all the information I had been given the night before. The sun couldn't come up any sooner. I was itching to call the fellas to tell them everything. I didn't want to alarm them, so I actually waited until the next day to fill them in. How could this happen? How did I become so careless and forget to do the little things I would have normally done? I couldn't help but feel like I let myself and the team down. I potentially put everyone in harm's way. I was supposed to be the leader of the crew. This should've never happened.

I knew Risk was the first person I would hit up. I'd meet with him before the rest of the crew because he would be way more understanding. So I called Risk, knowing he would be up early. This kid didn't sleep much and was always checking numbers. He didn't play at all.

"Yo, son! We need to talk, like, right now!" I said with much urgency once he picked up the phone.

I told him to come see me or I'd swing out his way so we could talk. It was, like, six in the morning, and the sun wasn't even up, but I couldn't sleep with all I found out last night. Like a half hour later, Risk was on my doorstep. I met him at the door after I heard his music playing from a distance.

I opened my door and told him, "Let's take a walk and chat." As we began walking, I started spilling all the shit I heard in the last twenty-four hours. "Son, Sabrina's father had the drop on us."

"What you mean he had the drop on us?" he asked.

"This motherfucker knows about the dudes we put down for shooting Rock. You remember the dude that popped up out of nowhere? The one who claimed he knew Jason? Well, that mother-fucker works for Tony, Sabrina's father. He wanted to know about the shooting, so he had dude tailing us for weeks to see what was going on. The crazy part is, I would've normally checked with Jason about the shooter, but my mind wasn't there the next day, and I took his word for it. You know I never do that!" I practically yelled to Risk.

I was both nervous and angry at myself for being this exposed. "I'm fuckin' slipping. He knows we killed them dudes, but he doesn't know about the drugs or anything else. Well, he didn't mention it 'cause the Knicks game would have been the perfect time to say something. Like, he did it so smoothly, son. He wasn't mad or anything. He knows Jason and all. He said, in his line of business, people always need help like that. It was just a lot to grasp, and I didn't expect this shit at all," I continued to blurt out. My mind kept going in full throttle. I couldn't stop it at all.

Risk had a way with words and quick solutions that were never temporary. He didn't look or sound shook or nervous as he responded, "Okay, so let's look at the facts here. Shorty's pops knows about the shootings? He had to be cool with it because you're still standing here, talking to me, which indicates that he sees something in you, either with the way you act around his daughter or something, because no harm has come your way or our way. There's no issue here if you really think about it on a serious note. This man sent protection for us when we least expected it because he knows your level of importance to his daughter."

Risk continued, "Was it you slipping? Hell yeah, you was slipping by not thinking things over. Also, by not contacting Jason to see who the dude was after we clapped them dudes up. It was a lot of shit going on, so I can't fault you for that. I probably would've missed that piece of the puzzle, too, but you and I know you damn sure won't make the same mistake twice."

His words were slightly comforting. He was helping me process everything devoid of emotion while looking directly at me.

Risk said, "So you know what we're gonna do from here? Son, we are going to use this and hit the ground running with it hard. I honestly think you should have another talk with him offline again, maybe in another setting like that, and let him know who you really are. I mean, what can really happen by doing that? He already knows you don't mind putting in work if you really needed to, so let's use it. Think about it. You sit him down and tell him your plans for the future with his daughter, his most precious jewel. Then let him know what you're doing in these streets. He's bound to send crazy protection around us, son.

"There won't be much we'd have to worry about on the streets but getting these drugs off and expanding. He's going to find out sooner or later if you keep messing with his daughter anyway. No matter how low you are, that man has killed plenty of people. Trust me. I'm sure he'll find out. But I don't think it matters, though, honestly. He likes you. You've mentioned that before, so move with it like that.

"This is actually a great look for the team. I don't think we should tell Rock and them about this though. They might be a little more paranoid and less understanding about the situation than I am right now. This is an opportunity, and we have to take it. Trust me on this one, Steph. It's a good look, son. We good out here. Talk to that man," Risk concluded.

The picture started coming together rather fast after hearing Risk run everything back down to me. I no longer had the feeling of fear inside my body. Just like that, I was relieved from all the stress that I had accumulated in the last twenty-four hours. My next move would be crucial from whichever standpoint I chose. I was leaning more on the telling Sabrina's father everything than not saying anything. I trusted and valued Risk's opinion, and his words carried a lot of weight with me.

"The only issue we have now or *you* have now is, you can't do his daughter dirty because he's got the drop on you. I'm sure you've already thought of that though," Risk replied once more.

I had no intentions on doing Sabrina dirty. I loved her so much. I knew feelings did change in time, so I would definitely have to tread lightly. I would never want to hurt her feelings nor come up missing. I felt strange from the added pressure that just put on me. It was as if I held everyone's lives in my hand at that moment. Risk had a funny way of making me see things his way with a vividly painted picture. What was a man to do? I felt like I was now being forced to be with shorty even if I didn't want to end up with her. Not saying that was how I felt, but I was just thinking at a higher rate right now.

Risk noticed the look on my face. "Yeah, I know it's a lot to handle, but you brought us this far. I'm sure you got this. Just don't think about it. Keep doing what you have been doing."

It all made sense. Why would I even decide to change up now? Things had been going well, so there was no need to change them now.

Risk interrupted my thoughts again. "Let's go get something to eat. I'm hungry as hell. Stop thinking about the shit for real," he said, followed by a laugh.

I was sure I was truly overthinking it, as I did for a lot of things. However, I felt this topic deserved some extra thought. I was hungry, too, so I figured I'd go with Risk to get something to eat. Afterward, we could get with the fellas to go shopping for a little bit and hit the Tunnel that evening and catch some good vibes.

We haven't gone out to the Tunnel in a while. The funny part was, we weren't supposed to be in there at our age but we knew the promoters. The Tunnel was definitely a good look, too, but you really had to be fly out there. I told Risk my plans for the day and what I had matched up for us that evening. He was with it like I knew he would be. I was sure he was gonna show out too. I might need to cop a bigger chain and Jesus piece fuckin' with him!

"Yo, it's a dope mom-and-pop spot like a few blocks from here, son. I'm sure they're open this early. We have some time to kill before the sneaker and clothing stores open up, so it's no rush. Plus, I have some things we need to catch up on businesswise," I told Risk.

We decided to walk to the spot since it wasn't that far. On our walk, we started chatting about everything, especially the moves that we had been making. I knew a few dudes that were trying to bubble things out in Coney Island. They were really getting money, but I wasn't sure about it. I wanted Risk to run some checks on them before I gave the okay. I'd known them for a while, but I always run checks on people; you could never be too cautious. Risk agreed to do so. It was looking like we were really tryna supply the whole city with drugs. We had damn near every spot in this big-ass city.

We moved a little different ever since Rock got shot. I didn't let Risk or none of the front-line brothers of mine touch products. I became extremely cautious of surroundings and anything that didn't feel right. Risk didn't like the rules as much because he was more hands-on with things, but he knew where I was coming from. We didn't know if there were dudes still out there ready and willing to harm us. Our name rang bells in these streets, and dudes knew us.

It was funny because the same dudes that gave us the spark off the benches copped from us now. As we approached the restaurant, my hunger grew more intense. Risk had never been here before, but I knew the food was good and he'd enjoy it. After a few minutes, our orders came out. The food really hit the spot, and as we let our food digest, we continued our conversation. I asked him what was his plans for college or after school were. All of us were smart, so college was definitely in the works.

"I know you're tryna go to St. John's, so I figured I want to be close to the money. Business is my thing, so I'll probably stick around the city just to make sure shit goes smooth. I don't want us to have any issues. So wherever you go, I'll be close behind, son," he said.

I laughed and nodded in a sort of agreement with him. I wondered if he knew that I was really serious about going legit and leaving all this shit behind. The smart ones would get money and get out. We'd been doing this for years, and sometimes I wondered if we'd all make it out to the end.

These were the questions I asked myself daily. I knew this life didn't love us, if I was being totally honest with myself. I'd seen it take some good people out of my life, my father being one of them.

I'm not gonna be next, I thought to myself.

I was often in deep thoughts like this, and it was scary at times. I switched my thoughts back to the present day and how fresh I was going to get for tonight. I told Risk I was going to get crazy fresh on the low for the night. I knew he already had some shit up his sleeve. This nigga be fresher than the old heads that came before us, but it was still on some regular shit. He knew not to draw too much attention to himself, but he also knew how to steal the spotlight without trying. When you saw him do it, it was a sight to see.

After sitting, eating, and sharing a bunch of laughs and jokes, we decided to hit Jamaica Avenue up and finally do some shopping. We started walking back to my block to get the cars to head out to Queens. I didn't feel like driving, so I threw Risk the keys and told him to drive the Beamer. I made a few calls to the fellas to let them know the move for the night and where we were going to be at.

When we got to the avenue, everything started feeling like déjà vu, like this day had happened before. Tyesha appeared in front of me again—this time, in a different location. It was on the same area of the Coliseum block instead of in front of Gertz Mall. It was weird because I still didn't call her even after our last encounter. The look on her face said she was either eager to see me or she was tired of me playing hard to get. Either way, I played my usual role.

As she approached, I started to greet her. "What's up? How are you? What are you doing out here again?"

But instead of answering my questions, Tyesha had some questions of her own. "So you're just gonna stand there like I didn't tell you to call me and you didn't?" She looked good as fuck tryna tell me off in front of Risk.

"I didn't know I was obligated to do such a thing. We go together? Nah, I didn't think so. So relax!" I replied.

She thought she had control of the situation, but she sure wasn't ready for that type of response. She had a look of hurt or feeling played on her face after what I said. I didn't want to take it to that level, so I brought her back to a medium comfort zone. That way, I could play with her head a little.

"I was a little busy since we last spoke. I'm sure you could understand that, but if you're serious, I'll get with you either tonight or tomorrow after I come from the club."

She smiled, and I knew I had her right where I wanted. I wasn't sure if I was going to move on it, but I knew how to keep the pot warm at all times. I just didn't want things to get sloppy, and she tried some funny shit with Sabrina, especially after all Risk just told me. I should tread lightly, especially since Sabrina's father knew who

I was. I didn't care about that or her feelings at the moment. I wasn't worried about what her father might do if he found out I hurt his daughter. I had the whole ordeal under control. It was no reason to think otherwise.

Tyesha inched closer to me and kissed me for a brief second. She probably thought her soft lips would fuck me up, but I played it on a greasier level. I grabbed her ass while kissing her back and then bit her bottom lip while clutching her throat in an aggressive manner. I then pushed her away to fuck her head up even more. The look in her eyes said it all. She looked like she wanted to run and tell everyone she knew about the whole ordeal. She was gone. I really fucked her head up because she thought she had control of the situation. Tyesha had no real idea of what I was capable of.

Her defenses were down, and she suddenly became the prey instead of the hunter. All I thought was, *Damn, I'm good at this shit.*

I slapped her on the ass as I walked away, leaving her helpless. Her friends were far in the distance at this point. I told her I'd hit her line later on that night and she better be up.

Risk started laughing as we made our way inside the Coliseum. "Son, you got a way with bitches. She didn't even stand a chance after that move, but she didn't know that."

"Not a chance at all!" I replied as I dapped him up. "She thought I was gonna let her win this round like last time, but I had different plans. She looked good as fuck, son. I can't front."

I mean what was I to really do on that note? I was seventeen years old, and I was not a regular nigga. These chicks knew that even without me being flashy about my business. I was seriously considering her offer.

"I need to get my chain polished for tonight, son, while we are out here," I told Risk.

He replied with a hand gesture and a nod, letting me know he had to do the same. Tonight was going to be ill. I could feel it already.

CHAPTER 26

As I pulled up to the Tunnel, the illest club in the whole Tristate area, I could feel the bass from the music vibrating outside. There was a crazy line at the door that wrapped around the block. There was heavy police presence to keep the order, as the Tunnel had a reputation for getting live every once in a while. I circled the block twice to check for my boys and to see who was standing around. While most people came to go into the club, there were niggas who were notorious for jacking whoever they felt was shining too hard.

After pulling back around, I saw Rock and the rest of the crew standing outside of their cars in a lot. I pulled in, dapped everyone up, and slid the parking attendant a bill to make sure our cars were good. We then all proceeded to the side entrance of the club.

"Yo, Steph, your cousin will get us in, right?" Rock asked.

"I'm not tryna look mad dumb walking up to the entrance with everyone in line for him to be like, 'Nah, son.'" I gave him a look, and everyone started laughing.

"Oh, aight then. I was just checking', son!" he responded with a chuckle.

As we rounded the corner, we could hear the beginning synths of "Superthug" by Norega blaring out the open club doors. As the beat dropped, there were some girls on line that started dropping to the ground and moving their asses like they were on the dance floor. A couple of dudes got behind them, and it was like the party was just as hyped outside as it was on the inside.

I heard somebody yell out, "Yo Steph!" which snapped me out of my observative state.

I looked up and saw my cousin Jay at the door, working security. He gestured for me and my boys to come to the front of the line. As we started moving through people, we could hear complaints from niggas, wondering why we were getting to jump in front of everyone. We weren't concerned with that at all as we kept moving to the front. As we approached, I noticed a couple of police officers were at the door with him.

"Yo, Steph! What up, son?" Jay said, greeting me with a pound. He turned to the cop standing near him. "These five are good. They're with Jay. They are a couple of his artists."

Oh shit! Jigga is here tonight? This is gonna be bananas!

The first cop looked us over. We certainly looked the part of artists. We had on expensive clothes, Pelle Pelle and 8-Ball leather jackets. The latest Uptowns or Jordans were on everyone's feet. Not to mention the chains we were wearing around our necks. I felt nervous, and I was sure the rest of my brothers did, too, but we knew how to play it cool. We didn't say anything. We just stood there, looking kind of bored, like we were used to this kind of hold-up at club entrances.

The second cop spoke. "Well, kind of small for an entourage, and they all look kinda young."

Fuck! I thought. *We not getting in! Leave it to these bitch-ass city cops to hate on—*

Right then, a group of guys walked up behind us, jewelry shining and with an air of confidence. It was the Mobb Deep niggas from Queensbridge. John was cool with the brother of one of the guys in the crew because they hooped together in AAU.

"Yo, what up, Thunn?" one of the guys said to Jay as he exchanged dap with him.

"What up, P!" Jay said. "What's good god? Y'all performing tonight, right?"

The cops were watching everyone, but they didn't see the look exchanged between Jay and P as they were talking.

"Yeah, Thunn. We going to tear this shit down tonight word to muva."

P looked at us for the first time and halfway nodded in our direction, as though he recognized us, but we weren't that high on his radar.

"Aren't those Jay's people? They performing tonight, too, right?"

Right then, I picked up on the vibe. Jay was basically asking P to vouch for us to get us past the police officers. P was looking out for us! My nigga Jay. I could always count on him. I made a mental note to send him a pair of kicks, as a thank-you later on in the week.

"Yeah, that's them. They were just about to walk in when y'all walked up," Jay replied.

Right then, the second cop, who was closely following the exchange, interjected, "Yeah, yeah, gentlemen. Carry on the convo inside. This is a fire hazard. Move along to the security line. Ten more seconds, and nobody is getting in. You guys are holding up the door."

We all dapped up Jay and moved into the building. As I walked past Jay, I gave him head nod that said, "Good looks, my nigga." He understood exactly what it meant. The security check went pretty quickly. The cops seemed familiar with the Mobb niggas, so they lazily ran the metal detector wands over them. They barely checked us as well since we were with them. On the contrary, regular patrons had to turn their jackets out, take off their shoes—the works. I wasn't with that and was glad Jay came through for us in the clutch.

After we got through security, our groups parted ways but not before we thanked P for holding us down.

"Nah, no doubt, shorty. Jay is my man, so it's nothin'. Y'all keep holdin' it down."

And with that, his crew headed in one direction, and we headed in another.

The music they were playing was live as fuck! I could see DJ Funk Flex from Hot 97 spinning from the booth. Behind him was some of the other NY legends of music, just chilling and talking. The vibes for everything was right. We were in the building, shining all crazy.

This was an ordinary night, but I could swear it felt like we won some type of award. The love we were getting in there from the older heads and some real street dudes was overwhelming. I felt like we were supposed to be there that night. The ladies were in the building, looking good—the perfect scene if you could imagine it, like something out of a movie.

"Yo, we're on top tonight, and all eyes are on us, son!" John yelled over the music.

"You feel that energy in the air, fam? This was definitely needed after the last few months of bullshit we've been through," Rah replied.

They couldn't have been any more on point with those statements. The last few months had been crazy for us, from robberies to murders. We weren't little kids anymore; we were living dangerously. There was no telling what the future held, but we were living for this moment. Rock was healthy. Risk was doing his thing, handling business along with John and Rah. The team was stronger than ever, and we all were getting money, lots of it.

Of course, this wasn't the life I wanted for me or my best friends. We'd known each other since the dirt, and these were the cards we were dealt. Luckily, we turned out to be the aces in the deck and not the jokers. No sooner did all these thoughts entered my mind than I saw a familiar face making her way over to me.

"So you weren't going to call me?" she asked.

The whole time I was just standing there, trying remember who she was.

Before I could think of it, Risk leaned over to whisper in my ear, "That's the shorty from the car dealership that sold us the moped and dirt bikes, remember?"

As soon as he said it, I automatically remembered who she was. I grabbed her hand and gave her a handshake while looking in her eyes. Shorty was bad as fuck, with a nice frame to match the dress she had on. I couldn't keep my eyes off her, but I maintained eye contact. I didn't want her to think I'd be calling her after this only because she had this tight dress on. I was definitely gonna call her, but I didn't want her to know that! The ball was in my court once again, and I moved as such.

"Tavia, right? Nah, I didn't forget about you, ma. I've been busy, out here tryna get that money back you took from me for them bikes," I replied with a grin.

I wanted her to know I knew exactly who she was. She was a grown-ass woman, maybe twenty-three or twenty-four. She looked mad good, and she knew it. I was intrigued by her beauty and how she carried herself. She didn't seem like this was her type of crowd by the way she spoke at the dealership. However, everything wasn't always what it seemed from the outside. I sure didn't seem like a big-time drug dealer, but I was. She was amazed that I remembered that transaction and her name.

"I don't forget much. You helped me out that day. How could I forget that?" I continued, all while looking to accentuate my statement. "I still have your number, and I'll probably get with you in the next few days, if you keep looking like that!"

Her cheeks became rosy, and I knew for sure that sealed the deal. I leaned in and pulled her closer while still holding her hand. I hugged and kissed her on the cheek before letting her go.

"I'mma hold you to that," Tavia replied as she pulled out a pen and paper. "Just in case you forgot the number, here it is again." She hugged me again, and her soft skin brushed against my face. She walked away to enjoy her evening, leaving the scent of her perfume in the air.

As soon as she walked off, everyone started dapping me up.

"Sooooon! You already got a bad shorty. How does this nigga keep bagging these joints with no effort? Where the fuck was I when he bagged her? You're greedy. You need to share, nigga. This nigga is the new-age Goldie!" John yelled out.

We all started laughing. I couldn't even respond 'cause I was damn near choking from laughing so hard. John had *it* though. My man could make anyone laugh with no effort at all. I loved that about him. He was cool as the island wind but serious about his business—an ill combination.

"Let's get some drinks, and we'll all be baggin' chicks tonight 'cause there's plenty in here!" I said as we started heading toward the bar.

The Tunnel was packed, and if you were here, you were definitely getting to the money. Everybody was laid back and chillin' for the night. There was no beef, and everyone was looking to have a good time.

I knew I told Tyesha I was gonna check her tonight, but after a few drinks, that might not be the move. Sabrina was heavy on my mind after a few shots of Hennessy. I just wanted to see her face when my night was over. A lot of chicks were on me because of the vibes I gave off or whatever it was, but Sabrina had always held me down. She was real special to me, and I couldn't have asked for a better chick by my side.

How did all these thoughts come to mind in the middle of the club? Why did your feelings appear when liquor was involved? I'd probably had way too many drinks 'cause I was definitely sauced. I just continued dancing and had good-ass time, leaving all my thoughts in the back of my mind. The team was bent, too, and nothing else mattered. The lights came on, and I was hoping I'd be able to drive home. I was bent, but I wasn't gone to the point I didn't know what was going on around me. My pager was blowing up from Sabrina and Tyesha, and I needed to make my way home. I was hungry as hell, so I told the team that we'd grab something quick to eat before we went our separate ways.

I was doing about eighty on the FDR, tryna make it home in one piece. I was really feeling myself tonight. I didn't know if it was the liquor in my system or what, but I felt different, in a good way. Sabrina was still blowing up my pager as I pulled up to my parking spot on the block. The stars were out, and the night was still feeling nice. I wanted to enjoy it a little more, so I went upstairs to grab my cellphone and headed back outside to call Sabrina. I rarely carried my phone because I didn't like people keeping tabs on my movements. I dialed Sabrina's number to call her back while I sat on the trunk of my car. As the phone started to ring, I realized it was a surprisingly quiet night.

"Where have you been? I've been paging you all night!" Sabrina yelled, interrupting the peacefulness of the night. She was speaking so fast it all seemed like one big-ass sentence, and I was too messed up to not even laugh.

"Babe, the fellas and I went to the Tunnel tonight. I told you this. What's the issue? You knew this already. What, you missed me or something?"

"Yes, I did. You know I missed your ass. I need to see you, like, right now. What are you doing?"

"I'm outside, sitting in the car, enjoying the weather, thinking about a bunch of shit."

"Well, I'm coming over. You can talk to me as you think."

On a normal night, I would have told her to wait for me or I'd meet her halfway. But tonight, I was so fixated on the sky I just sat there and waited for her. As I sat there, I thought about a bunch of shit. I was turning eighteen soon. Graduation was right around the corner, then my next moves. Sabrina walked up, and I stumbled off the car to greet her. She didn't seem bothered that I didn't walk or drive to her. Maybe it was because she saw me stumble just now. She hugged and kissed me, and she put her head on my chest. It was like she was listening to my heartbeat or something.

"What's the matter, baby? Did you have fun?" she asked.

"It was mad fun. I needed that tonight. I'm good, just think-ing about future events and my birthday along with graduation approaching us soon."

It was good to just sit and talk to Sabrina during moments like this. She always seemed in tune to my vibes. As we went into the house, I knew it would be a good night. I was still feeling nice from earlier, and I had Sabrina there. I couldn't ask for much more.

I needed a shower, so I grabbed some things from the room. I placed my jewelry on the dresser along with the remaining stuff I had in my pockets. I grabbed some boxers and a wifebeater and headed to the shower. A few minutes into my shower, I heard the bathroom door slam open. It was Sabrina, and she started yelling at me in Spanish while holding something in her hand.

Once I noticed the piece of paper in her hand, I knew exactly what it was she was yelling about. I only had a few seconds to think and get my shit straight before matters went from bad to worse.

"What the fuck is this? You go out to bag other bitches? Who the fuck is Tavia?" She was speaking in fluent, fast Spanish, but I caught her drift. This wasn't the first time she'd caught me in a jam like this, so I had to be on point with my response.

"First of all, don't go through my things while I'm in the shower. If you wanted to go through them, you could've done it while I was just in the room." I was hot, so I continued going off on her. "Secondly, if you must know, that's the shorty that sold me the mopeds for Risk's little brother a while back. She gave me her number because I told her I needed some more stuff. She deserved the sale the first time we did business. I couldn't see why a second exchange wouldn't have the same outcome. You're welcome to throw it away, if it's that serious to you. It's not even that deep."

I knew I had changed her mind when her face changed from extreme rage to a look of foolishness. I was sharp and smooth with my words. She wasn't used to being handled this way, which was crazy to me. I knew her father had game and must've put her up on it.

Maybe he did, but it was different because it was coming from me. Either way, I liked the fact that I could flip the script on her with ease. She didn't second-guess anything I said to her. She still looked cute with her "I'm embarrassed" face. I loved it.

"I'm sorry. I just don't like you talking to other women at all. But yeah, I have a problem with the number, so it's going in the toilet," she replied as she pulled the toilet lever down.

I stood right there, watching her flush Tavia's number away. I wasn't sure if she was looking for a reaction or to see if I gave a slight fuck about what she just did. I simply shrugged my shoulders and kept staring at her. I was cool with her throwing away the number because I had the original in one of my sneaker boxes. So she might have won the battle, but I was gonna win the war.

She didn't know this at all, but I knew it was dangerous to send her home sad or mad. I didn't want her feeling crazy about our relationship because of how dangerous her father was. I played the game properly. I was in too deep, and hurting feelings wasn't a part of my forte. Sabrina had a hold on me, whether I wanted to admit it or not. It was a different feeling when I was around her.

I could have any woman I wanted, but the feel I got from her was special.

Now I had this beautiful girl standing in front of me, ready for me to claim her soul. I was going to give her exactly what she wanted. I knew she wanted me to love her body down and take full advantage of her in ways others could only imagine. The look in her eyes were fierce as she took it upon herself to join me inside the steaming hot shower.

I grabbed her by the neck with a swift motion, leaving her little room to breathe, but clutching her with the slightest hand. I knew how to control her, and her body spoke a language that I only understood. I knew how to make her cringe from the things I was doing to her. I pulled her closely, and my lips met hers, activating the electricity between us.

"Fuck, why are you doing this to me? How can you have so much power with so little effort, baby? Did you have this effect on the women before me?"

I had answers for all the questions she asked, but my goal was to fuck her head up. I wanted her to yearn for the love and lovemaking I provided her and would provide her for a few lifetimes. I opened her legs, giving her a sample of what I was offering. When I entered her, she let out a sensational sigh. She clutched my neck with one arm and dug her nails into my back with her other hand.

She knew she was in trouble within a few strokes of our session. I could tell from the way her body kept shaking. I was hitting the right spot to get the results I wanted. Sabrina was feeling so good under the warm water. She started sucking on my neck, telling me she loved me and that I better not ever give this dick away. I began grinding into her pussy to make her cum harder for me. I loved looking at her face when she started cummin'. It was by far one of the best faces I'd seen because it was mixed with nothing but passion and love for just me.

The Hennessy had my mind and body in a different space. I knew this wasn't going to end in the shower. I wanted more, and I told her to hurry up and meet me in the bedroom.

CHAPTER 27

The last few weeks had been busy on many levels for us. We were finishing projects, taking finals, and preparing for graduation. Business had hit a different stride, and I had touched more money than I could have ever imagined. I started thinking more intensely on a way to get out. I had more than enough money to go legit and the smarts to carry along with it. I received my acceptance letter into St. John's University, and I couldn't describe the feelings of excitement I had. I was about to fulfill my dream of attending the university I always hoped for.

I was happy with life, and I had great people in my corner, pushing me to continue being who I appeared to be in their eyes. Sabrina was happy because she was accepted into all the colleges of her choice. She hadn't made a decision on where she was going yet. I knew she wanted to be close to me, so I was all for whatever school she chose.

I was sitting in my final class of the day and started thinking of the good times I had in school. I didn't want much to change, but I expected growth. Rah and John were in class, kickin' shit, talking to the shorties as usual. Rock and Risk were sleeping, as always. We finally made it and didn't have much more to do. This was our last week of classes, and we had no worries at all. In all honesty, I wasn't sure why we still came to class. I guessed just to sleep or get through the day, which was a short one at that. I only came because my homies were there. Also because it was the last few days and something crazy always happened when you were not there. I wasn't tryna miss any last-second memories all 'cause I stayed home.

There were some joints in class whose futures I wondered about. Like, were they going to college or were they gonna get knocked up quick fast? As I glanced them over, there were a few I knew I could have if I really wanted them. I knew it because of how they acted around me. Everyone knew I was with Sabrina, but a lot of the chicks didn't care about that at all.

They'd try to get at me if they could find an opening. I wasn't giving many opportunities, although I loved to flirt. I deemed that natural, but I didn't see myself with none of these chicks. They might be a good fuck, but I wasn't testing many of them.

The bell rang in the distance, and I got up to exit the class. Before I could get out my chair, one of the chicks in class walked over to me.

She was quiet and stayed to herself most of the time. I never really saw anybody fuck with her because she had a crazy mouth and hands to back it up. We'd spoken before over the years but nothing major like that. I was quite shocked that she came over to speak to me.

"Why is everyone so scared of you? You've never given me that kinda vibe. I was told not to talk to you, so of course, that made me more curious. You carry sort of a dark, mysterious look to you, so I wanted to know more. I know you have a girlfriend, but I still want to kick it with you. You can tell me things you may not want her to know. Here's my name and number, just in case you didn't know who I was. I'm letting you know now."

I read the name as though I didn't know who she was. It read "Ariel" with a diamond at the end. She surely had me intrigued to know more about her. I felt like she was looking into my mind and soul without permission and demanding I gave her more. It was very appealing, as were her looks. That whole interaction was aggressive as fuck, but I liked it.

"You're tryna get me killed, I see. But that was probably one of the best approaches I'd seen in a while. You got straight to business. I'm not sure why you waited all these years to really speak though. I might just call you off the strength since you didn't come at me like you just wanted to fuck. I respect that. I might let you in my mysterious mind, after all. But for now, I'm going to meet my shorty and end this conversation. She always seems to catch me when y'all approach me like this, then I look like the bad guy," I said while laughing to mellow the mood back out. I wasn't sure about the situation at all, but I definitely liked it because it was different.

"I never said anything about getting with you. I got a nigga. I just wanted to see what your mind was like. That's it!"

She was mean as hell, but I knew I could have her too. Her mouth was saying one thing, but her facial expressions told a different story. I was really good at reading body language and vibes. I knew if I applied pressure, she would be singing a different tune. I played the game on her level, though, and read between the lines. She might have a man, but something brought her to me in that specific moment. She sounded like she'd had that on her mental for a while.

"Okay. Cool. Then we'll chat later on today when I have free time. I don't want you to beat me up. I've witnessed a few fights of yours, and I don't want no problems, ma," I replied with a smirk while holding my hands up.

I was definitely low key kicking a bit of game to her. She pushed me as she laughed and walked toward the door. I stuffed the number into my pocket and left the classroom to meet up with my team. They were all laughing as though they had seen the whole ordeal.

"Son, I don't know how you do it, but I'm tryna to be like you when I get older," John said. "You sit in the back of the class and barely open your mouth for anything, but these chicks flock to you. What you be doing, son? I need to learn this method."

I started laughing because that was exactly what I did—stayed to myself. Ladies must love quiet dudes.

"It does seem that way, huh? Chicks love quiet niggas, the guy everyone wants but doesn't give everyone the time of day. I think it's like a reward when they finally get them, because not many get past the surface."

"Well, nigga, I'm about to follow suit. I'm never talking again," John replied, laughing, and we all joined in.

As we traversed through the hallway, I saw Sabrina walking toward me with her usual smile. Nothing was out of the ordinary.

I expected that familiar face on the daily basis, as we did the same thing after class was out. Sabrina gave me my normal hug and kiss as I watched the fellas meet up with lady friends as well. It was time to get something to eat. I was starving. I asked Sabrina what she wanted because I knew she was hungry too.

"Whatever you want to eat, baby. I'm cool with that," she answered with her usual response.

It wasn't really an answer, but I knew she was going to say it anyway. I was feeling for pizza today, so I told her that was the move. I let the team know that was what we were doing as we exited the school and headed to our cars. As I looked over at Sabrina in the passenger seat, her skin was glowing from the sun, and her hair was blowing in the wind. In that moment, she looked mad good, even better than she usually did. I couldn't help but tongue her down when we stopped at a red light. I had to let her know exactly how I was feeling.

Chicks loved that shit. It made them melt. She'd definitely been holding me down for the last year through it all. Although I loved her for that, I still hadn't shared everything with her. I was just waiting for the perfect time to do so. I knew that time was approaching rather quickly. I just couldn't continue to hold this partial truth from her any longer. Not only did she need to know; she deserved to know.

Shit, who knew? She might be rocking with it. It might entice her. All these thoughts just helped me make up my mind. I knew when I was gonna tell her. I figured this moment would be dope. I was getting too wild; she was my calm to a lot of things, and she didn't even know it.

The light hit green, and I saw Risk take off, racing everyone. I knew what time it was, but before I could even get going, Sabrina said, "You better get him, papi."

I looked over with a smirk on face. "I'm on it, baby!"

She was a thrill seeker; that was for certain. I was sure she'd been in cars before with dudes speeding crazy. I was sure she didn't have that level of trust with them like she had with me.

I took off, switching lanes, getting my speed up. All I could hear was Sabrina laughing, as she put her hands out the sunroof. I noticed her home girl Ashley, who was riding with Risk, doing the same thing. If this was a scene from a movie, it was perfect. Rock, John, and Rah shot past us, holding their middle fingers in the air. I wasn't about to be last as we hit the freeway.

I started getting tunnel vision on where I was trying to go while switching lanes. I started gaining more and more speed. Pretty soon, I was leading the pack like I was back in pole position. I slowed down to let everyone catch up. What a time to be alive! We were living life! I could see the exit we needed to get off at for the pizza spot. It was really time for us to slow down. Police be lurking mad heavy around the blocks, leading up to the spot.

We all got to the pizza shop and ordered. As we sat down with our slices, we started taking and laughing about the race we just had. We continued eating, and I realized we had to get moving. I had to check with the connect to see about this new shipment. I figured I'd give Sabrina some bread and let her do some shopping while we went to see Jose. It had been a minute since we saw each other face-to-face, and it was long overdue. As I handed her some pocket money, I told Sabrina I had to handle some stuff but that it shouldn't take me too long. She didn't have a problem with it, and neither did her friends. She would be occupied, so it was perfect timing.

We decided to leave my car and take Risk and John's car. Shortly after, we arrived to the spot, and we were met by the usual faces.

"Mister Steph and friends, long time no see. Business is going well, I presume, because the money never stops nor do the drops."

"Business is doing very well. I just wanted to touch base with you to see how things were moving on your end and show face. I know it's been a while, but it's always good to pop up every now and then to shake things up a bit. You know?"

"Funny you ask. I have more product coming in this Friday, and I need you and your crew to take on a bulk of the load. I'm talking twenty to thirty kilos extra on top of your regular orders. Can you handle that much weight, manito?" Jose asked.

That was a heavy load but I knew I had the bread to get it. I could even front the rest of the crew, if they didn't have the whole amount due for the load. I looked around to check and see if they were in agreement with the heavier load. Everyone shook their heads, signifying they had the money. They knew they could make them bricks disappear with ease, or could at least get the money. I turned back to Jose.

"That looks like it's a go for that. I'll make sure the money is correct Thursday evening. As for the drop Friday, same spot and location as before, right?"

"*Si, manito. Este tiguere* always comes through in the crazy times for me. How's your girlfriend's father's situation going?"

I could feel Rock, John, and Rah looking at me, as they didn't know what he was taking about.

"Everything is good on that level too. Thanks for asking."

He could tell from my facial expression and the way the guys looked at me that I hadn't told them about Sabrina's father. He fucked up, and I knew I had some explaining to do as soon as we left. I shook Jose and his people's hands as I made my way toward the exit. As soon as we reached the exit, Rock started off the Q&A session I knew was coming.

"Steph, what the fuck is going on? How does he know about your girl and her father? What is it that you didn't tell us?" he asked as they all huddled around me, looking confused as hell.

"Sabrina's father worked for him back in the day. I saw him and Jose talking a while ago when I was making a drop. I didn't want to speak on it until I found out how he knew him. He was one of his henchmen back in the day, so he gets busy. No, he doesn't know about the business we conduct. But that dude that was there when we killed them dudes, Sabrina's pops was the dude that sent him to watch over us, not Jason. Oh yeah, he knows Jason too. So yeah, he's no threat. If anything, he's a helping hand. I kept it low because I didn't want this crazy feeling y'all giving me right now back when I found out," I explained, trying to smooth over the bubbling tension.

Rock looked stunned with all the information he'd just received. He also looked relieved that it wasn't bad news.

"Damn, I didn't know homie was connected like that. He had our backs and didn't have a problem with us killing anyone? That's ill, son," he replied.

"Nah, he seemed proud that we handled it the way we did. It kind of bugged me out when he told me too. I know it's crazy, but we're good, son. I got us if we have any problems on life, kid."

The crew seemed content with the news I told them, so I knew I wouldn't hear about this again.

"I kinda now want to thank him for looking out for us and mainly me because he didn't have to send any arms for that. That's crazy love, kid," Rock said.

"It's already understood, son. I'll send the word to him in the right setting. Don't even worry about it. As for Sabrina, she doesn't know shit about anything. I want to keep it that way until I feel it's the right time. Understood?" I replied, looking at each one of them in the eyes to highlight the seriousness of the conversation.

Every one of them nodded in agreement. I reminded them to have their money ready by Thursday evening. I told them I could front them some bread if they needed everyone because I didn't know their financial situations.

"No one here is to make any drops. The money goes to the location we always drop at. Then you send your team to pick up and unload the work," I reiterated.

The plan had always been very simple. After Rock got shot, I didn't want my guys getting their hands dirty. Once we agreed on everything, we went to meet back up with the girls.

On the way back, I started thinking this was a lot of weight to really handle. If we were cutting it like we'd been doing, there was no need to even continue moving weight. That alone was more than enough to retire with. I was not sure how everyone felt about backing out of the game, but I knew I was planning an exit sooner rather than later.

Sabrina called Risk's car phone to let me know she had taken the car and the girls to a different shopping spot. She said she would bring the car over later that day if it was cool with me. I didn't have a problem with it. I trusted her, and she didn't know about the burner tucked in the stash box. It was probably better that way so she wouldn't freak out.

I told Risk to drop me off at the crib and let him know where the girls were. He could spread the news to Rock and John so they wouldn't waste time trying to find them. I already knew what I was going to do when I got to the crib. I was gonna hit up the shorty Ariel that gave me her number in class. I wanted to see what she was talking about. Something about her had me intrigued to the max.

Normally, when I got a number, I'd never call, but I was breaking my rule for this one. I got to the crib and told Risk I would get at him later. Before he left, I told him I wanted to talk to him on a different level later on. I headed inside and hugged and kissed Grandma. I told her about my day and how excited I was with graduation coming at the end of the week. She expressed how proud she was of me and that she couldn't wait to see me walk across that stage.

After I got settled in my room, I took out Ariel's number and called her. I wasn't sure if it was a house phone or her cell phone. When a woman answered, I asked if I could speak to Ariel.

"This is her. Who is this?" the person on the other line answered.

"The nigga you gave your number to today. Fix your attitude. You don't have to sound so mean on the phone too, shorty. I don't normally do this, so consider this call a gift. How was your day?"

"Shut up. You're the mean one. And you fix your face. You think no one can read you, but I see who you are. My day was good. How about yours?"

I wanted to know more about this person she allegedly knew. "So who am I, Ariel? Since you know me so well, who am I? You must've had eyes on me for some time. You seem to think you know me better than my immediate circle."

I wanted to lay the round work early in this conversation to get some answers.

She didn't take long to respond at all. "You're a smart dude. It can come across as arrogance, but nevertheless, you're extremely smart. I can tell you have some well thought-out goals, too, but that's not who you are. You're dangerous because chicks be on you all day long and you don't budge. You act like that because you know what you're capable of. I know how to handle niggas like you. You think you have all the game in the world, but you don't."

I laughed because she was partly right. What she didn't know was, I already thought about this conversation in my head a few times earlier today. I wasn't dangerous or arrogant like she claimed I was. I knew she had spent some time watching me. I wanted to know who told her not to talk to me, though, so I asked her the million-dollar question.

"Chris told me not to fuck with you. All that did was make me want to get to know you more. That alone made you more appealing because I wanted to know why he said that to me."

"Damn, not Chris. I'm cool with him. We've spoken in passing many times. Why the hate on me? I must've talked to someone he liked in the past or something, but that's crazy."

I was really digging her vibe and energy on the phone. She was mad easy to talk to and wasn't really mean. She just stayed to herself and fucked with people who were just like her. I did my research on people too. I was good at reading body language, especially facial expressions. Shorty was definitely digging me. I could tell she was. If she wasn't, we wouldn't be on this phone, kickin' it the way we were. I guessed I was digging her too. If I wasn't, I wouldn't have called her to find out more about her.

"Where's your man at? Because I know you have one. You can't look the way you look and not belong to someone," I inquired.

"I belong to no one, but he is at home right now! And your girlfriend, Selena, where is she?" she replied sarcastically.

"You tryna be real funny. Sabrina, which I'm sure you know is her name, is out with her friends now," I responded while correcting her sarcasm and laughing at the same time.

I could tell Ariel was ill from the little conversation we were having. I knew if nothing was to come from this, she would definitely be a great friend and somebody I could chill with. Only time would be able to tell that. Shorty was tryna get to know me on a deeper level. She wasn't settling for my regular, nonchalant answers. Maybe she did see something deeper in my eyes that made her ask questions. Either way, I still wasn't budging on letting her know everything about me just yet. It wouldn't be fair to move that way when my girl didn't even get put on to my lifestyle.

I still wanted to see if I could get her for real, so I asked a different type of question.

"What if I kissed you and started undressing you. What would you do?"

"We aren't on that level, so I can't answer that for you. But if we are fuckin' with each other on that level, I'd follow your lead," she replied with no hesitation.

That was all I needed to hear. I knew I could have her and the response she gave me was to throw me off. I'd seen niggas get at her a few times, and she would dismiss them every time. I believed she was faithful, but something must be off in her relationship if I was getting this kind of energy from her. I never asked for her number; she gave it to me. So I didn't know what they had going on.

I didn't care about her nigga though. He meant nothing to me. I knew how to move in situations like this. I'd been in this position before. I didn't rattle easy. I was rockin' with Ariel's vibe for sure. Sabrina would kill me, though, if she knew I was on the jack with another shorty. I had to move accordingly if I was going to chill with her to see what her head was really like. I didn't need any drama in my life at all.

"So what made you talk to me today? You had mad time to ask me these questions throughout the years. I don't bite. I'm friendly as hell. I know you said I look mean, but I'm really just low key, and I stay to myself."

"Honestly, I like that you don't make noise and are very quiet. You remind me of someone I know. Plus, all the girls want you, and they can't have you. That's appealing too. If I wanted you, I could have you. I'm sure if it too."

I started laughing into the phone. I admired her supreme confidence, but she didn't know me that well. I let her have her moment though. I knew the ball was in my court and every move that would be made would be on my terms. She definitely made the initial approach, but I was calling the plays from here on out.

"Gotta love a chick with confidence. Well, since you had this all planned out in your head, we will see where this goes. Maybe I'll test this theory of yours soon. But let me get off this jack before shorty comes in this house and finds me on the phone and kills both of us. I'll see you in class tomorrow. I'm sure you'll have plenty to say then too."

"Okay, I don't want to get you killed. I'll definitely talk to you tomorrow. That's cool with you?" Ariel asked while laughing.

I agreed and hung up the horn. No sooner did I hang up the phone than Sabrina walked in my room. She had a bunch of bags while I lay at the head of my bed, waiting for her to show me what she got.

"Baby, I missed you! Look what I got. I picked up some Uptowns since I know you feel about your Uptowns. I didn't see these in your collection. I figured I'd bless you with them and an outfit to match."

I opened the box, and to my surprise, there was the new orange, blue, and white mid top joints with the bubble checks staring at me. Sabrina definitely knew my style 100 percent.

"I saw this earlier, too, and I was going to pick them up later on in the week. You definitely came through in the clutch with these, baby," I replied with a kiss and grabbed her ass.

"That's an early graduation gift, baby. I have another surprise for you after graduation for you too. Just wait and see!" she said.

I didn't like surprises at all, but I knew she wasn't going to tell me before she was ready. She was good about keeping things quiet from me. Now she was going to have my mind wondering what it was she had for me. Hopefully, it was something I wanted or didn't have already.

CHAPTER 28

Graduation day finally arrived! I was having so many mixed feelings and emotions. I finally made it, and I did a great at it! I got accepted into the colleges I wanted to go to, so I was on top of the world. Life was definitely good at this point, but I wished my parents were here to help me celebrate this major accomplishment. I wasn't supposed to make it. Most kids my age with my circumstances didn't make it out the city or past the age of twenty one. They either ended up in a casket or with a felony. I was doing well for myself, at least to the naked eye. Every kid wanted their parents to witness a great moment in their life. So I woke up with all these mixed feelings about the day, but I was still very happy. I was so excited to walk across that stage and say I made it.

Even with all the excitement surrounding graduation, there was something else weighing heavily on my mind. I had to make sure the drop was made before lunch and everything was in play before I walked across the stage this evening. I hit Risk up. Something like this had to be confirmed and then reconfirmed to make sure it went off without a hitch.

"Make sure the numbers are correct. I know you said you checked already, but this is heavy, kid. You know I've been like this recently, son. You know how I get," I said, trying not to stress him out, but also making sure he understood my position.

"We're good. No worries! I'll hit you in a little while, and I'll let you know everything," he replied.

I hung up the jack and proceeded to wake Sabrina up with a kiss on the forehead. I didn't know what it was, but her face excited me when she woke up. She was bad without makeup on, and her eyebrows always looked done. I thought the eyebrows and smile did it for me at that very moment. She got up and kissed me on her way to the bathroom. As I watched her fat ass swing past me, I couldn't help but tap it as she made her way out the door. I really loved her. There was no doubt about that. She practically lived with me now.

I wasn't the lovey-dovey type, but I didn't mind cuddling or being around her for long periods of time. She wasn't a headache, and we didn't argue at all. Or at least we didn't argue much. I didn't see a need to ever argue. You should just say what you had to say, and then we could keep it pushing. No ill feelings needed. That way, we could go back to what we knew. It worked for us.

I threw on some LOX, DMX, and Noreaga to start off my day. I knew exactly what I wanted to wear to graduation, so I took it out of the closet. I knew it was going to be a crazy day. Suddenly, my mood switched, and I was thinking happier thoughts. I thought that Sabrina being there and looking at her face when she woke up made everything feel so good.

A few minutes went by, and Sabrina returned from the shower. She was in just a towel, and her hair was still dripping wet. I wanted to make love to her when I saw her strut over to me. Her body was glistening, and she had a glow to her naturally. She must've picked up on the vibe, as I grabbed her and started kissing her. I told her she was gonna need another shower once I was done with her.

I yelled out to her, "Graduation sex!"

As I took off her towel, I kissed from her neck and down her body. She smelled so fuckin' good. I couldn't help but want to devour her. I wanted to make her body speak to me in a different language. I started grinding like I was trying to make her forget that she knew English. I had done this many times before, but today felt different. I could hear her pussy talking to me, so I dug in a little deeper while biting her neck.

Sabrina responded as expected. She had one hand on my ass, pushing me in to her. She started telling me how much she loved me in Spanish. That shit was driving me crazy. Hearing her speak to me in Spanish drove me into a different gear. She was truly my weakness, and her facial expressions were so appealing. As I looked down at her face, I continued to stroke her *chocha* with the music playing. At this point, the music didn't even matter. I had tunnel vision, and her body was the only thing in sight. I didn't know who or what was playing.

I was holding on to the moment when she said, "Papi, I'm about to cum. Oh my gosh, you feel so good. Let me feel you in my mouth, baby, please."

I knew what it was; she was tryna avoid cummin'. I didn't budge at all though. I kept going and hitting them exact spots to release all that wet goodness I loved. Moments later, her body started shaking, and her eyes were going in the back of her head. I knew she was cummin' hard too. I swear it felt like a trigger because once I felt her body shaking and climaxing, my body started to cum too. I never wanted to cum because she would be looking at my facial expressions, just as I often did to her.

She had a gift, though, because it didn't take much to get back hard. All I needed were some kisses from her soft-ass lips, and I was ready to go. She knew she turned me on like crazy and loved that it didn't take me much to get back to that point.

We had a busy schedule ahead of us today, and I couldn't partake in any extra rounds. I had to get a cut, make sure the birds flew in, and graduation was later on that evening.

"I love your nasty ass. You be tryna kill me with all that shit you be doing. That shit be feeling so amazing, but get up 'cause I gotta get back in the shower now. You play too much," Sabrina said, fake annoyed.

I knew better though, not after how I just gave that ass the business. I laughed and clasped on the side of her, kissing her with my arm still wrapped around her.

"Get up, ma. I know you gotta get your hair and nails done before tonight. You need anything?"

"Yep, you're paying for it all, but I'mma lie here for a minute. You just took the life outta me. My body is still shaking. You better not ever give that shit away. I'll kill you!"

I laughed, but I knew she was very serious. My phone rang, and it took me a few seconds to answer. It was Risk telling me everything went smooth and asking me what time we were meeting up for the barbershop.

"Give me about a hour, and I'll meet you at the barbershop. I have to make sure shorty is ready for tonight too. I'mma drop her off then head that way."

"Smooth, I'll check you then," Risk responded, and I hung up the horn.

CHAPTER 29

"Stephen Jones."

Although it was my name, I almost didn't recognize it. It was like an out-of-body experience. Everything from the last few years seemed to flash before my eyes—my crew, me getting the girl, getting the plug with Jose, Miami, getting accepted into St. Johns, and finally, graduation.

I began to walk across the stage. The crowd began roaring when they heard my name. I looked at my section of guests and all the people that were screaming for me. I fuckin' made it! I couldn't believe I fuckin' made it, son!

My homies were going crazy, whistling and yelling my name. The ego boost that came with the celebration was irresistible. I had to repay the love that was being shown my way.

I took two steps across the stage. Cheers and whistles began in earnest. I hit them with the first few moves of the Harlem shake. The roar was deafening. I took a bow to show my appreciation to the people who showed up to celebrate my achievement.

When I finally reached the principal, she reached out to shake my hand and leaned in to whisper in my ear, "Don't do that again, or else you won't get your diploma." She was smiling but looked dead serious.

I knew she was extremely proud of me. I could see it in her face. The crowd's reaction said the same thing. I was winning. I felt like I was on top of the world!

Accomplished—that was all I could think to myself. Grandma was so happy. I could see her crying tears of joy as I exited the stage. I knew this night was going to be one I wouldn't forget. After our ceremony was over, the team and our girls took pictures to record these memories for the future. I was proud of everyone. This was big for us. I knew the graduation party we planned was going to be so crazy. I told everyone to go change and we would meet up in a few hours.

Sabrina's parents were waiting for us off in the cut. I walked over, and Tony gave me a firm handshake, followed by a tight hug. Her mother hugged and kissed both of us, and I could feel the love from both exchanges. They were proud and honored to have me in their daughter's life, and I shared the same sentiments. They both kept telling us how proud they were of us. I wasn't one for joyful moments like that, but this felt right.

I could tell that Sabrina's parents wanted to celebrate more with us on our night, but they knew we had plans. They gave Sabrina her balloons, a card, a gift, and a few more congratulatory words before they left. Sabrina was hyped. I could see it on her face. She gave the gift to her parents to hold for later since we were going out. She didn't want to be worried and have to keep an eye on it all night.

Sabrina said goodbye to her parents, and I kissed my grandmother, who still had tears in her eyes.

"Grandma, stop crying. We did it! You helped mold me. This one is for you," I told her while smiling.

She smiled and thanked me for being a good kid and not giving her a hard time. As I walked her to her cab, I told her I wanted my favorite dinner tomorrow night.

She kissed me on my cheek and said, "Treat the pretty girl right. She's special. I can see you love and care for her. Just take care of her through it all."

I had no idea where this was coming from, but I felt every word she said. I knew that gem would come into play soon, so I appreciated hearing it from her. I put it in my mental Rolodex for future use.

"I will, Grandma, I promise," I replied while kissing her once more. I opened her door and gave the cab driver money to take her home. I told her I loved her and would see her later as I closed the cab door.

I booked a room for Sabrina and me that evening, and I had a surprise for her. As I walked over toward a few people I knew to congratulate them, I saw Ariel making her way to do the same.

"Congratulations. I hope we can still chill and be cool too," she said.

The look in her eyes said she wanted to fuck, but I dismissed it. Sabrina was in the distance, not far behind, and I didn't need a scene at all.

I casually replied, "Oh, no doubt we definitely will. I'll let you know when. I have your number."

She hugged me and put my hands on her ass, which was softer than I imagined. "Don't wait too long," she responded and kissed me on the cheek.

I immediately got nervous because I didn't know who peeped that slick move. It was swift as fuck but still too bold. She didn't give a fuck at all, and that showed it. This night was already getting crazy! I was definitely going to get to know her throughout the summer before my fall semester started.

Shorty smiled back at me with a devilish grin as she disappeared in the distance. I knew she was hoping to fuck my head up, and her mission was accomplished! On the low, I liked it because of the boldness. I smiled back and shook my head because I knew she was trouble. When I turned back around, Sabrina and I locked eyes as she made her way toward me.

"Who kissed you on your cheek? Don't get fucked up."

I froze for a moment and then responded, "Huh?"

"You have lipstick on your cheek," she replied with an attitude.

Damn shorty really tried to set me up just now. That was why she smiled the way she did. I had no time, and if I stuttered, it would look like I was lying. I had to think fast.

"I don't know, babe. Probably from my grandma," I blurted out.

She wiped my face as I said it and gave me a look. She then kissed me, and we continued on with the night.

I told her after we got out of our gowns and put on our regular clothes that I wanted to talk to her and show her something. She had no idea what I wanted to talk about, but she agreed. As we made our way to the car, I couldn't help but palm her ass as usual. I planned on wearing the outfit that Sabrina bought me earlier this week. It felt like it was meant for me to do it like that. I was nervous because I didn't know how she would react to this sit down of ours.

After a short drive, we arrived at the hotel in Midtown. It was one of those hotels you'd see in movies, the ones you'd expect Richard Gere or one of those famous white actors to stayed in. The front desk attendant seemed a little suspicious of two nonwhite teenagers staying at such a fancy hotel. She made that clear when she asked us for our reservation.

I anticipated this might happen, so I clarified as soon as I saw her getting ready to question me. "It's our graduation night, and my uncle looked out for us on getting this room."

A knowing smile spread across her face as she nodded. "You guys just graduated, huh? Very cool uncle you have, Mr. Jones." Very cool, indeed. She didn't even know the half.

We got our room keys and headed to our room. As I opened the door, it was hard to contain my excitement. The room was ill as fuck. It was large and had a separate bedroom and living room area. The ceiling-to-floor windows had a view of Midtown, with the Empire State Building directly in front of us. There was a chair and table nearby. I looked at Sabrina, playfully smacking her on the ass.

"You see that table? Get familiar with it. We aren't spending any time on the bed tonight."

"Shut up, bighead. You might not even be getting any pussy tonight. So you might need to get familiar with the couch," she replied, laughing.

We both laughed and then continued checking out the room before getting ready for the evening's events. We showered, changed, and I grabbed my shines and was ready to go. Normally, I would've tried to fuck her brains out, but tonight I was on a different vibe. I figured I'd do things differently for a change.

I was waiting on the sofa when she came out of the room. It was as if I was seeing her the first time. She wasn't fine; she was beautiful. Gorgeous even. The way her red Armani dress was hugging her hips and ass made me want to say "Fuck this event tonight" and immediately get her out of that dress. I was ready to fuck her like I was trying to make a baby.

As long as I had her on my side, I was good. She was complementing me like crazy right now with her sex appeal. Her walk was mean, like she knew she was the shit. She took her shades out of her purse and put them on her face. She looked so dope. I was eating all this up. She looked like a grown woman at this point, with her hair done to perfection.

As we left the room and began to walk down the hall to the elevator, I turned to her. "We have a pit stop to make before we meet up with the crew," I told her.

"Where are we going? I thought we had to be there right now."

"Don't worry. I got everything under control," I assured her.

The drive to the spot was quiet on my behalf, but what I had to tell her was very important. I kept this secret from her for too long. If we were going to take our relationship to the next level, it had to be done. This was a major part of my life. I either had to put her on or end things, and the latter wasn't an option to me.

We pulled up to a gated entrance that I had to put a code in to enter. I glanced over at Sabrina. She looked slightly confused as to why we were at a storage complex and not a club.

"Where are we? This wasn't what we had planned," Sabrina asked, sounding slightly perplexed.

We arrived at my compartment, and I entered a second code in order to open the door. I grabbed her hand as we entered. The lights came on as we stepped inside, and she saw all the boxes.

"Open one of them up," I said.

She was hesitant but did exactly as I ordered her to do. She uttered an audible gasp when she saw the contents inside. "Babe, what the fuck is going on? Where did you get all this money from?"

It was a question I had waited for her to ask me for some time now.

"I can't keep this from you anymore, baby, because I love you so fucking much. I sell drugs in varieties, baby. I'm not going to lie. I'm not nickel and diming either. I'm the head honcho on my team. I run all this city on the low. Ninety percent of the coke you can find on the streets is from me and my team."

I paused to look at her reaction. She looked stunned as she took it all in and tried to process it. I continued filling her in.

"I've been hustling since I was twelve and have a really good knack about getting money. I don't plan on being this drug-dealing motherfucka forever, but for now, this is who I am. I have millions saved up, and I'm planning our escape. I'm just trying to play things right. I'm sorry I didn't tell you, but I didn't want to lose you. I don't or didn't know how you would react to me being who I am. I guess I hid it because that's all I know."

Sabrina still looked shocked as she squeezed my hands tighter and looked into my eyes. "Damn, baby, that's a lot to put on someone's plate at once. What if you get caught. Then what? Have you thought about that?" she replied with a look of concern. "Listen, I still love you. I'm not sure why, but you kinda just turned me on. I guess you wasn't lying when you told me you were the boss. Do you remember that when we first met at the bus stop?"

"Nah, you said I was the boss. I just went with it," I responded while laughing. "I'm not going to get caught, I promise. I don't do the pitching, and I don't touch none of the stuff. Only thing I touch is the money when I put it in here. This is for us. If you want me to stop right now, I'll give the reins over to Risk, and we can fade into the sunset."

Sabrina smiled and replied, "I did say you were the boss. Damn, you have a good-ass memory. You sound like you have a plan, and you've yet to get caught. If you hadn't told me, I wouldn't have known at all. I guess that's a good and a bad thing. What else could you, or would you, keep from me? I mean, you kept this away from me for so long."

In my mind, I wanted to tell her more, but her father's history wasn't my business. It also wasn't my place to tell her about it. I'd let him have that talk with her. That was a different book whose chapters I didn't feel like revealing.

Instead of that, I just answered, "Nothing. I just felt this was the perfect time to tell you. No more secrets."

"Good. No more secrets!" she said as she leaned in for a kiss.

"I don't care how mad you ever get with me. You better not ever tell anyone about this or me. If something was to happen to me, not saying it will, remember the codes you saw me press to enter this place. Everything here is yours. Just make sure my grandmother is good. That's all I ask."

"Stop talking like that! I don't like that kind of talk. You aren't allowed to leave me alone. You made it your business to make me fall in love with you, and that was scary enough. If you could do that, I always wondered what else were you capable of. This right here takes the cake."

I felt so relieved of that burden. I had been holding it in for so long. It felt good to finally be able to talk to my girl about my life. I kissed her a little bit longer as we made our way to the exit.

She looked me really deep in my eyes and said, "I really love your nasty ass. You better not ever leave. You aren't allowed to leave me. I'm going to tell you that again and again if you try it. You're stuck."

I laughed because she sounded like a crazy chick but I liked it. I knew she meant every word by the way she looked at me. I pulled her closer to me as we walked back to the car. She must've felt the connection because she put her arm around my waist and invited herself further into my body. I opened the passenger side of the car door and let her in. As I walked around the car, she made eye contact with me the whole way, smiling.

I got in the car and remembered there was something else I had to tell her.

"Oh yeah, I have a gun in the car, too, but it's in a stash box. I'm the only one who knows the code to the box. So if something were to happen with me, it's the same code as the combo to the door, with a few twists and turns. Okay? I'm just getting it all out now," I told her while laughing.

She shook her head with a smirk and asked to see it. She had never seen a gun before. I wasn't shocked that she didn't see one. It made sense because her father was the lowest dude I had ever met. I showed her the hammer but took the magazine out. There wasn't one in the helmet, so we were good.

At that moment, I felt like I was turning my good girl bad. She started asking me questions about how much coke cost and where I got it. It was intriguing to say the least, but I didn't want her knowing much about this lifestyle. I wanted better for her. That was probably why I hid it for so long. She didn't belong in this world.

"How much money do you have saved up?" she asked.

"Millions. I'm waiting to do this legit. I want to have different spots and businesses to wash this money and make it legal."

Her eyes got wide when I said millions. "So I've been making love to a millionaire for a year and some change now, huh?"

She was beyond intrigued, and I could tell from all the questions she was asking. I told her I would explain everything to her in the morning. She had enough surprises for the night. Actually, I just wanted to get to the spot to celebrate the occasion at hand. I wanted to be with the people I loved and trusted the most—my girl and my brothers. Work could wait.

She agreed and sat in her seat, staring at me as I started driving. I was moving in and out of lanes, trying to get to the party quicker. Biggie's "Hypnotize" was blasting from the speakers, as I headed down Ninth to the Meat Packing District. The vibe from that song, from the beat to the lyrics, summed up my current state of emotions. Tonight couldn't be going any better. The crazy thing was, I felt that way earlier, and now I feel like the greatness turned up a notch. I glanced over at Sabrina, and we made eye contact. She grasped my right hand as it was resting on the middle console. No words were exchanged the entire ride, but then again none were needed.

We arrived at the spot, and the street in front of the building was lined with cars. The small parking lot behind the building, where I arranged for my boys and me to park, was also packed. I saw one of the bouncers I knew standing out front. I rolled the window down and called him over. Before I could even ask him anything, he answered my question.

"What up, G? Yeah, I already know about the parking lot. But I got you. I lined off a couple spots in front of the club so y'all could be out front. Why not show off the whips, right?"

I couldn't front. It absolutely made sense. I agreed with a nod and low key slipped him a $100 bill as a tip in a handshake. As I maneuvered the whip into the parking space, I see all my homies parked up, enjoying the summer night. I knew it was going to be a crazy night. Everyone here either graduated or was on the same vibe that we were.

As soon as Sabrina and I walked up, Rock started passing us drinks. Sabrina and her friends were looking good as hell. They were wearing designer dresses or skirt/blouse combinations with Louboutin or Gucci heels. All of us guys were also similarly dressed. It was either Armani, Versace, or other Italian fashion house suits and loafers. Each one of my brothers had their shines on, and we were turning heads in the spot.

We soon after made our way into the party. Sabrina started dancing on me, already feeling the mood of the night. It was crowded as hell, but I wasn't complaining. I was gonna get bent and have a good time with the people I deemed family.

A few songs in, with a few drinks in my system, I was ready to completely get loose. I was getting fucked up, and so was Sabrina. I was gonna destroy that pussy when we got back to the hotel! I looked down at Sabrina to pass her a bottle, but I noticed she wasn't drinking.

"Yo, ma, it's our night tonight! Let's turn this shit the fuck out. Grab a bottle!" I said, extending the bottle toward her. "Let's get this shit going!"

She still didn't take the bottle from me. Instead she gave me a deep, piercing look. "You remember I told you I had a surprise for you? Well, congratulations, baby. You're going to be a father!"

I looked at her with a hyper shocked face. "You're serious, babe? For real?"

I didn't know what to do or how to feel. I was happy but everything started running through my head. How would I be as a father? Am I ready for a child? Who wants to have a father that's a drug dealer? Will she put everything in good for me? Am I killing her dreams with this baby on the way?

I had a bunch of questions, but this wasn't the time to ask them. I was super happy because I was bringing new life into this world. Even better, it was with someone I loved and cherished more than anything in this world. Everything would work out. I was sure of it.

I suddenly felt super happy with those thoughts that just entered my mind.

"I'm so happy, baby. You're gonna be a great mother. I'm sure of it," I assured her, grabbing her hands.

I yelled to Risk and Rock, the two that were the closest to me at the moment, "Yo, my niggas! You guys are gonna be uncles! I am about to be a dad!"

The love they showed me was unreal. Immediately that jumped all over me. They started giving hugs and daps and spraying champagne all over me and one another. They were more hyped than me, like they knew it was coming.

As we were celebrating, out of nowhere, I saw in my peripheral vision three dudes in black hoodies and skullies lurking. Immediately, my warning sensors went off. Something wasn't right. They stood out from everyone else at the party. Their black sneakers and Timbs and hoodies contrasted starkly with the high fashion of everyone else in the building. Something just didn't seem right.

They pulled out guns and started pointing in our direction. I did what was natural to me and pushed Sabrina out of the way. No sooner did I push her than the shooting started. I saw Risk get hit in the shoulder as he was trying to duck down.

Boom! Boom! Boom!

I heard the shots and the bullets ricocheting off the walls and tables. I looked over and saw Sabrina was crouched down behind a sofa. She was screaming, and as soon as she made eye contact with me, she started rushing toward me. I got up off the ground from where I was lying and ran toward her.

"Get down! Get down!" I yelled to her.

Suddenly, I feel a sharp burning sensation as a bullet slammed into me. I immediately fell to the ground. The gunman then reached down and popped my chain off my neck.

He shot me again and yelled, "This is for my brother!"

As I lay in a puddle of blood, watching the people screaming around me, clinging for dear life, all I could think was, *How'd I get jammed up like this?*